THE EAST GERMAN SPY MISTRESS

NATALIA PASTUKHOVA
AND PETER MORRIS

BROWN
DOG
BOOKS

Published under licence by Brown Dog Books and
The Self-Publishing Partnership Ltd, 10b Greenway Farm, Bath Rd,
Wick, nr. Bath BS30 5RL

www.selfpublishingpartnership.co.uk

ISBN printed book: 978-1-83952-508-7
ISBN e-book: 978-1-83952-535-3

Cover design by Kevin Rylands
Internal design by Andrew Easton

Printed and bound in the UK
This book is printed on FSC° certified paper

ACKNOWLEDGEMENTS.

As with my first novel – *The East German Police Girl* – the Cold War anecdotes of both family members and former colleagues have provided much of the bed-rock in creating this story.

Also to my co-writer Peter Morris, without whose linguistic talents and first-hand knowledge of the subtlety and humour in the British Army, this tale would have lacked both colour and balance.

PROLOGUE

Aziz, in a grubby jellaba, squirmed on the hard wooden chair.

Through a barred one-foot square window in the thick-walled cell, came a shaft of dazzling light from the mid-afternoon sun, which struck the earthen floor before diffusing itself.

Two squaddies, who stood by the door, came to attention as Major Dardry entered.

'At ease.'

'I demand to know why I am here? There is nothing wrong with my work permit!'

The Major sat himself down on the opposite side of the trestle-table and smiled.

'No, I know there isn't, Aziz. You're here because I think you're a communist agent.'

'Hah!' The Arab gave a snort. 'I hate them even more than I hate the British.'

'Poor communists. But … nice shiny silver? That might tilt the balance?'

'I work for my living.'

On the table lay the items found on the prisoner; a worn leather draw-string purse, a large filthy handkerchief, a box of matches and a note-pad.

'Let us chat a little about this work ... and your "friends".' Dardry, in a short-sleeved pale-khaki shirt, took a packet of cigarettes from a breast pocket and placed one between his lips. Then, as a seeming afterthought, he added, 'Do you smoke, Aziz?' He offered one to the prisoner.

Aziz hesitated. If this officer thought that a cigarette would soften him, then he was even more stupid that he looked. He took one and gave a brief nod.

Dardry put a hand to his other breast pocket then patted it. 'My matches must be in my jacket. We can use yours. You don't mind?'

The first two failed to strike, but the third burst into flame and he lit their cigarettes.

'Must be damp,' muttered the lined swarthy face. 'The cement-mixer splashed me a lot earlier.'

Dardry nodded, then threw the box of matches to the corporal. 'Keep hold of that, Owens.'

'Sir.'

'Hey, they're my matches!' Aziz stared to rise.

The private strode forwards and thrust him back onto his chair.

Dardry took a long thoughtful puff and eyed his quarry. 'A compatriot of yours came here recently. Having pledged himself to bat for the enemy, he then turned himself in. He also had a box of matches ... of which around half seemed to be duds.'

'I told you, they're damp.'

'And the "duds", once dipped in water, produce an invisible ink.'

The Arab's brow had moistened perceptibly. 'I know

nothing about any "cryptography".'

'That is writing which cannot be read. This is steganography, writing which cannot be seen.'

Aziz's chest was rising and falling rapidly.

'Anyway, to avoid any mishaps on your return journey to your family, I suggest you lay a few cards on the table.'

'You crafty bastards. About what?'

'Well … you could begin with Tatiana Unikova?'

'Is that Giselle Bisogno?'

'Yes. I think so.'

CHAPTER ONE

On a July afternoon in 1952, Captain Archie Stanton walked briskly into the shadowy vault of Berlin's Charlottenburg Railway Station where the train for Brussels stood at Platform One.

The cheery young officer took a window seat in one of the cream and blue first-class carriages, where in open-plan interiors the seats were grouped in fours with a walnut-topped table separating each facing pair.

A stylish lass in her twenties with coiled corn-gold hair also boarded and sat opposite him.

He greeted her with a *'Guten Tag, Fräulein,'* and received a coy smile in exchange.

'King Farouk deposed,' stated his newspaper's headline. 'Sailing today for Europe in his yacht ... ' Stanton had seen him once in a Cairo club with a pretty Syrian coquette.

A whistle shrilled, their engine's up-blasts echoed under the station's overall roof and with jolts and clunks they swayed over numerous sets of points to emerge from the blue-tinted geometrical shadows out into the sunshine.

A hint of *N'aimez que moi* – a slightly astringent pre-war perfume – drifted across from the dishy and sinuous blonde.

A lean craggy German – at least he carried a paper-back entitled *In jener Nacht* – strolled up and sat down beside her.

'With his throne usurped by Colonel Nasser, the play-boy King – accompanied by his new wife, chef, barber ... ' The girl stiffened abruptly, the toe of her shoe striking Stanton's shin.

Peering over his paper he saw her twist sharply, exhale with some emphasis, then slowly regain a calmer pose.

The thwarted Hun glared at the drab olive-green British Army uniform, with its shoulder pips and Sam Browne belt, his eyes ablaze.

Taking a deep breath Stanton switched his gaze to the window.

Outside a pall of pale sunlight outlined signal gantries and girders in smoky greys, beyond which stood the gaunt outlines of blackened bombed-out tenements.

His family's estate in Dorset had also suffered during the conflict. Trainee saboteurs billeted there had for instance, cleaned their boots on the Sanderson curtains.

The game-warden had now though restocked the carp pond and he looked forward to cycling and jolly talks with his sister, to trout stuffed with chopped chestnuts and to brandied apricots with frothy coffee, all pleasantly remote from the tawdry delights of Berlin.

The classy neatly-dressed lass suddenly shuffled again and turned pink.

A stunned Stanton growled in a threatening tone, 'Lassen Sie sie allein.'

The big-boned thug returned a hard stony stare, before casually lighting a cigarette. It gave off the whiff of that dreadful Bulgarian tobacco which the Germans had used in the war.

A flat rural landscape had replaced the gutted six-storey city dwellings. Run-down farms with dead apple trees and lean cows drifted by mingling with a trail of smoke from the engine.

The girl's pale complexion and her limpid hazel-grey

eyes exuded an authentic delicacy, scarce in these dreary post-war years.

Beside a stream a gnarled rustic fished and a covey of birds flew out of a bush.

The train slowed. Barbed wire, guards and obstacles known as 'dragons' teeth', marked the East-West German border. The first stop was Brunswick.

The blonde asked her neighbour to excuse her. She swung her handbag onto her shoulder and moved off along the gangway. The train drew in to the platform, a porter shouted *'Braunschweig'* and Stanton saw her alight from the end-balcony of their carriage.

The German, in his dark reefer jacket and goose-dung shoes, snatched up his book and left.

As the train restarted, a puckish-looking dark-haired lass appeared, shoved her knapsack onto the cord rack and sat down opposite the Captain.

Her milk-white skin and rosy cheeks were homelier and less studied than her predecessor's and her jacket bore a small Belgian flag.

Stanton recalled his father once telling their Belgian *au pair* to buy his wife some coloured flowers and the silly girl had returned with cauliflowers.

In Egypt, Farouk's wine cellar was being 'evaluated' by the 'liberators'.

The German reappeared and sat nonchalantly down beside the Walloon.

Whilst unwrapping a cheese bap, she started unexpectedly and looked crossly at her pinchbeck neighbour, before readjusting her position.

The intervening table prevented Stanton from seeing

what this cadaverous brute was up to.

The German, in his mid-forties, had a longish face with a colourless oval mouth and a missing lower front tooth.

As the train had become quite full before leaving Berlin, his sitting beside the first lass had not seemed strange, but what of this return?

In the fading twilight, the dim lamps of farms and villages slid sleepily by.

At Hanover their brakes ground and squealed as they halted in a loop short of the station. With irritation the ogre leapt up and leant out of the window opposite, peering down at a man beside the track who was tapping the carriage wheels with a long-handled hammer and swinging a red lamp. Without warning the train lurched – they were changing engines – and he hit his temple on the frame of the window whose upper half he had wound down. Smoke from a passing engine engulfed his head.

Back in his seat, as the train drummed over a girder bridge, the doll-like girl suddenly spun round and shouted, 'Allez-vous-en!'

The bad-hat went rigid at this flare-up, then sensing a confederacy among the other passengers, left.

As they steamed into a dismal Liège, the flickering gas lamps depicted the 'Boche' stepping down onto the platform. He tripped over a suitcase and gave it such a kick that those nearby fell back.

Doors slammed, the guard waved his green flag and the train moved effortfully off.

Stanton, with a smile like the sun trying to ripen barley, asked the spirited girl – in good French – what the 'Kraut' had done?

She eyed him primly for a few seconds, then relented. 'He kept touching the front of my thigh.'

'That is unpardonable,' Stanton sympathised.

What sort of deficient persona behaved so? Many had suffered, yet still exercised self-control.

'His custard and crimson ticket – I saw it when the guard clipped it – denotes its issue in the Eastern Zone.'

At *The Chew-Chew* café on Weymouth station, two days later, Stanton thumbed through *The Daily Sketch*. A short article caught his eye; 'Prostitute strangled in Liège.'

His toast, honey and tea appeared, served by a girl with an unaffected yet perceptive cheeriness.

Ah England; cobble-stones, faded shop awnings, enamel adverts for Hudson's soap, mail sacks on platform trolleys ... so homely in contrast to the scarred minds and mistrust on the Continent.

In Liège, a parlous-looking fellow had been sighted in the Bressoux district, described as tallish and missing a lower tooth. Probably he had boarded the midnight train to Antwerp. It was news chiefly because his victim had once been the mistress of a corrupt Vichy minister.

On the local train, as pastures and byres drifted by, Stanton pondered his own shortcomings with girls.

A 'masher' some called him; a show-off; but scared of close ties.

He alighted at Maiden Bodwas and with his kit-bag took the lane to Udcot Manor.

Larks with his young nephews and bibulous frolics with his sister Alice, beckoned. It was good to be on leave.

*   *   *   *

At Antwerp's Albertdok, Walther Coburg embarked unobtrusively onto an Estonian cargo ship. Two crew members had defected from the *Narva* and he was to replace her missing First Officer.

Having off-loaded her cargo of Baltic spruce, she sailed out from the Scheldt estuary and northwards to the Arctic Circle to rendezvous with a heavy Russian ice-breaker which would lead her – together with eight other Eastern Bloc merchant vessels – via the North-East Passage, to the Pacific.

It was August and the ice was at its thinnest – although still thick – but the ice-breaker *Rurik* ploughed on steadily through the Kara Sea, creating a channel through which the freighters followed her in line ahead.

Then one dazzlingly white minus-thirty-five-degree morning, the ship in front of the *Narva* drifted to a halt without warning. First Officer Coburg – the officer of the watch and sipping tea on the bridge – rang 'reverse engines' on the engine-room telegraph and awaited an acknowledgement. To his surprise and annoyance, none came.

'What are those bastards down there doing?' He yelled unavailing abuse down a voice-pipe before sending the radio operator scampering down numerous companion-way ladders to the engine-room to kick the hell out of that dozy Latvian engineer.

It was too late. With three or four feet of ice on either beam, Coburg dared not steer into it for fear of tearing open the half-inch thick plates of the hull and so they rammed the ship ahead. The dilatory engineer, belatedly reversing the engines, then contrived to take a blade off the propeller on some submerged spur of ice.

Coburg sought out this buffoon – who posed abstractedly with his hands in his deep square dungaree pockets, a whiff of vodka about him and a ludicrously curved pipe – and broke his jaw.

Via the Trans-Siberian Railway, a shackled though still autocratic Coburg arrived back in East Germany in November 1952.

In Stralsund, a Board of Inquiry blamed him bluntly for not ensuring that the duty engine-room artificer was at his post. The hairs on his ears rippled.

'Whilst having the honour to command the People's cargo vessel *Narva*, you exhibited indolence and thus incompetence,' declared the chairman. She sentenced him to six years' hard labour.

An incendiary anger surged through Coburg's being. His whole life seemed to be one chain of unmerited mishaps and calamities.

Despite this, after six months of breaking road-stone, he was mysteriously released, given a poky flat in Erfurt and a job driving a bread van.

On Sundays, after this unexpected parole – which no one explained – he would often sit in the park opposite his flat, watching the town's subdued human stock shamble by.

Under the lime trees lay the gaunt rusting hulk of a Tiger tank with its turret upside-down beside it, having been blown off by its own ammunition exploding. What had destroyed this steel monster? What terrible blow had pierced its mighty heart? It had been left there by the communist authorities to remind the native East Germans of their utter defeat.

Fifteen years before he had been a guest of honour at a Hitler Youth girls' camp – black skirts, grey blouses with red and blue triangular flashes, a log fire, jacket potatoes, a blonde lass reading a tale about a Valkyrie ... they had felt like gods and goddesses. And now these same girls – reduced to drudges – were shovelling mounds of rubble into wheelbarrows across the square to earn an extra Pfennig or two.

Life was dreary, clothing wretched and food both sparing in quantity and poor in quality. He had once lived in a castle, been served at table and gone on childhood holidays – or 'whizzes' – to Switzerland and Italy.

Then in the summer of fifty-three, he found one day that his bread van had been loaded – by some casual oversight it seemed – with an extra tray of buns and cakes.

Between the copper foundry and the bus depot, he dropped them off inconspicuously at his lodgings.

That evening – armed mentally with this fare as a bribe – he strolled to a dingy bar or *Stübli* called *Der Knabe*. Here, amid pre-war photographs of flying boats and racing cars, an ancient zither, dim lights and an old barman serving watered-down ale, whores sometimes lurked.

One sat there, almost he could have believed, lying in ambush for him. She swivelled round on her bar-stool, threw him a north-south eye-balling, crossed her legs provocatively and gave her name as Lisa. He bought her the prescribed Schnaps and after ten minutes of trite formulaic dialogue, asked her round to his flat. The two pool players paid them no obvious attention.

In his first-floor pad, he asked, 'Do you want me to recite some cloying and over-abundant flattery?'

'Not particularly.'

She actually was quite striking and well-cared-for for her class. 'Anyway, it's here in unspoken form.' He indicated his trouser fronts.

She batted her eyelids. 'Payment is more to the point.'

'True. Excesses pall. Surfeit dulls the delight. Besides, you know you're beautiful, don't you? After all, you're a girl.'

She looked at him warily, though with a hint of heady insolence.

Oily fumes from a paraffin heater tinged the air.

'I've no money, but I can feed you.' He waved a hand at the wooden tray of confectionery.

'A perk of working at the bakery?'

'Quite.' He pointed to a Danish pastry and then to a spot below her midriff, 'So, that sticky bun in exchange for this sticky bun?'

Hesitantly she accepted his barter; one bun per shag with coffee thrown in.

He tried to muster a brief charm, which however soon evaporated to expose the raw physical bones of their contract.

And so for two hours she coddled his pine-cone mechanically and slid said hefty arrow into her quiver six times.

He hated her for having bits of anatomy which he lacked and above all, for *knowing* that she was curvy and alluring.

After their final climax, in the faint glow from the retorts at the gas-works across the back alley, he glimpsed above her cream chiffon bra, a seemingly unperturbed face ...

and craved to fetch a knife and mutilate this conceited piece of flesh.

Immured in grim ruined East Germany, were such reckless instincts so rocky? Urinating on an American flag in public might be excused, but ... dare he slash this conscienceless sin-immune slut? A sixth sense whispered and warned him that there was something singular about her ... and those pool players?

They shared the dregs from the coffee-pot – they were still on rationed ground acorns then – and played cards for a time.

She remarked, 'I've grown used to acorns. I think I prefer them?'

'I doubt they'll be on sale if the real stuff ever returns.'

'There might be a market?'

'Of one.'

The ritual ended and she left, Walther escorting her down to street-level where sure enough – in the doorway of the cobbler's opposite – lurked two plain-clothes watchers, probably *Volkspolizei*, the so-called *Vopos*.

Back upstairs Walther picked up a 1930's adventure novel from a shelf full of such books which had come with the room. After one page, knuckles rapped firmly on his door.

He opened it to view the usual Trilby-hat-topped faces above those predictable belted large-lapelled Ulster raincoats. One held up a warrant-card. 'Police. May we come in?'

He waved them in, not that he had any real choice of course.

'I half-suspected you'd planted her.'

The senior officer of the duo smiled faintly. 'So you have keen instincts? Not that you did when we placed the extra bread-rolls in your van this morning.'

'Bread-rolls?' He feigned an amateurish look of bewilderment.

The second policeman stepped into the kitchen recess, lifted up the wooden bakery tray still containing five buns and held it in front of Walther who shrugged as if to say, 'All right. You win.'

The policemen each took a bun and began chomping.

'So, what's the penalty? Is it a capital offence?'

'Most things here are,' admitted the chief drolly, 'and yet ... we could overlook the matter ... ' He paused so that Coburg could digest his position.

'What do you want me to do?'

These past-masters of oblique-communication spoke thoughtfully. 'Your file suggests that you might be guilty of killing young women. Gisela ... '

'Who?'

'The girl you've just stuffed. Gisela had instructions to scream if you attacked her.'

'Lucky I controlled my alleged proclivities then?'

Again the senior policeman smiled slightly. 'Very lucky. Pitfall number three avoided ... but perhaps you will soon be given other opportunities?'

'Go on.'

'Your full name is Walther Willibald Hesse-Coburg? Yes?'

'I haven't used the "Hesse" bit since the war.'

'Very sensible. And you're originally from Lynfels ... is that a castle?'

'Sort of.'

'Sort of?'

'A small one, but yes.'

The callers switched to a more serious tone. 'You are to travel to Leipzig tomorrow … in fact we have a railway warrant and an address for you here. We do not know exactly what they want ... that you will discover after you arrive, no doubt.'

'No doubt.'

The *Vopos* each took another bun. 'Have the last one,' the Chief said cheerfully to Walther. 'Good night.'

*　　*　　*　　*

Walther Coburg took a tram from Leipzig's *Hauptbahnhof* to the address given to him by the *Vopos*, arriving at a large boarded-up villa in a drab but leafy suburb.

He was cursing what appeared to be a mistake when a lean grey-faced man in plain clothes climbed out of a car with military plates on it, scrutinised Coburg at a distance and then beckoned to him. Without a word he drove him a long way out of town to a disused airfield beside a lake.

He parked the vehicle beside others on a section of weed-split and abandoned runway, before leading his sweat-moistened passenger past a desultory sentry and huge coils of barbed wire to a sparsely-furnished though airy reception office. Here Coburg faced a hard-looking girl in shirt-sleeve-order military attire, perched behind an antiquated typewriter.

In East Germany, pleasantries with governmental factota were considered quite unnecessary.

She studied the card given to her by the driver, made

a brief internal telephone call and then stiffly led Coburg up two flights of stairs. Here she knocked on a grey door.

In a spacious well-furnished office, he stood erect and attentive in front of a woman seated at a broad dark-green steel desk.

She wore a brown skirt, a soft cream blouse and a neck-chain of irregular brass links. Her hair was blonde and her face shrewd but not unfriendly.

'Thank you, Ute.'

The girl left.

'Sit down, Herr Coburg.'

He did so. 'Thank you.'

Through the wide floor-length windows of this the old control tower, he glimpsed a young girl rowing a scull leisurely on the lake in the afternoon sunshine. The oar blades were red with white chevrons.

'It's quite a pleasant spot here,' the mystery blonde remarked. 'This airfield was built in 1937 so it's well-constructed. The central heating still works for instance.'

'Indeed, Comrade.' No clue so far, he thought.

Farther out across the lake a dinghy tacked back and forth in a light summer breeze. 'That's Herr Engel, our Minister of Foreign Affairs,' she added as the solitary yachtsman reefed his main-sail.

Coburg was forty-eight and she thirty-four, quite neatly turned out and – though one might not go the whole hog – not unattractive.

She gave him a cursory smile. 'You don't recognise me, do you?'

He stared at her. 'I'm afraid not.'

'I'm your cousin ... Ulrica.'

'Ah, Ulrica Catharina zu Lauenburg?'

'Very good.'

A secret sigh of relief, even a spark of hope crept into his mind. He had experienced enough snakes; time for a ladder.

'We met at a number of family weddings in the twenties ... though I was only a child at the time.'

'It seems like another world.'

'It *was* another world.'

A corporal knocked and brought in a tray with coffee and some open cheese rolls.

Ulrica rolled a pencil back and forth between her two sets of fingers, then; 'So, in Erfurt, "The knave of hearts, he stole some tarts"? Two very different flavours?'

'Well ... there were no goddesses to supply my needs.'

She shrugged with a watery porcelain-doll smile. 'No one is entirely self-sufficient.' After pouring out some coffee, she added, 'Anyway Walther, I have a job for you.'

'Something preferable to breaking road-stone?'

'Well, more colourful at least ... you speak English and Italian, I believe?'

'The Italian's rusty. Ulrica ... I may call you Ulrica?'

She peered reticently at her mildly unctuous subordinate. 'When we're alone, yes.'

'And drop the "comrade" stuff?'

She eyed him as if to say, 'What do *you* think?'

'Ulrica, what is your actual job?'

'Um ... espionage operations in northern Europe.'

'That sounds quite high-flying?'

She rocked her head non-committally from side to side.

'Am I going to be a spy?'

She pondered this. '"Spy" suggests someone covertly placed ... long-term. You would be more of a "difficulty-solver" ... one of a perhaps blacker dye ... sent abroad for short spells.'

'To kill?'

'Well, the tasks would vary.'

'Good. I like action.'

His prominent Adam's apple bobbed above a shirt collar two sizes too large, as fire surged through his bones and sinews.

Ulrica wore a calm outer demeanour which hid from the unfussy observer, a somewhat callous indifference to life.

'I chose you because you seem to have the required attributes, because we're related and later ... '

He leant forwards. 'And later?'

She hesitated. 'I'll explain when the time comes.'

They talked a little of childhood holidays. He recollected that on the French Riviera, he had seen a French battleship at anchor – white in the dazzling sun – with bunting and a huge *tricolore* drooping at her stern and on a nearby fort, heraldic pennons flapping.

She had recently met a most captivating French *contre-amiral*, his dress and manners a sharp contrast to Walther's cheap suit and harsh-featured mask. Her cousin was indeed a debased minor aristocrat, a man demeaned by a vindictive war, a savage world and his own perverted lusts.

He detested the 'what-ho' pith-helmeted British, ditto the supercilious slimy French; he was too proud to dig pit-coal or sell goods and so spent his days throwing rough ineffective lances at the sun.

Ulrica discerned his psychological scars.

'Do you ever wear a uniform, Ulrica?'

'Seldom ... We had enough of those under both Hitler and the Kaiser.'

From an initial bearing of inscrutability, there now came hints of a milder side to her nature; the scent of warm soap-suds, a glass of brandy and a more forgiving spirit.

'I can see you've suffered, Walther.' She exhaled. 'Sociable interaction can have a redemptive effect ... and sexual affection softens our hearts.'

Discountenanced by her insight, yet not wishing to disclose his abhorrence for dark barbarians say, or his antipathy towards elevated and pretty girls, he said lamely, 'I have fought those I loathed ... and lost. So no point in attacking again with even weaker forces.'

Ulrica restrained a grimace. 'Anyway, step one; you must undergo four months of basic training.'

'I understand.'

'First come some political lectures. These will increase your understanding – though not your enthusiasm – for the theory and methodology of socialist world domination.'

He helped himself to a second bun. 'I admire your scepticism.'

'It's pretty ubiquitous ... if a senior Party member rolls up, we just switch to the set socialist-Eden flannel.'

He smiled.

'Also, do *not* mention to anyone that we're related.'

Such remarks underscored that their dialogue was not being recorded. 'You're a dark horse, cousin.'

'Not really.

When I was fifteen, I fell in love with the young

blacksmith in the village ... but of course could not meet with him. Once he came to the castle to hot-shoe a horse and my mother saw me give an involuntary tremble ... so she understood. He was garrotted near Saint-Lô by the *Résistance* in 1942.

So I have just had men, poor miserable men ... sad really, but such is life.'

Walther nodded. 'Had the war not upset everything, you might have been a genteel or even a clinging society wife.'

She frowned humorously. 'That sounds equally awful.'

'Who's the girl there sculling?'

Ulrica turned and watched. 'Oh, Sabine ... she's the Minister's daughter.'

CHAPTER TWO

Her mother being half-Finnish, Hayley Ellyard sailed on a cargo boat to Helsinki in June 1953, for a spell with her hunchbacked Uncle Oskar, a tobacconist there.

This well-to-do twenty-three-year-old from Sussex, had in the spring been caught shop-lifting. Before the magistrates, she had worn a dog-collar with a black skirt and blouse and clutching a Bible had claimed to be a Minster in 'The Idaho Immersionary Tabernacle'.

The local press reporters though knew her, for on a protest march, she had borne a placard, 'Disarm the whale'.

When her American accent went skew-whiff, their paralytic laughter was met with mouthed obscenities. A quarter-page photograph of 'Priestess Ellyard' adorned the next day's front page.

Her grandmother then persuaded her to do some voluntary work in a local hospital, but when caught half-undressed in a linen cupboard with a radiographer, she was thrown out.

This was the last straw. Her parents packed her off to Uncle Oskar.

She helped in the shop, improved her Swedish and went on cycle rides with Per, a neighbour of her own age.

'What's your job?'

'A fisherman.'

'Which fish do you catch?'

'Herring. They're easy ... like girls.'

'Like *some* girls,'

'I avoid the snobby ones.'

'They too have their weaknesses.'

'But ... they take time.'

'You're in a hurry? So leave the salmon? Go for the tiddlers?'

'Stop taking the Pisces.'

They went into a shabby café.

'Some girls have trouble catching boys,' he said.

'So I've heard.'

A shower of crumbs fell onto her skirt. 'Shall I help you brush them off?'

She gave him a meaningful smile. 'It's good bread. The French are crazy about bread.'

'And love.'

'And what about Finns?'

They exchanged pithy stares, then she slurped her milkshake.

He moved close to her and they snogged.

He sampled her drink. 'Sharing; it's a social lubricant.'

'Not a sexual one?'

'The same idea ... it facilitates interaction and reduces pain.'

They went to his waterside cabin and made love.

Uncle Oskar, peering beneath his bushy brows and over the wiry spectacles perched on the tip of his nose, said, 'I hope Per isn't taking liberties with you?'

God, he was as hung up about sex as people back in England.

Oskar said, 'I have a friend. He knows of a forthcoming "cultural exchange" to East Germany. Have you ever visited Germany?'

Hayley – bored with weighing out shag tobaccos – said imploringly that she would love to go.

Next day, for the consideration of one hundred under-the-counter Havanas, the tobacconist fixed it up.

He was glad to be rid of this hot-potato niece.

*   *   *   *

The De Havilland *Dominie* flew eastwards over the Hadhramaut towards Muscat. This rugged commercial biplane, though able to carry six passengers, had only two on board; an Indian who ran a sisal plantation in Tanganyika and a curvy young lass from West Germany.

Stephen Tennant, the pilot, had once been in the Southern Rhodesian Air Force.

Sophie sat sideways-on behind him and looked ahead.

'The altimeter says eleven hundred feet. That's wrong surely?'

'That's above sea level.'

'Oh yes.'

'Why are you flying to Muscat?'

'A local sheikh plans to make a film.'

'And you're hoping for a *rôle*?' A roll on a mattress, he wondered, sensing her to be a bit rough.

'Yes.'

'It's unusual for a girl to travel alone in these parts.'

'Someone's picking me up when we land. Besides, it's exciting.'

'True. Life needs a few dabs of courage.'

'My agent in Mainz offered me the chance … he said it was out of the ordinary.'

27

Her jacket, which she had removed, lay on the deck. He spotted its label; 'Cottbus Kommune S.H.'

'Aden is still a British Protectorate?'

'It is.'

'Do the Yemenis not want to shake off those colonial fetters?'

'Well ... schools, hospitals, training for administrators and engineers ... a gradual path to independence is more or less implied.

Who's collecting you?'

'Dennis Hoar. A shipping agent. Are we on time?'

'The wind's behind us, so we should be early. What's the film called?'

'*Gretchen in Arabia*. They might give me the titular rôle.'

'Title *rôle*,' he corrected her, unless her contribution was to be her tits?

They landed forty minutes early on the short airstrip in a cloud of dust.

Cottbus was in the Eastern Zone of Germany, an area historically far earthier and less developed than the Rhineland. The Iron Curtain had fallen fortuitously on a line which was also a cultural divide.

'So, the Queen of Sheba arrives ... but there's no sign of King Solomon. Do you want to join me for char and wad?'

They crossed to the small control tower and a cluster of tin sheds.

Tennant wondered if success in such auditions required spending time in bed? Or could she be working undercover in other senses?

                    *   *   *   *

On the outskirts of East Berlin, a score of young Westerners
with ill-defined but anti-establishment leanings were
lodged in a mansion which had once been the home
of a nineteenth-century industrialist. The ravages of the
functional hatchet men – walls knocked through and
corrugated-iron annexes tacked on – had though distinctly
lessened its charm.

Each day these 'Neophytes' hiked in pine forests, then
at tea-time, ate fluffy pancakes and peppered kidneys
and listened to Philippics tinged with Red incense. These
stressed the evils of a morally-posturing though secretly
bellicose West.

Kurt Hauff quoted Goethe. '"Theory is grey", we need
action. On your return home, do *not* join the Party. Take
a job in education or in broadcasting … we have friends
placed to help you.'

This tough-looking character – in a loose red shirt and
dark grey Lederhosen – appealed to Hayley more by his
muscular physique than his being an acolyte of … was it
Bad Linen? Well, some such name.

She sat next to him at supper, which consisted of weak
coffee and a slice of rye bread with blueberry jam, served
on dark green plates with gilded double-headed eagles.

Scandinavian girls then still wore white knee-length
socks, which Hayley was wearing and which Kurt found
sexually alluring.

'Good evening, Hayley.'

'Good evening Kurt. I liked your talk. Have you always
been a communist?'

His English was fluent though accented. 'No. My family were quite Bohemian … amusing, a bit anti-authority, but not serious political warriors.'

'Did Else say you're from Berlin?'

'Augsburg.' He whispered, 'I like your socks.' His knee touched hers.

'I had an art-book about Berlin in the twenties … with that sudden craze for reckless behaviour.'

'I was only a boy then, but indeed, the old Puritan values were cast aside and a devil-may-care spirit seized everyone … or at least the younger generation.'

'Headbands with yellow ostrich feathers, patterned silk skirts?'

'A very pretty aunt of mine had a capricious streak, but in a foolish moment married a botanist, bore him four children and lost her looks.' He felt a hand on his thigh.

There were no second helpings.

Kurt, who studiously ignored the garrulous cross-eyed girl from Bolton sitting opposite him, went to see Larisa Alexandrovna Lysenko.

As the initiates settled down to play Skat or read the papers, Hayley was summoned to Comrade Lysenko's office.

She knocked, entered when bidden and sat down.

'Who told you to sit down?'

Hayley stood up.

Lysenko had not achieved her present rank by ignoring impertinence.

They studied one other.

'Discipline is necessary.'

'I understand, Comrade.' A note of meekness.

'Extra blueberry jam has to be earned.'

'You saw me?'

Lysenko eyed her equably. 'Sit down.'

Hayley complied. 'I don't really like jam ... except in exams ... I used to cheat when I could.'

Larisa gave her a look, free of subterfuge. 'We're looking for "covert insubordination". My father became a secret communist after the *Okhrana* shot his brother. Then ... opportunities occurred.'

The Russian smiled with a hint of conceit, lit a cigarette, pinched her eyelids together, tilted her head back and blew out a thin ribbon of smoke.

'Do you know what a Thespian is?'

'Someone who comes from The Greek isle of Thesbos?'

Larisa gave Hayley a more human smile. 'Very good ... Lesbian, Lesbos ... yes.

You have to act, to dissemble ... and be steadfast.

What does your father do?'

'A geologist ... well now he's a director.'

'Which company?'

'Burmah Oil.'

'And you?'

'I've just finished university. I read theology.'

'Theology?'

'I wanted to go to Oxford ... and as few apply for theology now, it was a way in.'

The G.R.U. officer looked impressed. 'You have some intriguing qualities, Hayley. Talk to Kurt.'

Although attracted by this arena of false lights, Hayley noted that despite their superficial style and elegance, both Kurt and Larisa were discernibly coarse. What she did not perceive, was that they saw her as also discernibly coarse.

In Kurt's cramped attic room, he took the armchair and waved at the bed. 'Sit down, Hayley.'

His left eye drifted outwards, a squint which made the axis of his gaze hard to ascertain.

He un-inverted two tumblers. '"Vodka" is the diminutive of "voda" ... Russian for water.' Liquid glugged.

'Let us talk about ambitions ... and talents.

One of my uncles was a scrivener in the Kaiser's navy and another what was then known as "a deputy cofferer" ... just office workers really who were not allowed opinions.'

'So no concord between heart and work?'

'Exactly. Social democrats, were by the start of the First World War hovering in the wings, though given no voice.'

She nodded, though this sounded boring. 'I would like to be a saboteur ... more exciting than a typist in an insurance office.'

'True, but ... hasten slowly.'

He extinguished the centre light and they clinked glasses. Hayley sipped the liquid, coughed, inhaled, then spluttered.

'Oh dear. Some tomato juice with your vodka?'

'No.' Her eyes watered. 'I react to tomatoes.'

'You turn red? Well, that's what we want?'

She smiled through her tears. 'No, I *become* a tomato.'

He moved onto the bed and sat beside her, a forefinger stroking her neck.

'I want to join the cause ... prime bombs, not fiddle with lipsticks.'

'The Iliad tells of how – with the gods' help – the

Greeks stepped over some sleeping Trojan sentries and then destroyed them from behind.'

Suddenly he seized her tightly and kissed her forcibly on her lips.

She surrendered. It seemed churlish to refuse. When flat, she undid his Lederhosen and fumbled his swagger-stick. Was he rough though? She determined not to let it show ... she could take it ... and afterwards ... 'Oh Kurt ... è *tutto finito*?'

When daylight awoke her, she fought to dispel an uneasy desolation which had deftly invaded her. But she could play *Kriegspiel* too and scoff at the cherry on last night's cake.

He asked quite unemotionally if she could remain in the East for a time?

'I would need to telephone my uncle.'

*　　*　　*　　*

Hoar drove Sophie up into the arid, jagged, honey-hued foothills.

Outwardly the ancient fort consisted of rough unbonded stones and purply-grey mud bricks baked hard by the sun. The tops of a few palm trees rose above the parapet together with a thin aerial.

The native lookout climbed down from the rampart to lift the hefty cross-bar which secured the crude wooden gate from behind.

In a stone-walled chamber, made moderately comfy with a scattering of rugs, couches, a desk and an ornate coffee-table, she met her contact.

Habib bin Alawi – in a baggy blue *sirwal* and a loose coarse-woven shirt with a cord round its waist – rose. 'Sophie Nebel?'

Habib showed her a ring. A marking indicated its gold to have come from the Sachsenwald mine in the former German East Africa.

She held out her left middle-finger with its twin.

He waved her to a seat whilst indicating a spread of biscuits, cheeses and fruit.

'I travelled once on the old German metre-gauge railway, which runs inland from Dar-es-Salaam.'

A manservant poured coffee and a pair of birds with blue and yellow plumage, chirruped softly in a cage of shiny silver wire.

'The English are our enemies, yet we have to speak English. It's so bizarre.'

Habib shrugged, sat down and lit a *chubouk* or Turkish pipe.

'Do the British ever cross the border?'

'Historically they did. A platoon of British or Indian infantry would come over … to eradicate a few "brigands" … but today the native levies – though British-officered – are unreliable.'

'But they have regulars in Aden?'

'Yes, but … with U.N. observers and uncensored reporters prowling around, they daren't risk it.'

She detached a cluster of grapes. 'Busy-bodies have their uses?'

Habib dismissed the servant.

'The two crates arrived safely?' Sophie inquired.

'Yes. The *Rosa Luxemburg* anchored off Shuqrah on the

fourth and a fishing boat brought them ashore.'

They heard a vehicle growling down in the valley.

Habib said, 'That'll be our friend. He has an expensive girlfriend in Tel Aviv.'

Sophie lowered her voice. 'A further consignment of weapons is conditional upon some action.'

'A watched pot never boils.'

'No pot does … unless someone lights a fire under it.'

'My frogs are nearly ready to creep out from under their stones … '

'So no inter-tribal feuds … yes? Adhere to the plan and no bluster.'

Habib put cheese on a biscuit. 'So thump the Brits … or you will be "cheesed off"?'

She gave him a laconic nod.

A young Englishman was shown in, clad in a clumsily arranged Arab get-up.

Wine was poured. He raised a glass. 'To Habib and his *saray*.'

He gave Sophie a packet of microfilms and Habib an envelope detailing British Army dispositions in Aden. This renegade was callow and with an affected languor. Both Habib and Sophie tacitly despised him.

The visitors left.

Habib had six male servants – drawn from his own tribe – and three concubines. The imams encouraged asceticism, as leading to a purer life, but Habib held to a more colourful philosophy.

Behind a trellis lay his harem. Outside their pavilion and dressed in bright linen skirts and silk blouses, the two Uzbekistani girls played a board game, 'The Astrologer', beside the rock-ringed pool, whilst the Turkish girl, lying face-down on some cushions, watched a butterfly explore a clump of grasses. They lived pampered yet empty lives.

Habib chose Yulduz.

Next morning Sophie flew out of Muscat.

The plane stuttered on its approach to the airfield at Aden, before landing short of the runway.

She climbed down the ladder, but whilst walking from the plane, a bullet zinged past her ear and she threw herself to the ground.

A fellow, in native garb and aiming a rifle, stood behind a prickly thorn bush and fired twice more, each round throwing up a spray of earth beside her.

The 'rebel' – whom no one seemed eager to catch – escaped.

An R.A.F. flight lieutenant strolled up, picked her up, smiled and asked if she were all right?

'I think so.'

'This happens now and again ... these Yemenis are so volatile.'

'Where's my bag?'

'My sergeant's just taken it to the bar for you.'

'I must have my bag!'

'Don't worry. It'll be safe.'

* * * *

Near the village of Nietsovo, five English-speaking girls were lodged in the former Convent of the Transfiguration with a cadre of fairly high-calibre instructors.

In the tiny wooden church, with its skewed cross and

a darkened altar triptych, the girls slept on sacks. Hayley's pseudonym was 'Elissa Bontoft'. They had not to reveal their true names to one another.

A weather-beaten G.R.U. brigadier addressed them, wearing an oversize cap and a double-breasted field great-coat. His narrow eyes peered out from his ruddy face, which had a bulbous blue-nose. 'We have a common foe. We have a bond!'

Crack-of-dawn P.T. with Alena preceded simple clear-cut lessons. One, surprisingly, was on Russian folk-tales. The Russian word 'gromit' cropped up, meaning it seemed, 'destroyed'. Pushkin was quoted with this archetype of the stolid Russian peasant:

'Give me the good life,
Give me a good wife
And a large bowl of cabbage soup.'

They learnt the printed form of the Russian Cyrillic alphabet.

The pseudo-moral gambits of Western so-called democracies were unpicked, as was their celebrated 'equality'.

The summer was hot and dry. They dined *al fresco* on apple-flavoured tea from an antiquated samovar, coarse grey bread, tinned mackerel, purple soup and stodgy pastries.

Some blackbirds in a nearby thicket kicked up a racket.

It was all quite an adventure; hinting at something celestial yet patriotic.

Under a blue sky – tinged green as it neared the skyline

– they crossed a ravine via a precarious foot-bridge. By a shady wood they learnt how to fire and maintain the simple and reliable Makarov nine-millimetre pistol and to set explosive charges with a simple detonator and a clockwork time-fuse.

Ioanna, the stout small-arms instructress, said, 'Early morning is the ideal time to strike. The body's steroids are at their lowest then, so the mind feels jaded. This is one element in the "dawn attack" concept.'

On their last day, the quintet were taken to the village of Kotadnoe, where a wizened crone owed Colonel Kulak of this outpost of the Sanprobal Training Camp, a favour for arranging a hospital admission for her son.

As she served up pancakes with butter and caviar, a young G.R.U. officer caricatured the supposedly typical habits of British agents.

'They're all Oxbridge types, "good chaps" and they contact one another with such code-words as, "Good morning old chuff. My hedgehog loves carrots. Does yours?"

You can spot them a mile off.'

A corncrake gave its approval.

Returning on a deserted road, hemmed in by dark woods, Gosia, their driver mentioned that for road-stone, slag from a Czech uranium mine had been used.

'Does it glow in the dark?' asked Hayley.

Alena smiled. 'Soviet ingenuity. It saves on street-lights.'

Next day Hayley was on a train back to Finland.

CHAPTER THREE

In Eastern Libya, inland and surrounded by desert, lay the airfield of El Adem and here were stationed units of both the British Army and the R.A.F.

Eight miles farther south – in a natural depression – lay an oasis known locally as Al-haql al-noor and there, hostile activity was afoot.

A string of camels – brindled tawny with buff and relieved of their sumpters – knelt in the coarse grass and snored, whilst a magenta hue from the setting sun glimmered through the palm trees.

Their drivers kicked over the camp-fire embers and the sibilant babble of Sabir – a mix of Berber, Arabic and French – ceased.

With the lessening light glinting on their cartridge belts, ten baggily-clad fighters moved off.

The temperature began to fall, whilst above them, a myriad stars popped up. The moon would rise soon after midnight.

By one-thirty they had found the tangled barrier of barbed wire which ringed the airfield.

At a point remote from the main camp – but not too far away from two parked aircraft – they slid a length of stiff rubber cable-ducting beneath the jumbled steel strands. It contained a plastic explosive dubbed C4 by the British and PE4 by the Americans.

Originally made in India from hollowed-out bamboo stems filled with gunpowder, such devices were known as 'Bangalore torpedoes'.

When exploded, it would break the wire by hurling it into the air and snapping it.

Nazim – their bearded leader – substituting hand flourishes for words, waved his co-zealots to withdraw and to lie flat.

He pushed a six-inch length of British No. 11 time-fuse into the grey putty-like explosive and lit its far end with a match. Crab-like, he withdrew.

He put his fingers in his ears. Their imam – a leper with a numb arm and a green turban – had forecast success.

The cord spluttered brightly before fizzling out. Unbeknown to this cur, a plastic charge – unlike black powder – could not be detonated by a burning cord. His lips curled with curses.

Najam crept forwards and prodded him.

A desert golden hyaena – its pointed ears sticking up – was watching them.

Suddenly it howled; a long clear bay.

Sharif took aim with his antiquated bolt-action Lebel rifle and shot it.

Half a mile away, in the darkened control tower, Flying Officer Hall heard the distant crack.

On cold nights, rocks could split and sound like discharges, but as the magnified circle of his Kershaw binoculars made a *tour d'horizon*, he spotted a slight movement in the thin moonlight. 'I spy black hyaenas.' He nodded to Flight Sergeant Houghton. 'Blue sector.'

Houghton picked up the red telephone beside the green-pin-pricked radar screen and rang down to the guard-room.

Both the guard and the control tower had received a tip-off; 'Bandits expected tonight'.

From No. 3 Hangar – the one also used for film shows and magic-lantern lectures – the two stand-by infantry sections, resting but ready, mounted a Bedford three-tonner and a Saracen armoured troop carrier at the double and sped off.

Nazim swore and bade his men cover themselves.

Brakes screeched.

This desperado was still scooping sand onto others when the Saracen's searchlight came on and lit him up as by the light of day. The infantrymen debussed and took up firing positions.

Nazim – known for his caprice and fury – called on Allah, as he struggled to draw its pin and lob a grenade.

Whilst Lieutenant Needham fumbled to unholster his revolver, a single shot rang out. A young squaddie calmly lowered his rifle.

The .303 round hit Nazim's upper chest, its impact numbing the entry-point, so that in his last seconds he felt nothing.

The other flattened, sand-buried infidels lay stock-still, each nose and two eyes hidden by a ridge of sand or a low thorn bush.

The barbed wire was too dense to allow the defenders to advance. They could lasso neither their mutilated enemy nor his archaic seven-millimetre model 88 Mauser rifle.

'We'll drive round at daybreak,' said Needham.

'There'll be nothing there by then, Sir.'

Private Platten dragged the Bangalore torpedo from under the perimeter wire. 'It's that grey U.S. plastic ... which the C.I.A. are said to be smuggling in to the Algerian rebels.'

Corporal Boyd added, 'Like the helicopters the French have ordered for Indo-China … and which never arrive.'

Eisenhower's policy then was for all colonies – of any country – to secede.

Platten knew all about explosives. He had mined bridges in Malaya to trap or blow up Chinese communist forces, often attaching so-called 'ripple' detonators to the charges, so that if someone jumped into the stagnant water to check the bridge's piles, the splash would set them off.

'Sir,' Boyd addressed the Lieutenant, 'blowing a hole in the wire must mean others are nearby … but lying doggo.'

Needham was not only militarily inept, but he often overruled subordinates who were competent. 'No. A mat couldn't hide over there.'

'Sir?'

'The others – if they exist – have fled.'

'Sir, Hartley and I could stay behind – stealthy like – and watch?'

'No.'

They switched off the searchlight and returned to camp.

From there wiser heads despatched two Meteors at first light to search for and strafe the fleeing caravan.

*   *   *   *

Ulrica sipped her coffee in a smart art deco Monegasque coffee-house.

It was January 1954 and outside, snow covered *La place du palais*.

A vintage Benz car with the name 'Aurelia' on its side left the palace.

At the railway station, she had lingered in the *Salle d'attente* to be sure that the other four passengers who had alighted had dispersed.

A pretty Sicilian songstress, swinging her pale-yellow skirts and petticoats, sang an Italian air accompanied by a gaunt violinist. A tambourine with red and green ribbons lay on a chair beside the wood-burning stove.

The waiter served Ulrica's waffles with jam and cream and offered her a newspaper.

An inside article caught her eye. In Upper Galilee one Aaron Amos – a shopkeeper from Tzfat – had been killed by an anti-personnel mine.

In the Suez Canal Zone, Arab nationalists buried their charges two feet down, because British mine detectors could pick up metal objects as far down as eighteen inches. In this remote part of Israel though, a mine could be hidden just below the surface.

Amos had met his grisly end beside a shrivelled fig tree on a stony track bordered by furze. In the distance snow had glistened on Mount Hermon.

The Israeli Police had established that a Palestinian girl wearing a black shawl dusted with the powdered spices of her father's warehouse had passed that way an hour before, but used a parallel path.

The violinist began a light *capriccio*.

A grumpy Canadian tourist – staff in hand – had also trudged that way, but some Bedu waifs had called, *'Sayed!* Booby-trap.' The shabbily-dressed older lass with a proud nose and a cerise-coloured *fichu* had held out a hand and the hiker had handed her a half-shekel.

She pointed to three squarish stones on a rock, which were evidently a clue.

This article could be of use. Ulrica tore it out and slipped it into her bag. The violinist saw her. She dropped a two-franc coin into the tambourine.

She trod through ankle-deep snow down a side-alley in Monaco-ville, to where she had an appointment with a high-class coin dealer. Erich Neumann – who still wore wing-collars and exhibited cloistered habits – ushered her to a tiny office above his shop.

Taking her hands from her white fur muff and knocking the snow off her boots, she climbed the narrow stairs.

A dusty grandfather clock in a shadowy alcove ticked and a plump cat purred as Neumann dispensed two shot-glasses of *Cointreau*.

'I saw the sign on your door; "*Nous cherchons une vendeuse. Anglais obligatoire.*"'

'Indeed. Many Americans call these days. My old assistant only spoke French … and had a white face and hair, as if a bag of flour had exploded.'

Ulrica smiled. 'And why a girl?'

The numismatist shrugged. 'Charm perhaps?'

'The French tongue is … clear yet lacking in nuance.'

'Perhaps its clarity is its attraction?'

Neumann had been a petty officer on the battleship *S.M.S. Thüringen*, which towards the end of the First World War had been taken over by mutineers in the Schillig Roads. The officers had been incarcerated and the Red flag hoisted. Amid the chaos, some torpedo boats had threatened to sink the ship.

After the Armistice, he realised one night that he was being watched by *Reichswehr* agents in *Der Kummer*, a sailors' tavern in Kiel, but he escaped to the railway sidings and stowed away on a goods train.

'Are you still a communist?'

'Not at all. Actually very few of us were ... we just couldn't stand the appalling conditions.'

Ulrica nodded. 'And the overbearing officers?'

'And so Provence ... fragrant green trees ... hedonists in Italianate villas, artists at their easels on the littoral.'

'The *cognoscenti* ... supposedly.'

Neumann smiled. 'Perhaps we're all frauds to a degree?'

Ulrica took out a cache of Carthaginian gold staters and Phoenician silver shekels.

Neumann studied them slowly with his eye-glass. 'Nice pieces. Very nice. Museum grade.'

Her pose, though restrained, hinted at strong reserves of character. He offered her a fair price to which she agreed.

He wrote out two cheques to be drawn on an account with the Italian bank, Banca Etruria; one to Erwin Bachmann; a second to Monika Steyr.

She reflected that she might have been an honest Saxony land-owner's wife, but fate had made her a crook.

On the train to Genoa, Walther came to her emotionally tired mind. Most murders are down to jealousy, hatred or money. Walther though, the enigma, perhaps loved hating women ... or did he just envy them?

Back in her H.Q. near Leipzig, she handed a sketch to their forger. 'Jutta, print some fairly crude blank receipts with this heading.' It read, 'Gallery Amos; Zahab Alley, Jerusalem Street, Tzfat, Israel.' 'And *not* on Eastern Bloc paper.'

CHAPTER FOUR

'Four, three, two, one, zero.'

The tail ends of the missile's four booster rockets glowed a reddy-orange and then ... whoosh! *Red Duster* number 131 streaked up into the sky, leaving a widening trail of white vapour in its wake.

Within thirty feet of the ground, the missile had broken the sound barrier of 720 miles per hour. Within three seconds it had reached Mach 2.2 – that is 1600 miles per hour – the solid-fuel boosters had fallen away and its two *Thor* ramjets taken over.

A group of visiting R.A.F. top brass, immured in the camouflaged control tower, watched it arc across the clear July sky, its deep dull roar gradually fading.

'Lower frequencies travel farther,' remarked Group Captain North.

Girls in blue-grey uniforms sat perched on high metal swivel-chairs with head-phones on, adjusting dials and watching blue and red lights on grey metal consoles, whilst boffins in white coats eyed phosphorescent squiggles on cathode-ray oscilloscopes.

The cohort of high-ranking observers pondered these technical marvels as the twenty-five-foot, one-ton projectile – with two trapezoidal wings sited half-way along its fuselage – disappeared over Cardigan Bay.

'I can barely understand how my Jag's twin carburettors work,' muttered Tug Orr-Ellis.

Doctor Gorton, Ferranti's electronics expert approached, stepping over thick multi-coloured bundles of wires. 'This is *Red Duster* prototype XTV-5.'

North – who was shepherding the guests – added, 'The Air Ministry last week officially named it *Bloodhound*.'

'What about the ignition failures at Woomera?' queried Wing Commander Mainland.

'That flaw has been rectified … though the press have been informed otherwise.'

Tug asked, 'To mislead the enemy?'

'Or a sop to keep the *Manchester Guardian* readers happy?' Sir David intoned.

The bespectacled Gorton stuck to science. 'It now has CW radar, which is harder to jam and is not distorted by ground "clutter".'

'"CW"?'

'"Continuous wave". It replaces the earlier "pulse" radar.' He explained gruffly.

Using a note-pad, he sketched out how long-range surveillance radar would cue the missile's target-engagement radar.

Mainland knitted his brows, whilst Stackhouse puffed out his cheeks.

'We must exhibit our seniority,' whispered Sir David afterwards, 'if not by understanding, then by grace and etiquette.'

Tug winced. 'Treading on thin ice there.'

'In some cases, yes.'

Mainland smiled. 'Are men ever *truly* mature … or do we just bluff it?'

'Well … time for lunch, gentlemen?' North enquired.

*   *   *   *

At the main gate of the Army's Aberporth Rocket Testing Range, Sergeant Stubbs, Corporal Hawley and Private Hale were on guard duty.

The red and white boom was down and behind neatly trimmed verges, dense coils of barbed wire lay between the railings and the hedges of the camp's boundary.

Private Hale on sentry-go stood 'at ease', holding his Lee-Enfield No. 4 rifle at the prescribed angle, with its butt on the ground.

Across the road, a gaggle in scruffy jackets and woolly hats sat on damp corn-chaff mattresses atop inverted tea-chests. A drooping banner declared, 'Peace not War'.

When a soldier entered or left camp this incongruous crew would shout stock taunts.

Of the seven, the public-school hormonally-active libertine was the real snake in the grass. Perceiving Hale's furtive interest, she kindled it with sly pouts and a subtle writhing of her rather plain though feminine physique.

'"Peaceniks" is apparently the new word for this shower,' said Stubbs to Hawley, 'doing good on behalf of the dumb.'

'The illusion of altruism, Sergeant, is usually just a failure to detect motive.'

Stubbs gave a snort.

Hawley quoted Yeats.

'I have heard that hysterical women say,
They are sick of the palette and fiddle-bow.'

The beady-eyed Stubbs was watching the sorceress as she pushed her hair back, dimpled her cheeks and fixed

Hale with her cold sparkling eyes.

As she advanced, Stubbs tucked his brass-capped blackthorn baton under his arm and strode briskly up to the red and white boom.

'Careful 'ere, lad. Witchcraft's afoot.'

Hale trembled.

The lean, almost bony soubrette approached. 'Good morning, inflexible robots.'

'Good m-m-morning, Miss ...?' Hale stuttered.

'Nina. And your name?'

'Private P. Green,' the Sergeant answered for him. 'And "green" is the word.'

Her pettishly-formed mouth wore a restrained smirk. 'Some "wizard-prangs" are visiting today, we note?'

'Would you like a "wizard-prang"? It might give you something else to think about?'

She narrowed her eyes meanly. 'You're an anachronism, Sergeant.'

'Preferable to being a mischief-maker.'

'But not a sword-rattler, it seems?'

'Anyway "Nina", this anaemic squaddie 'ere, is ill-equipped to tackle devious anarchists.'

'He might embarrass you?' She gave a cruel white smile. '"Conduct prejudicial to good order and discipline." Queen's Regulations?'

'A useful charge.' Stubbs' stare equalled hers. 'Your claque yonder is an ill-assorted bunch?'

'Thinkers are not stereotypes, Sergeant.'

'Brains are signalled it seems by fake ragged skirts or holed trousers?'

'We irritate you because we don't fit into a box.'

'Would that be Pandora's box?'

She sighed with emphasis then winked at Hale.

'Leave Private Green alone,' Stubbs said sharply, ''E doesn't need your "critical intelligence" to disturb 'im.'

'Oh dash!'

The Sergeant had had enough. 'You've a distinctly "country-house-set" accent for a ragamuffin?'

'Blame Cheltenham Ladies' College. But as well as Latin, we were taught to *ask questions*.'

'Who's "we"? You and the lice in your underwear?'

She reddened. 'Piss off. I can be crass too.' Her next phrase – which may be skipped – demonstrated this.

As a battered red van appeared, labelled 'Argosy Potatoes', she stalked angrily back to her creepy-crawly wispy-heretic 'friends'.

'Boarders repelled.'

'Yes, Sergeant.'

'*And* we annoyed her.' Stubbs exhibited a hard-to-define smile. 'Take your goggling eyes off her.'

'Sorry Sergeant ... though she knows she's eye-catching.'

'Well don't reinforce it, you bone-head.'

The van stopped and several of the demonstrators scrambled aboard.

Hawley jotted down its number, make and colour.

One bearded old activist remained. His sandwich-boards read; 'The wrath of man worketh not the will of God.' He wore a dirty oilskin of an angular cut and moved with a limp.

Stubbs turned on his heel. 'Who's 'e, Hawley?'

'"Mr Drake", Sir?'

'Drake?'

'A lame duck? In oily green plumage? Sir?'

'Speak only if something worthwhile enters your head, Corporal.'

'Being religious, he could be "Mr Shepherd", leading his flock ... Is that wool or dandruff on his shoulders?'

Stubbs crossed the road. 'Good afternoon, Sir. You didn't accompany the others?'

'Er ... no. I have to catch the two o'clock bus to Newcastle Emlyn,' he croaked with a soft sing-song Welsh accent.

'Where have the others gone?'

His left arm had a twitch. 'To Cardigan. To eat fish and chips and watch a game of footer ... except for Nina. She's catching a train to London.'

'Is she your ringleader?'

The unkempt face disputed this. 'No ... though she pays for the tea and butties and talks plenty.'

'There's a sort of manic certitude about her.'

'"Swiftness does not win the race."' He quoted the Good Book.

'I'm Sergeant Stubbs and I'm addressing Mr ... ?'

'Heddwyn Inir Jones; a preacher at the Elim chapel.'

'Good afternoon to you.'

'I do not wish anyone ill, Sergeant ... '

'I'm sure you don't, Mr Jones.'

'But ... you understand ... honest service to one's fellow men sometimes means contesting their viewpoint?'

'I do understand that.'

Stubbs sensed that this needy-looking fellow rarely ate a square meal. 'Would you care for some lunch Mr Jones ... before your bus comes?'

'Er ... that's most kind, Sergeant.'

'I'm about to be relieved ... I'm sure we could conjure up an extra plate of stew.'

*　　*　　*　　*

In the Officers' Mess, the R.A.F. visitors were joined by Colonel Trewick – the Camp Commandant – who recited grace.

'O God, who lends us life, lend us also grateful hearts.'

'Amen.'

They sat down and lunch was served by girls of the Army Catering Corps in their cinnabar-edged dark green jackets and skirts, whilst green linen napkins were being spread on laps.

The most senior of the visitors – Air Vice-Marshal Sir David Fairweather – sat to the Colonel's left.

'I recall that grace at Repton, Colonel.'

Trewick looked surprised.

'You were two years below me.'

'Ah, indeed. "Boney" Maloney chose it. It's Shakespeare.'

'"Boney" did not refer to Napoleon ... he was just "bone" idle.'

'That was old Smithy. He had names for everyone.'

Tomato soup laced with brandy and cream formed the starter.

'He called me "the tin miner"?'

'Based on "By Tre-, Pol- and Pen-, you shall know Cornishmen"?'

'Quite.'

'But your accent is ... Borders?'

'You've a good ear. "Trewick" is a Northumbrian name. There's an old saying; "When Harry Hotspur went a-reiving, the Bewicks and the Trewicks were the first to saddle up."'

'When the tithe or the sheep tax failed to bring in enough silver?'

Trewick smiled, but dissembled.

The main course was Dover sole, new potatoes and broad beans. Plain meals were the order of the day.

Mainland mentioned the Soviet parallel to *Bloodhound*. 'It uses a liquid propellant and is based on the Third Reich's "Wasserfall" project. It's NATO codename is "Barbara".'

'The future of air warfare is increasingly model-based,' submitted North.

'Human courage though, still must play a part?' Trewick countered.

'Perhaps more in the Army.'

'The first trial of this *SA-1cx* took place in 1952, but it fell over on launch and exploded ... in spite of being designed by German engineers.'

'*Wunderbar.*'

'A firework display?' queried Stackhouse.

'A Catherine wheel or a girandole?'

'A shuper shizzling shpectacle,' frothed Greenwood.

A reticent humour ballooned.

'There's a song, *Wunderbar Barbara in her Wonder-bra.*'

Even North cracked. 'Well, it clearly went "tits-up".'

'And perhaps an extra train to Siberia?'

'The cove in charge is German-Jewish ... or *was*.'

'Doubly unfortunate ... a tiny pogrom?'

A large solid silver candelabrum – taken during the

Crimean campaign – stood in the centre of the table. Its incused legend read; 'Sebastopol 1855.'

'One hundred years ago,' observed Group Captain Stackhouse. 'An era of consensus ... of common outlook.'

'Meaning?'

'A more natural coherence in our society ... not riddled with faction or polemic?'

As the circulating sauce-boat of Hollandaise sauce reached him, Trewick said, 'The clock sadly cannot be turned back. Tight-knit medieval societies and suits of armour are out.'

Sir David offered an olive-branch. 'We are I think, between two worlds.'

Tug took up the baton. 'Folk-lore and magic give character, not logic.'

North mused, 'Even if technology is spiritually a golden calf, it is still necessary ... to face down the Red Terror of Muscovy.'

Tug disliked this fellow's gold-rimmed spectacles, his thin nostrils and his 'Bay Rum' after-shave. A slight frost loomed until he remembered that one ought at least to *appear* magnanimous.

A sturdy girl sergeant finished decanting white wine into their conical glass goblets.

Trewick stood up and proposed an impromptu toast. 'Gentlemen, *anglichanye*!'

All grinned, rose and raised their glasses. '*Anglichanye*!'

*   *   *   *

Stubbs escorted Jones to the Sergeants' Mess, where another sergeant rolled an eye-ball over the ham-bone in rags.

'He's my guest thank you, Mr Baynes.'

Stubbs and Jones sat down with bowls of lamb stew.

'My Grandfather was a Methodist minister ... and I played a B-flat trombone in the chapel band ... but I've not heard of this "Elim" set-up.'

'"Elim" is an oasis described in the Book of Exodus. It had springs and palm-trees and lay between Egypt and Canaan ... between captivity and the "Land flowing with Milk and Honey"; so a resting place on the journey to the Promised Land.'

The listener attended closely.

'I feel that my place is in the Army. It's unfashionable ... but if you can *think*, being unfashionable is inescapable.'

'There are indeed false prophets ... self-flatterers ... who bow to the baalim and propose a do-as-you-choose cliché-stamped freedom.' Jones speared a piece of meat.

Despite his infirmities, the preacher spoke with a decorous and artless gravity.

'And the more intuitive are despised like spam fritters?'

Jones paused in his chewing. 'Good teachers will always rebut catchwords.'

On a rough stone wall beyond the window, a bullfinch stood with the burst of red on his breast and black and white wings.

'The wonders of God's creation.'

Two dishes of rhubarb pie and custard – pale yellow with a reddish swirl – descended, courtesy of Mr Baynes.

'Thank you, Daniel.

Mr Jones, can I ask you about your "associates"?'

The *bijou* vinegar-bottle Danish hoyden it seemed, had cleaned windows until her cannabis fags caused her to fall off her ladder and break an arm.

Stubbs nodded. 'And Nina?'

'Her real name's Hayley ... Hayley Ellyard. I saw her picture in a local newspaper.'

Stubbs cocked an eyebrow.

'Last month ... June ... climbing up a drain-pipe ... she fell and gashed her leg.'

'A drain-pipe?'

'It was in Ebbw Vale ... some flats beside a slag-heap.'

'How appropriate.' Stubbs sipped his water.

'It was allegedly a Tory M.P.'s secret love-nest.'

Stubbs gleaned that Nina came from a village in Sussex, where a tablet in the church bore a dedication to her great-grandfather, a pew-opener there for thirty-one years.

'She sees it as degrading that someone in her family should be so craven as to scrape to the gentry.'

'Pews were like boxes then?'

'Some were reserved. The squire's family usually had the front one.'

'The driver of that potato van held the door open for Nina, I noticed.'

'He's called Sandy ... he worked on a kibbutz once.'

Stubbs was making mental notes.

'I tried to learn Biblical Hebrew once, but found it too hard.'

'You would probably need lessons?'

'It was not the script, but the verbs.'

There was a pause. 'When you see your peace-activist

friends again, it might be wise *not* to mention this meal?'

'I could not be dishonest, Sergeant.' Jones eyed his host curiously, almost with disappointment.

Despite this *faux pas*, Stubbs's instinct told him that Heddwyn would stay mum.

Outside a dark green six-wheeled Sentinel lorry with white lettering on it – 'G.P.O. Central Stores Division' – was about to leave and Stubbs heard 'Newcastle Emlyn' spoken.

'Could you give Mr Jones here a lift?'

'We're not allowed ... ' the driver began, but on glimpsing a proffered packet of *Senior Service*, added, 'but maybe I can risk it. Hop in.'

*　　*　　*　　*

Lunch ended, lips were dabbed and this dyed-in-the-wool company moved through to the bar for 'bracers'.

Sir David eyed a large varnished wooden propeller, which according to its brass plaque had been shot off a German A.E.G. bomber.

'The anti-aircraft regiment now based here were stationed near Beauvais in 1918, where they shot it off an enemy intruder,' expounded Trewick.

'But what's so special about *this* propeller?' Sir David queried.

'Well ... it's all they ever shot down.'

The Air Vice-Marshal looked up in surprise. 'Goodness ... perhaps we *do* need *Red Duster* then.'

'If successful, it's to be deployed to defend the new V-Bomber bases?' Trewick inquired.

'Yes. Progress has been slow. They began on it in 1949 … six years since.'

'Rocketry design hiccoughs?'

'That side has gone quite smoothly … more the novel electronics … and some bureaucratic delays of course.'

'All pioneering stuff.

Did you see in yesterday's paper, that a former Southern Rhodesian Air Force officer had been killed just outside Salisbury … with an old hunting spear?'

Sir David, who was naturally sincere, said, 'Rumour says that a communist agent – thought to be East German – did it.'

Trewick frowned. 'Why?'

Fairweather side-stepped this question. 'The killer escaped, supposedly on a lorry under a load of coffee sacks.'

They circulated and David drew Stackhouse who talked about the new Gloster *Javelin* all-weather night fighter.

'The *Gladiator* was the last Gloster I flew.'

'I've never flown a biplane,' said Stackhouse simply.

Trewick, guided perhaps by some obscure destiny, encountered Tug Orr-Ellis.

'A drink, Wing Commander?'

'Oh … a brandy and splash please, Colonel.'

They approached the bar and Trewick ordered. 'Did you have a pleasant journey down?'

'Yes … just those pacifists at the main gate hurling some spurious balderdash at David and myself as we drove in.'

'That's par for the course. Does "genuine balderdash" exist?'

'Perhaps in the Army?' Tug cocked an amused eyebrow.

Trewick smiled benignly.

The wizened bar-steward measured out two singles before adding some bitter cherry and lemonade.

'That little bald guy kicked our rear wheel and bellowed something at us.'

'He,' remarked the Colonel, 'was a boxer in his youth.'

'A boxer? Did he work for a parcels company?'

'What? Oh yes. Very funny. Someone else asked, "Was he a paper-weight?"'

They laughed and clinked glasses. 'You're on good terms with Sir David?'

'I was his navigator in the war ... for three years we flew Halifaxes.' Tug sipped his drink. 'It creates a bond.'

'Naturally. Do you still fly?'

'No. I'm in "Communications" now at High Wycombe.'

Trewick looked bashfully down at his well-polished shoes to cover a hiatus.

'Have you seen this?' He led his guest to a framed fading sketch of a huge butterfly amid some succulent vegetation, drawn – the label stated – by Baden-Powell in Turkey in 1909.

The visitor examined it without result.

'In the butterfly's wings are disguised drawings of Ottoman artillery emplacements.'

'So! A real Boy Scout,' murmured Tug. 'The Turks were the baddies then. No tiresome caveats. And no apologist home-grown non-patriots.'

'True,' the Colonel acknowledged. Yet though disenchanted with post-war Britain, was there something falsely two-dimensional about Tug? Was he using it in some way as a pretext? 'Today we face *avant-garde* charlatans ... '

'Who hate this country … and who drop shiny "window" whilst urging us to lower our guard?'

Trewick thumbed his left ear-lobe. 'Humanity though will hopefully win through … so the unprincipled ought not to cause us undue alarm.'

'Feudal allegiances finally ebbed away in the twenties … my father pins it exactly to 1926. Now it's all business and economics … which creates an incipiently restless society.'

'Yet we survived the Conquest and the Reformation. History is never static.' Trewick cleared his throat, hid his suspicions and smiled. Perhaps he had just read too many Agatha Christie novels?

CHAPTER FIVE

In Lincolnshire, Stephanie Chalk switched off her sewing-machine. She had – after many snags – finished a costume for her niece who was to play Cordelia in King Lear.

She stood up, stretched and on tip-toe, touched the ceiling.

A clock chimed two-thirty and her Border collie padded up to her.

'Goodness. Is that the time?

Walkies, Jack?' She pulled on her coat, boots and mittens and took him out for an unusually late walk.

The village of Haxey lay under a clear if sombre sky and a burnished coppery half-moon shone shyly. They passed dark sleeping cottages, crossed a steeply-cambered road and headed up a track sign-posted 'Nun's Cross Farm'.

An owl hooted and the dog's ears pivoted.

Then came the low growl of a diesel engine, which seemed strange at this hour.

Stephanie, who was quite bonny yet curious in temperament, stopped beside an old moss-encrusted obelus and looked out over the ghostly allotments.

An excavator was digging a pit, watched by three motionless figures.

Then a rabbit hopped by and Jack gave a rough, sharp bark.

The thinnish young woman glanced round and glimpsing the watcher, nudged her two loose-limbed Yahoo-like companions. They all turned and strode towards the road.

A frightened Stephanie ducked into a thicket, held Jack's mouth shut and looked up at the crystal stars.

*   *   *   *

Sir David Fairweather and his wife Marion sat on their verandah in Higham Ferrers.

He folded up his Sunday paper.

'Some Labour parliamentarians are calling our new anti-aircraft missile "provocative",' he remarked. 'Given that it's defensive, that's illogical.'

'I doubt that worries them. Being seen as rebels adds a dash of colour to their drab lives.'

Sir David spread salted butter and Cooper's marmalade onto a slice of toast taken from the cracked Coalport china toast-rack.

'Outlaws tend to be popular … I suppose because we're all cheesed off with paying taxes and such … but I sense a more sinister design in some of this anti-defence rhetoric.'

Marion wrote short stories for magazines. 'If we lived in the Middle Ages dear, we might applaud the sheriff for curbing reprobates who wished to rob us or shoot arrows through our windows, but script-writers never choose that side of the story.'

David's expression was of dry amusement. His outlook though was firmly anchored in an England of thirty years before – the *status quo ante bellum* – 'O' gauge tin-plate toy trains and Sunday-school plays where Saint George kills the Turk. 'Perhaps I'm over-reacting. As Geoffrey Mainland says, "We have to 'adapt'."'

And yet he did not really believe it. Serious concerns within the British military about fifth-columnist politicians existed. Both Trades Union leaders and duplicitous Oxford intellectuals wished it seemed to affiance the country to haywire or gilded horizons; to menacing tombstones; brutes ruling the timorous; the crème de la Kremlin.

Recently a leak had led to a newly modified radar destined for Fassberg in West Germany and due to be trialled there in a *Canberra*, being stolen *en route*.

Their daughter Sally, came out.

Marion stood up. 'Anyway dear, open your new book and don't upset yourself.'

Self-assured and wearing mud-streaked riding boots, wide navy jodhpurs and a faded red satin top, Sally asked, 'What's it about, Daddy?'

'Railway signals,' said Marion, nonplussed.

Sally smiled the knowing smile of youth.

Her horse was slothful and flabby. David called it 'Göring' or sometimes other epithets. 'Off you go dear. Dig your spurs into that barrage balloon.'

Sally gave him a peck, before she and her mother left.

Fairweather had been to early Communion, his faith underscored by two close scrapes in the war. He believed also that the Bible kept society lowly and honest.

An endless bombardment of false weights and trite sentiments were urging the populace towards a more leisurely, yet subtly degraded existence.

In contrast to pre-war days too, life had become markedly utilitarian. Marion had advertised for a maid four times since 1947, but domestic service seemed to be no longer anyone's cup of tea.

Tug rolled up as arranged to draw up a plan for a squadron reunion dinner.

'There's a Temperance Hall near Barry Island which is spacious and attractive,' said David. 'It has a wooden disc too, which calculates when you've had enough to drink.'

'And some samples to test it with?'

David grinned.

'Surely the only possibilities are, "Not enough" or "Too much".'

They set off for *The Grey Heron*.

Leaving Higham, Tug had to brake sharply to avoid a crazy motorcyclist. 'Shall I climb out and fold up the drogue-chute?' asked David.

Then a fox slunk out of a coppice and the Jaguar C-type had again to skid to a stop. The animal paused and peered back over its shoulder, briefly static in that distinctively vulpine pose.

Tug swore. 'I recently flew out to El Adem. Sahara-dwelling golden hyaenas apparently creep into the camp to scavenge.

Squiffy landed a *Beverley* there and squashed one with its undercarriage ... buckling the sproggle pin.'

'Lucky he didn't slew off the runway.'

'These animals – like foxes – are not it seems, in the habit of looking upwards.'

'A Blackburn *Beverley*? How long is the runway?'

'Three thousand yards? A foot or so of ferro-concrete on top of a similar depth of hard-core I guess.'

'Built by the Italians?'

'Yes. They say you can chase these hyaenas in a Champ or an R.A.F. fire-tender and shoot them, but it's hard to locate their lairs. They need a good tracker dog.'

'A bloodhound?'

They drew into *The Grey Heron*. Inside, Tug's eye-balls locked on – not too discreetly – to the serving girl's boobs.

'Twin carburettors?'

David gave him a disapproving frown.

Tug ordered and asked the girl her name.

'Belinda,' she said without enthusiasm.

'You're a pretty lass.'

'What are you buying me for Christmas?'

They sipped their drinks and found a table.

'No anti-cyclone developing there. It's called "punching above your weight". You're twice her age.'

'That means nothing.'

David unzipped his jacket. 'How's Ellinor?'

Tug's Swedish wife, a professional singer, like Belinda wore close-fitting blouses which displayed her elevated breasts to good effect.

Tug sighed. *'La bella sirena*? Don't ask.'

She had a finishing-school type charm, but David also thought her quite decent.

Two plates of bubble-and-squeak were placed before them. Belinda gave Tug a wry look. 'Is that your Jag out there?'

Tug winked.

She smiled and waltzed off.

Fairweather had seen ex-colleagues go off the rails. The anti-climax at the end of the war had drawn some into risky schemes – hoping to revive their fortunes – or in others an emptiness had led to excesses of Speyside whisky, poorly masked by a show of counterfeit jollity.

'Tug, old friend,' said David earnestly, 'keep away from dodgy girls.'

'Bright plumage and the dark side of the moon?'

'Precisely.'

'Stick with Miss Millstone?'

They ate whilst editing the list of names for the reunion.

'That Jag cost a tenner.'

David raised his eyebrows.

'My niece's husband ran off with his secretary. He cabled from Switzerland, to ask Emily – my niece – to sell the Jag and pay the money into his account. She said, "Ten pounds? We'll see how far they go with that."'

David had heard a similar story elsewhere.

Back on his verandah, as the descending sun shone through the hawthorn hedge, the Air Vice-Marshal pondered the *Red Duster* project.

On the Woomera Range in southern Australia – in the summer of fifty-three – it had been trialled unsuccessfully due to a defective igniting mechanism for its ramjets.

Now the production of this long-range high-altitude anti-aircraft missile had been awarded to The Bristol Aeroplane Company, its assembly being mostly at their Cardiff works.

His musings drifted to El Adem, the golden hyaenas and the phrase, 'a good tracker dog'. Could those Foreign Office traitors who were intercepting R.A.F. signals intelligence and relaying it to the Kremlin, be tracked to *their* lairs by a ruse involving this new non-canine *Bloodhound*?

The telephone rang.

'Higham Ferrers 32.'

It was Ellinor, looking for Tug.

'He left twenty minutes ago, Ellinor.'

'Oh, thank goodness for that. I was worried he'd gone to Tewkesbury again.' She did not elaborate.

David hesitated. 'Ellinor, does Tug have a niece called Emily?'

'Emily? Yes. She lives in Canada. Why?'

'Oh … nothing.'

With a sense of mutually unspoken doubt, the call ended.

The A.V.M. picked up one of Marion's magazines.

'How to knit a troll … hairy head, big feet, spraggly teeth and a lumpy nose.'

He grinned. Trolls came in all shapes and sizes.

CHAPTER SIX

The Emir Omar climbed the stone stairs of the old governor's palace in Benghazi. In the smoking-parlour or *selamlik*, amid the relics of Ottoman luxury and decadence, he adjusted the brass telescope.

Beyond an almond tree, he could see the level blue bay as through a fine silver dust and a steamship moored in the Old Port. It had a grey hull, a white superstructure, a buff funnel and a red ensign fluttering at its stern. Down its gang-plank marched a line of British servicemen, whilst a crane swung a net laden with kit-bags over to the quay.

Omar spat.

In this land of camels, coffee-pots, tents and sand, their current king – although of the Senussi tribe and so from the Libyan desert – had acted perfidiously in allying himself with the British. He had sullied the green banner of a purified faith.

The inhabitants of this still war-damaged town too, dwelt slothfully and dispiritedly. They lacked a champion, a *ghazi*.

He kicked an antique silver pitcher. Omar's angry yet self-pitying complex saw the Near East's many frictions as stemming from the old imperialist institutions and not from its bent post-colonial régimes.

He swung the telescope on its tripod. A bomb-scarred Italian storehouse, a Turkish bazaar, a courtyard with a small fountain of Saracenic design and the old Turkish fort swept past.

He shouted for his servant. 'Tahir! Coffee and cake

for the Emir!' He habitually used the third person when referring to himself.

An ancient green pennon, pinned to the wall, bore a phrase from the Qur'an embroidered in gold: 'The fear of Allah is the heart of wisdom.'

So far, his efforts here had accomplished absurdly little. Only five believers belonged to 'the veiled ones' – a sect of secret warriors – skirmishers or *tirailleurs*, who sought out and killed lone enemies.

Across the moth-nibbled carpet stood a grotesque Second Empire desk and on it, an antiquated brass telephone.

Omar sat down and dialled nought for the town's exchange. He asked for a number in Cairo. The American 'girlie' calendar on the wall read; September 21: 1955.

'Basil?'

'Mirador?'

'Greetings my friend. A British war-boat has tied up in Benghazi today.'

'A cruiser? A sloop?'

'*H.M.T. Empire Test.*'

'"H.M.T." signifies "Her Majesty's Troopship",' explained the Consul.

The Emir's balding and odd-shaped head settled back into a fusty and embosoming cushion. 'Men are coming ashore ... Air Force ... about sixty.'

'They'll be ground crew.'

'The lorries meeting them are from El Adem.'

'Understood. And thank you my good Lord of Araby. Stay tuned.' He cut the line.

Hamda, a servant girl with bulging eyes and a grey

tabard, brought in a fig cake and a tall brass coffee-pot which she placed on a small stove. 'Is that all, Excellency?'

The British had informers – *escrocs* – and hidden outlying sentries – *guetteurs* – posted around their bases. Why *did* he still use French words? The lingerie-wearing blonde on the calendar seemed to wink at him.

Out on the ancient crenellated harbour ramparts, a cannon boomed.

He knelt for midday prayer, his forehead and palms on the carpet. He was soon distracted though by the thought of his brother in the town's gaol. He dreamt of alchemy and broken chains or … bribes *might* free him?

Back in the summer, six prisoners had escaped through an old water tunnel, out into the dry gravel bed of a wadi. They were enemies of King Idris. The British had caught three of them and they had later been executed by the King's guard.

Ah, bribe money! The mystery of the British sovereigns lost off Susa! His son was taking scuba-diving lessons in Cyprus … a black wet-suit, blue cylinders, a red and grey rubber boat and other theatrical props … ah, and the *lovely* lambent gold!

Did he smell smoke? Was the couscous burning down in the kitchen? 'Hamda!'

He abandoned his perfunctory prayers, rose and poured himself a cup of strong Turkish coffee, eyeing again the semi-exposed boobs of 'Lynn', the enchantress on the calendar.

Violent sexual desires surged through him. How he craved to handle her frilly-clad, cozening, provocative, pale flesh … to probe her vulva.

Tahir appeared with the post. 'You are thinking of something bad, Sire?'

Omar's cold eye fixed him. 'I'm surrounded by gushing myrmidons. No one *does* anything!'

'*El mektub mektub,*' the old and seasoned manservant answered softly. 'What is written is written.'

'My uncle spied for the Italians against the Turks ... He was an *al-Fata* ... an anti-Turkish Arab.'

'But *you* are an Anglophobe, Sire?'

He eyed his butler.

'The British are less brutal.'

'But more subtle. You're a good man, Tahir ... too good.'

'You are kind Master.' Tahir was a 'haji'; he had been to Mecca. 'Beauty is more powerful than strength, Excellency.'

'How can that be?'

'In the film *King Kong*, the effect of the girl's loveliness exceeds the might of the gorilla.'

'Bah! A Hollywood sham.' Omar downed his coffee.

'Lynn' seemed to be watching him. She seemed to know. Ah ... *gardez le sourire.*

'My uncle, ruined by corrupt Turkish tax collectors, fought back. Copying documents in Abu Tucdah – when the doors of the Bab el-Kebir were closed for the night – he crept along the alleyways with an oil-lantern to his mistress – a French Red Cross nurse – and she smuggled the duplicates out. They had coloured matches – red and green – to use as signals.

He was caught, shackled in a dark cell ... and then shot.' Omar's eyes darkened.

'I had an uncle Sire, who was wounded in the Aqaba

episode in 1906 ... and then killed in the Turco-Italian War ... but these things are now a long way behind us.'

'Anyhow, enough.'

Tahir bowed courteously and left.

Omar took out a costly thirteenth-century glazed cup. It was dark green and inlaid with a gold pattern and four red Arabic letters which spelt the archaic word 'jawn' which might mean 'black', 'white' or 'pink'; the scholars were unsure. It had belonged to the Almohad Caliph Idris II al-Wathiq of Marrakesh.

He poured some good French brandy into this goblet, hesitated, scowled and drank.

*　　*　　*　　*

The Aeroflot flight from Zagreb touched down on the runway, bounced once then slowed, its propellers drawing up a flurry of dust as it passed the orange wind-sock.

Walther Coburg peered out over the shimmering wing of the *Lisunov* with its rows of tiny dancing rivets, as it swung round in front of Alexandria Aerodrome's thirties-style terminal building.

He had flown twice before, but still felt relief to be back on *terra firma*.

A searing dry heat – reminiscent of the infamous heat in ships' engine rooms in the Red Sea – engulfed this Prussian die-hard, as he descended the wheeled stairway. The hefty Russian stewardess bid him no cheery farewell, so he redirected his uncommitted gaze to a young girl's hour-glass shape.

As the sun dazzled his eyes, he reminded himself; 'I am

Egon Baus, born in Triftstrasse in Erfurt and now working in Leipzig.'

On this current escapade, he was under Russian control. Bizarrely they anticipated failure but with well-practised knavery, intended to twist it to their advantage.

His exploits had often ended in chaos or pursuit, such that the G.R.U. bozo who had briefed him had labelled him oh-so-wittily 'the bull-with-its-own-china-shop'. He had added, 'Might be useful this time.'

The eleven passengers crossed the sun-softened asphalt to the arrivals' hall, where the Egyptian immigration regulations were displayed in Arabic, English and French.

A stout police sergeant flipped open Baus's passport. He wore a creased uniform shirt and exhibited ill-kept finger-nails, unlike the Germany of the visitor's youth where all officials were spruce and orderly. He resembled more those moronic Soviet border guards until he spoke, when a vein of unwanted humour emerged. Glancing at the letters 'D.D.R.' on the newly-issued passport, he remarked, 'And your real name?'

Sweat beads broke out on Coburg's scalp.

Sergeant Hanne grinned. 'I haven't seen one of these before.'

'No? The German Democratic Republic has existed for six years. It was established in 1949.'

The Egyptian detected the visitor's anxiety. 'Coat collar not turned up?'

'Coat collar?'

Hanne handed the passport back. 'Forgive me Herr Baus – or whatever your name is – I watch too many third-rate movies.' He waved him through, before muttering to his colleague, 'An archaeologist, Nasir? I think not.'

It galled Coburg that his smoke-screen had fooled no one. As he strode to the baggage counter to collect his battered suitcase, he thought, 'Had we won, we would have livened up these slovenly fellahin.'

Lacking aplomb or composure, he could not mimic the old *de luxe* club traveller, nor did he look like a businessman.

In the concourse, he removed his jacket and eyed a brightly coloured *Pan Am* poster whilst waiting for his contact. An elegant air-hostess with a back-drop of a silver airliner on a palm-fringed airfield smiled artificially.

A gold and blue Tutankhamen death-mask clock gave the time as midday, whilst a japanned cartouche of pseudo-hieroglyphs, pinned to a stall, advertised tours. A money-changer thumbed some grubby notes whilst bronze coins dotted an ancient counting-board.

'Herr Baus?'

A girl, tall – partly due to her high-heeled sandals – slender and blonde, accosted him.

'Er, yes?'

She displayed a resourceful smile. 'Unna Engström. I've come to meet you.'

'How do you do. Er ... I was expecting a Herr Neufeld?'

'He took an overdose of bleach three days ago.'

'Oh.' Coburg faltered. 'Is there a correct dose of bleach?'

Unna gave a sardonic smile. 'Perhaps that depends on your opinion of the recipient?'

'Yes.'

'You're a German archaeologist?'

'Er, yes. And you? A Norwegian ... or Norman?'

'Swedish. I am to show you to your hotel and later – in the evening – introduce you to a Professor Nicolotti, an expert on North African excavations.'

In the forecourt they skirted a row of white rocks to reach a dented sun-yellow Ford Zephyr taxi, whose sun-blackened bony driver in a dirt-engrained jellabiya, leant against its wing. This curly-haired Nubian took a last puff on his cigarette, put Baus's case in the boot, climbed in and started the engine.

The tall craggy German sank into the taxi's back seat beside the delectable Swede. His eye caught her long well-shaped legs.

He tried to think of something to say besides, 'Will you go to bed with me later?' He said, 'The immigration sergeant I think, suspected I was an agent of some sort.'

'Don't worry, Herr Baus. Nasser's lot are pro-Soviet. The authorities won't trouble you.'

'Egon, please.'

'I take it there's a *real* archaeologist named "Egon Baus" in East Germany?'

'There is.'

They were silent for a time.

Under a chalky blue sky, stunted thorn bushes bordered the pot-holed road to Alexandria and beyond them lay a flat tawny landscape.

Ulrica's Muscovy counterpart had told Egon what not to do in Egypt. 'Trust no one. You can never reliably judge anyone in North Africa … a scheming and deceitful tribe.'

Unna – like all Europeans here – would be up to something too. Was she a communist? Most likely just sailing under a flag of convenience.

Her behaviour was cool. Her medium blue skirt and yellow blouse reminded him of the Swedish flag and her white socks gave her a schoolgirlish air.

'Where in Sweden do you come from?'

'Skåne ... or Scania. In the south.'

'Can we spend the night together? It might fox anyone who's tracking me?'

She tilted her head back and laughed whimsically. 'No. A meal's fixed though.'

'Professor Nicolotti I take it, will discuss sieves and trowels, trenches and pottery fragments?'

'You *know* what a trowel is?' She smiled teasingly.

Unoffended he replied, 'You're here to police me it seems, not please me?' So no cosy *dénouement*?

'We're going to a club later ... a floor-show. You'll enjoy it.' She patted his hand.

So a 'meeting place' not a 'mating place'. So much for all the anecdotes about Swedes and sex.

The traffic thickened and they passed some commercial premises. A pyramid of BP oil-drums floated by, then a tram rang its bell whilst old men played backgammon outside shabby cafés.

Unna spoke to the driver in Arabic.

This Alexandrian milieu – colourful, gripping, yet incipiently dangerous – contrasted sharply to the villages of East Germany, where small workshops and a humdrum existence lent a quiescent, almost medieval air to life. His nature had been forged by the solid feudal clay of Saxony, yet here the fleeting and insecure character of daily existence lent it a frenzied live-for-the-moment quality.

The older buildings had ornate façades, often with

colonnades or arched windows. The sweep of the famous corniche came into view. Through a slit-wide shot of the beach, he glimpsed a clutch of bathers frolicking, whilst in a basin yachts pitched gently at their moorings and beyond their masts lay the hazy outline of a merchant ship.

They stopped outside the Hotel Ptolemy, a faded puce-tinged block sleeping in the hot afternoon sunshine, its entrance edged with wilting pink tamarisks. Beside it were mediocre cafés and above them, flats with railed laundry-adorned balconies.

Unna led her charge between cars – parked at an angle to the kerb – to enter the cool mosaic-floored reception where Coburg – alias Baus – registered at the desk.

'I'll collect you at eight.'

'Isn't a cabaret a bit public for my meeting this "expert"?'

'I guess that's a part of the plan.'

Walther Coburg felt bewildered. Like a gibbon at the zoo, everyone knew him, but he knew no one. 'Still, keep your worries on a tight leash,' he said to himself as Aboud the porter took his case and ushered him into the cramped lift, with its gilt-edged mirrors and its concertina-like grid of sliding doors.

He tipped the polite baggage-carrier with his only coin and relieved to be alone, flopped down onto the bed.

The adventure stories of his boyhood did not entirely up-stage his own experiences. There spies pretended to read newspapers whilst noting which ships left harbour, before sending Morse signals from radios in attics, where say 'Two blue socks' might mean 'the second cruiser squadron has sailed'. His tasks so far had usually been similarly straightforward.

True, an odd fracas had occurred. On boarding the S.S. *Babylonia*, sailing to East Africa some months before, his pistol had been found and confiscated. Still, he had improvised and killed the renegade double-agent near Salisbury with a spear.

Then some deep-seated need conjured in his mind a craving for Unna, Unna with her springy goat-like gait. He saw her in a short navy gym-skirt and a white T-shirt. He wanted to master her. Turbulence and hauteur fought to overwhelm him.

Was Unna also a part of the plot to draw attention to his visit? Arabs were known to be crazy about blonde European girls. And would she let *them* be wayward with her … for favours? Hard to tell. He though, was clearly not as high on her fantasy list as she was on his.

'Unna, *meine nordische Nymphe*,' he whispered to the pillow. Then he grabbed it ferociously. 'I want to shag you!'

*   *   *   *

The Napier eighteen-cylinder marine diesels of the tank landing ship *H.M.S. Maldon* throbbed whilst cooling water spluttered from an outlet just above her water-line.

Hawsers had been secured to bollards on the stone quay and the Jimmy – a two-ringer – peered down over the fo'c's'le railings as the bow ramp was lowered. It grated on the sloping concrete hard in Tobruk's modest harbour.

From the taffrail of a three-masted xebec – moored to wooden piles which stuck out of the water – two natives with diagonally-set eyes, pretended to gaze down into the water to net fish. '*Roumis,*' one scowled, which meant, 'Infidels'.

Two soldiers with unshouldered rifles, stood on the seaweed-fringed breakwater.

In white uniform shorts and shirt – rather than the home-waters dress with a navy woolly and duffle-coat which he had worn on his motor torpedo boat in the North Sea during the war – the captain – a lieutenant-commander – stood on the bridge near the stern. Above him fluttered from a halyard, a plain yellow 'Q' flag and the flags for '3' and '2' – the ship's pennant number – which together made up the 'entering harbour' signal.

Under the direction of a warrant-officer, four long R.A.F. vehicles drove slowly down the ramp of the squarish grey-painted vessel and up the ribbed concrete to where an infantry platoon stood lined up in the 'at ease' position, beside two khaki-painted A.E.C. Matadors.

The articulated lorries – laden with mysterious equipment concealed under heavily-roped dull blue tarpaulins – were joined by a recce troop of armoured cars from the 16th./5th. Lancers which flew blue and yellow guidons from their thin whippy radio aerials.

The infantry remounted their tilt-covered Matadors at the double and the mixed convoy of buff and blue-grey vehicles moved off along this lack-lustre township's main boulevard, flanked by drab box-like buildings, knotted 'misht' trees and a sprinkling of sullen inhabitants, before picking up the dusty road which ran southwards into the shimmering heat of the Libyan desert and which after fifteen miles led to the airfield at El Adem.

In a scruffy café – formerly 'Il Caffè Rosso' but now

'Helmy's' – the two swarthy locals – Tariq and Makkawi – arrived from the harbour. They threw back bitter black coffees – one flavoured with a drop of vanilla essence and one with orange oil – and chewed dates dusted with icing-sugar to sweeten the dregs.

Zenab, the barmaid removed her interlocked thumbs from her belt and reckoned up the payment using an aged abacus with coloured leaden beads.

The twosome then ambled down a side-alley to the booth of Sameh the sandal-maker. Surrounded by stacks of wooden and canvas sandals and thickly-insect-laden fly-papers, he waved Tariq to his museum-piece wall-mounted telephone.

Makkawi tossed him a five piastre coin. It bore King Idris's effigy, their despised pro-British head of state. His subjects had been mostly pro-Boche during the war.

'Basil? Pascal here. We have watched the roadsteads at Tobruk and Derna ... as you told us and ... '

The shadowy 'Basil' replied, 'This is as I expected. Thank you, Pascal.'

Sameh offered them each a green marzipan ball from a small bronze dish.

'*Allahu akbar.*'

From the neighbouring booths came the aroma of hashish and the whiff of printing inks.

Between some poor hovels and an ancient orange grove, stood a mud-brick ochre-coloured mosque which Tariq and Makkawi entered. Once inside, they bolted the door.

Beneath the carved 'minbar' or lectern sat a *qadi* – or judge – from the Jazira, draped in a white ankle-length long-sleeved suriyah. He had been 'disranked' from being an imam by the theologians of Nishapur for praying to an angel named in the Qur'an as 'Harut' and who had supposedly taught sorcery to the Babylonians.

Together they descended some narrow steps into a cavern and here, amid black barrels and dim red lights, they burnt a sweet aromatic gum – a dark parti-coloured amber-and-brown myrrh – which smoked thickly and imbued the dry air with a sickly fragrance.

'A Russian agent is coming tomorrow. We are to put him up for one night and give him any needful assistance.'

'Payment?'

'Weapons. Six rifles with cleaning kits and twelve hundred rounds.'

'Ah, weapons,' sighed the *qadi*. 'Weapons are all the Soviets understand.'

'The King's fawning ministers cannot be ambushed with words.'

They ignited some beads of a fragrant gum called 'mokrotou'.

'And murdering non-believers is as sweet as raisins,' murmured Tariq. 'You must show indifference to the sufferings of others and also to your own sufferings, for the Prophet says, "Suffering is irreligious; it is a manifestation of self-importance."'

The two Beduin knelt on a worn pink and blue woven mat, shoddily made but pretty, where they lit a hubble-bubble.

They had a money-box with some old Austro-Hungarian Maria Theresa Thalers – still universally recognised as an unofficial currency – and two bundles of well-worn U.S. dollars.

'We have money for tickets and bribes and soon ... weapons.' The trio sat cross-legged in a ring and read from the Qur'an.

British administration had frequently won native acceptance by not imposing needless changes upon their customs, something which by contrast, had baffled German colonial pioneers.

In Libya however, the British had not been successful. Impartial supervision had not dented the morose and cruel touchstone of local superstition nor its silent extravagance of ill-will.

In Egypt and the Sudan, the memory of the harsh days of Turkish rule had bestowed on the British an air of seeming enlightenment. The Turkish governors had been licentious, corrupt and solely fixated on their harems and odalisques, whereas the British had done much to help poor villagers say, by drilling bore-holes for water or giving subsidies to plant sunflowers or corn.

Here though, there was no reverence or rapport.

Tariq took the rubber tube and drew on the mouth-piece of the hubble-bubble, so that the arcane mix of tobacco and hashish glowed with a bright corona.

'With these filthy invaders, we live as on Death Row,' rejoined the *qadi*, 'but without the joy of death to end it. *Allahu akbar.'*

Makkawi took the mouth-piece and inhaled so that again the lump radiated its fiery reddy-orange halo. 'Only cowards fear to fight.'

'And Basil, this "friend of Cyrenaica", may his communist mimeographs be used as toilet paper.

If I froth at the mouth, it is not rabies.'

The threesome drifted into a trance and oblivious to an adulterated world, began to wail.

CHAPTER SEVEN

East of Tobruk, sited on a low hillock, stood an ancient Byzantine watch-tower known as 'Al Mishwaz'. On a foundation of rough Cyclopean blocks rested courses of deformed weather-eroded sandstone ashlars.

A marsh lay to the west, abuzz with midges and the sporadic quack of ducks. Occasionally a mallard flew out of the reeds, trailing its webbed feet across the smooth still water. To the south, beyond a shallow fissured wadi-bed of grey pebbles, began the desert where now the horizontal rosy-orange rays of dawn were lending it a hue of burnt gold. To the east a shallow ravine forested with qaradh trees, provided cover and lastly, to the north, a scar of white beach separated the thinly ebbing sea-foam from dunes topped with combs of sloping yellowy grass.

An Austin Champ and a Saracen armoured troop carrier turned off the coast road and nudged their way into the gorge to hide in a cluster of low dark-green foliage.

Corporal 'Chalky' White scaled the precarious masonry of 'Al Mishwaz' and from its crumbling battlements peered down at the blue Mediterranean, the buff-grey deserted coast road and the patchy ribs of the scorched and scrub-dotted desert. A hot breeze – the *Qordofan* – blew from the south.

He recalled the dingy back-street of his boyhood home in Kendal – the hard times, the shortages – and why he had enlisted.

The telephone wires running along the coast and drooping between steel lattice telegraph poles, passed within a yard of this tower and leaning out over the parapet Chalky hooked a telesonic receiver onto one of the four wires. He repeated this feat, manoeuvring three further devices onto the remaining parallel wires.

A blue jay watched him before fluttering away.

At the base of the tower Staff Sergeant Roy Walsh unwound the drums of thin cable to connect the wires lowered by White to an amplifier in the back of the Saracen.

Sergeant-Major Ness – whose nickname was 'Lovely' – addressed his squad. 'Right lads, surveillance positions.' The sly pesky locals were skilled at creeping around unobserved.

Five privates in berets, khaki shorts, shirts with their sleeves rolled up, long socks and brown so-called 'ammo' boots, were to keep watch in the surrounding scrub.

Two were disposed *en échelon* to the west.

Gutteridge, festooned with bundles of pale grass, had dug a trench.

'"Birnam Wood shall come to Dunsinane."'

Hill lay prone beside a clump of tall green reeds. 'Think about your arc of fire, rhino-brain.'

'I was thinking about the vehemence of the sun, Sir.'

'From here,' Ness indicated a spot some yards to the right, 'you could enfilade the road for half a mile.'

'Ness found Matthews on the reverse slope of a bank facing southwards. 'Good position. Just watch the E.M.B.S.'

'The E.M.B.S., Sergeant-Major?'

'Endless miles of bloody sand.'

The east was the hardest to guard and the most likely direction of any covert approach. Badger lay in shadow beneath a dark oleander bush watching a green beetle climb slowly up a stalk until an unimpeded breeze blew it off. Seymour watched the ravine end-on, to spot anyone crossing it.

Back at the Saracen, Major Dardry lit a cigarette. 'The arcs described by telephone wires are not parabolic, Sergeant.'

'Are they not, Sir?'

'No. They're hyperbolic ... equations of the form $y = \cosh e^x + \cosh e^{-x}$ ... plus or minus a few constants.'

'Indeed, Sir,' replied Walsh, moving his eyebrows meaningfully to himself.

Major Dardry – of The Royal Corps of Signals – spoke fluent Arabic. Wearing ear-phones and resting a note-book on his knee, he sat in a canvas chair beside the Saracen's opened rear doors.

A flattish-topped samr tree lent him its shade.

Randomly tapped calls were usually mere gossip, but had thrown up the odd nugget. A Beirut journalist, ringing the editor of the Tripolitan *Sunday Ghibli*, had leaked a plot about an Egyptian assassin being sent to the Kingdom of Yemen or North Yemen as it was later referred to. This English-language weekly newspaper did not run the story, but a description of Nasser's agent was passed to the Yemeni court.

Corporal 'Topper' Jenkins brought the Major a cup of tea and a bully-beef bun.

'Jenkins, you're a religious man? What do you know about this tree?'

'It's sprouting plenty of thorns, Sir.'

'It's a "samr" tree, Corporal. They yield frankincense.'

'Do they, Sir?'

'Now the best frankincense – a very pale yellow, almost white variety – comes from the southern coast of Arabia, the so-called "Incense Coast". Once it was borne by dhows up the Red Sea to the Gulf of Aqaba.'

'Like the Queen of Sheba coming to King Solomon, Sir?'

'There's hope for you yet, Corporal.'

Jenkins gave a strained grin. 'Thank you, Sir.'

Suddenly the Saracen began to rock.

'Walsh!' the Major bellowed.

But it was not Walsh jumping onto its roof, but a slight earth-tremor.

'Er ... Jenkins, make sure the sentries have enough water.'

'Sir.'

An officer has his boots polished, meals served et cetera, but he must look after his men.

Dardry heard a crackle, then, 'Pascal' talking to 'Basil'. Hmm ... strange names.

At twelve forty, local time, on this Monday the third of October, the caller spoke of *H.M.S. Maldon* and her mystery cargo. Pascal, Dardry deduced, had to be in Tobruk.

'Basil' would be a code-name for some Warsaw Pact spoof, probably Georg von Collen, the East German Consul in Cairo. An amateur Arabist, he lived in the Bab el Louk, an old Arab quarter.

Their tracking of the consignment of *Bloodhound* missiles had been anticipated ... and yet 'Basil' sounded unsurprised, even disinterested ... as if he already knew.

Then someone spoke prematurely, before the caller rang off. 'Hey, Tariq, do you ... ' Click.

Major Dardry took a second cigarette from the packet in his left-hand breast pocket, tapped it, then on reflection, replaced it.

Only an occasional vehicle passed by on the coast road, but from an Arab *douar* – a huddle of tents – a mile to the west, came a man in a coarse dark-orange-coloured gown.

Hill raised his binoculars.

The telephonic *coup* had disclosed to Dardry that someone was tracking the *Bloodhound* deployment, despite possibly suspecting it to be a ruse.

This was convoluted and required thought. He muttered, 'They also serve who sit and ponder.'

Hill's target crept towards a small isolated farmstead with an Italianate villa nestling beside a copse of eucalyptus trees. Furtively he started to fill a bag with tangerines. 'These dollops aren't called "shites" for nothing,' thought Hill. Still, no threat to their operation.

'Walsh? Are any of our "friends" in or around Tobruk called "Tariq"?' queried Dardry.

The Staff Sergeant jumped down into their foliage-filled chasm. 'There's a Tariq al-Hanafi in Derna, Sir. His brother was one of the smugglers caught with those crates of rifles, back in June.'

Dardry massaged his jowls. Thirty early bolt-action rifles and two hundredweights of ammunition had been captured, supplied from Algeria by a disloyal *goum* in the police there.

A platoon of infantry had lain in ambush for two days

in an olive plantation. Then some baggy-trousered zouave deserters had advanced from the south with a string – or *cafila* – of shadowy camels. You did not step out and challenge these men ... unless you had a suicide wish.

Their leader had been al-Hanafi's brother.

When stealthily repositioned, the soldiers had quietly peered along the sights of their light-machine-guns and rifles and then the shooting had begun.

The leader's body had ended up with twenty-two bullet wounds.

'Al-Hanafi drives a green Panhard van, Sir.'

'Tell the men to embus, Jenkins.'

'Sir.'

As the Saracen and the Champ drove along the coast road back towards Tobruk, by a stroke of good fortune a green van headed towards them in a small cloud of dust.

Ness, driving the Champ, turned it broadside on, leapt out and flagged it down.

Under the evenly blue sky the van slowed sharply and attempted a hasty three-point turn. After two rifle rounds – one through a door and one through a tyre – it slewed into a shallow dry ditch.

The driver struggled out with a grazed and slightly bloodied shoulder.

'He looks nervous, Sir.'

'Let's pretend to be angry. Scare him.'

Tariq had a very Semitic face ... hooked nose, modest beard, a thick continuous eyebrow.

'Hands up,' Ness ordered. One arm rose.

Dardry strolled to within two yards of the scrawny savage, whilst Walsh padded him, found a revolver and a grubby letter which he handed to the Major.

'Haste and good work do not go well together, Tariq,' Jenkins observed.

'*Les Anglais … toujours la politesse,*' came the Arab's sour riposte.

'You are insulting the Queen's writ. We dislike *farceurs.*'

Ness looked baffled. '*Farceurs?*'

'"Jokers … idle bastards",' explained Matthews. 'A rough translation.'

Dardry took the lead. 'Who's "Basil"?'

Tariq pretended not to understand Dardry's fluent Arabic.

An elaborate silence followed before Dardry reiterated, '"Basil"?'

'I know no "Basil".' His extravagant dissent and one-handed gesticulating underlined that he *did* know.'

From the half-capsized van Walsh retrieved a dirty sack which when emptied produced a couple of hundred old silver budju coins and two wads of American dollars.

'What's this for?' asked the Major.

'For repairing the mosque in Tobruk.'

Dardry gave an ironic smile. 'Very likely.' He thumbed the U.S. one-dollar greenbacks. 'If you want these back, tell us who "Basil" is.'

The swarthy cur's long dark brow tilted gracelessly downwards in its centre. 'Tapping the Libyan Telephone Company's lines is illegal.'

'I doubt King Idris will object?'

Al-Hanafi spat violently.

'But his treacherous subjects do, Sir,' put in Walsh.

'The good master will evict the wicked servant.'

Another gelatinous globule hit the dusty road.

'Phlegm producing organs working well, Tariq?' Jenkins observed.

'We know the name of the Queen of Sheba, Corporal. Her name has recently been unpicked by some palaeographist. It's "Bilqis".'

'Sir.'

'But ... who is "Basil"?'

'No one knows, it seems.'

'We have here about a "ratl" of silver too. Now a "ratl" was a medieval Syrian measure of weight Tariq ... Did you know that?'

Tariq glared at him.

'Well, if you want it returned, you'll have to rattle your brains, al-Hanafi ... if not we'll use it to buy alcohol and pork scratchings for the mess.'

'His salivary glands have dried up, Sir.'

The Army's way was not to 'bag' a bandit, at least not for such as this. To kill or not to kill? The soldier's dilemma, which only God may truly judge.

'A penny – or half your money back – for your barbarian thoughts, Tariq?'

'Basil is the East German Consul in Egypt.'

'Name?'

'Von Collen.'

'Here's your silver. And how do you know His Munificence?'

'I don't. I was just given his number.'

'And?'

'And told to watch for your airplane *sayeds* landing equipment.'

'By whom?'

'Solly Isaacs.'

'Try again.'

'Xorios the Greek?'

'And again.'

'The Emir Omar in Benghazi?'

'Here are your dollars ... and we'll pull your van out of that hollow.'

Tariq, eyed the van's flat tyre.

'Drive slowly and you'll be all right,' said Matthews, a mechanic doing his National Service. 'Might need a new wheel afterwards, but you've money enough for that.'

Tariq scowled.

*   *   *   *

The hotel had seen brighter days.

From his narrow fourth-floor balcony, Baus peered down at the street below.

Children played in a sea-front park, whilst out in the bay a Blue Funnel Line cargo ship lay at anchor and behind her, the blurred outlines of level-luffing cranes twinkled in the late-afternoon sun, which threw a wavy greenish flare across the surface of the Eastern Harbour.

The tear-off calendar read; Monday the third of October, 1955.

Two days ago he had been in dreary war-battered Leipzig, now he was in giddy intrigue-ridden Alexandria.

An atlas recollected from his school-days had included a map of the Near East. It must have pre-dated the Italo-Turkish war as Libya had been coloured yellow, signifying

Ottoman rule. The sparse town names – Jidda, Madina, Beyrout, am Ma'an, Basrah, Aqabah and Stamboul – had been printed in now out-dated spellings.

Libya awaited him with few places to hide. If cornered he was to defect to the stuffy British. His Soviet controller – Colonel Zaharoff – expected this to happen. He had said, 'At El Adem, thermometer up but thumb-o-meter down.'

'As with Roman emperors at gladiatorial fights?'

'Quite.' He had given the 'thumbs down' sign.

'And then?'

'Then "Operation Eisvogel" comes into its own. You confess your alleged purpose ... but add in some hokum.'

'What hokum?'

'That will be drilled into you presently. A significant effect we anticipate, for a tiny outlay.'

'Am I the "tiny outlay"?'

The Russian had smiled sardonically. 'You win too ... ending up in the West?'

Walther had demurred, but Zaharoff was no fool.

'Prussian roulette. The bullet hits the firer.'

Coburg – or Egon as he now was – took a bath.

Amid the suds, conjectures about his cousin drifted through his mind. Ulrica went in and out of East Germany with surprising frequency and ease. 'Surprising' because her senior position in the H.V.A. made her seem too valuable an asset to risk abroad. There was more to her than just being a spy-mistress, but what? Life was one insoluble and endless labyrinth.

Making the best of his white shirt, red tie and third-class suit, he tried also to adjust his Teutonic mind to this city of eddies and quicksands ... and to Unna, lovely buoyant desirable Unna with her seeming Nordic purity.

He tried to picture her dour Lutheran upbringing; a wooden house beside a fjord; fishing in the inlet in the morning haze; helping to log young birches for fire-wood or scything hay on small slopes whilst herrings dried on poles and a distant sawmill buzzed. Would boys have kissed her in the churchyard?

At ten to eight, spruced up and ready, he heard a screech of brakes and shouts. Going to the balcony, he glimpsed in the dusk-pervaded street below, a dark green Buick *Super Coupé* with large red rear-lights. Dark figures moved towards it.

The passenger door opened swiftly and an elegant female leg emerged followed by a foreshortened Unna as seen from above. The shiny flying-saucer attempted to glide away, making a left turn, but after fifty yards machine-gun-fire into a rear tyre brought it to a halt.

Ringed by soldiers, its suited driver climbed out and stood in the surrender position with his hands on its roof. He was handcuffed and searched, whilst Unna seemed to have disappeared.

There was a knock at the door.

Baus – a rugged but frightened monolith – sweated as he opened his door cautiously.

Unna forced her way in quickly, breathing rapidly.

'What's happening?' he asked.

'Egon, I need to leave something with you.'

She extracted a beige envelope from her blue leather shoulder-bag, stood on a chair and dropped it behind the wardrobe.

'What is it?'

She spoke decisively. 'A ploy ... a safeguard.'

'For whom?'

'For me. It won't incriminate you.'

'But ... '

'You're an Eastern Bloc agent. The government here's pro-Soviet and anti-American. You're untouchable.' She made an effort to smile at him. 'Give me a minute to recover ... then we'll set off to the cabaret.'

'That envelope ... '

'I'll explain later.'

Another mystery-stuffed woman. Everything was like trying to take hold of jelly.

As they left, Egon knelt and reached round the door, placing a tumbler of red juice just behind it.

*   *   *   *

A bristly golden hyaena sniffed its way slowly across the sand-dusted limestone plateau beneath a three-quarter moon.

It crept into the shadows beside a buff-painted hangar whose lower part consisted of concrete and whose upper sections were of steel. He was heading for the swill-bins at the rear of the cook-house.

At the main gate of the combined Army and Air Force base at El Adem, the flag-pole stood stark and bare as the Union Jack had been lowered at sunset. Nearby two R.A.F. Regiment sentries kept watch beside the guard-house.

Beyond a row of dusky brown canvas bivvies, some pre-fabricated wooden huts and a semi-underground concrete air-raid shelter, lay a large apron with white-painted stones along one edge. On this, the M.T. or motor transport square – which consisted of oblongs of concrete divided by joints of black pitch – were parked in a neat line the four blue-grey R.A.F. low-loaders, debarked from *H.M.S. Maldon* that morning.

Beside them two soldiers in khaki-drill shirts, shorts and berets and each shouldering a Lee-Enfield No. 4, walked slowly up and down on sentry-go.

'You're quiet tonight Stockley.'

'Well ... I thought of a couple of interjections, Corporal, but they were not of my usual high standard.'

'Interjections? A big word.'

Whilst re-tethering a tarpaulin which had slipped, they had taken a peek under it.

'Corporal Stafford, may I speak?'

'If it's funny or useful boy, then proceed.'

'Why are we stood 'ere guarding this 'eap of scrap iron?'

Stafford looked at the low-loaders with their odd-shaped cargo. 'A good question, indeed ... if it is scrap iron? What we think is junk though, the top brass might see differently?' Then he added, 'But they usually misjudge things ... like that sortie last Tuesday ... "Oops! Slight hitch chaps ... no map."'

'I'll bet you two bob Sir, this stuff's nothing.'

Stafford replied, 'I'm not a gambling man ... Hey, look!'

Stockley saw the hesitating hyaena too. He knelt and took aim at about sixty paces.

In the Officers' Mess they heard the shot.

The junior officer on duty – deserting his filet mignon, new potatoes and cabbage – darted out onto the verandah followed by others including the Cumberland Yeomanry's Colonel.

Stafford ran up to the verandah rail, saluted and pointed into the shadows by the water-tower.

'A hyaena, Sir. Dead.'

Colonel Goodman's face was thin, almost gaunt, with slightly bulging thyrotoxic eyes and a measure of natural nobility. With little self-conceit, his speech was unflowery and sparing. 'Very good, Stafford.'

Stafford saluted again and departed. Most of the officers drifted back to their home-style fare – for they ate no native dishes – though Goodman stayed awhile and gazed at the R.A.F. trailers.

Having been informed by Dardry of the telephone call between one 'Pascal' and the East German Consul in Egypt, it seemed likely that the Ruskies had both taken the bait and yet knew the game; strange.

The moon was high up over the desert, its harsh treacly light passing over the tops of a few palm trees.

Could an enemy agent physically come to such a barren spot and not stand out ... unless he were already here?

As a young man Goodman had spent many evenings seated outside a tent beside an oasis with a red fire fed by camel dung, sipping 'shay bi nana' – mint tea – and watching tiny green lizards before sleeping on a rough 'angareb' mat, whilst the camels snored and shuffled, each tethered by a rope or so-called 'agal'.

The older officers were not interested in the twentieth-century's obsessions with motive or such digressions as 'explorations of conscience', but rather wished simply to anchor their lives to solid colourful truths. They liked landscapes and seasons and thought it vaguely godless or even foolish to delve too deeply into the 'whys' of life.

'Intellect' was for dried-up souls, for the seekers of artificial non-light and for those who enjoyed misleading themselves.

These officers in turn were exiled by modern leanings, their laurel wreaths those of an increasingly disregarded page of history.

*   *   *   *

In the warm evening air, they walked to the cabaret club.

The ochre-rendered tenement blocks had heavily-barred ground-floor windows. On a balcony a Copt quietly chanted his evening litany.

At the entrance to *The Blue Ibis*, fairy-lights twinkled in an arch of cypresses.

A Moor in a white dishdash and a black cummerbund, gave a modest bow.

'Good evening *Aenisa* ... and *Sayed*.'

'Good evening, Nagi.'

In the open-air venue they chose a table to one side, near some bushes with leaves of a deep pink.

Unna eyed the menu. 'The cook's Lebanese ... so the food's good.'

'I am very hungry,' Egon admitted.

'Did you not eat on the plane?'

'It was Russian.'

'That means "no", I take it?'

'Correct.'

A stiff, almost robotic, *suffragi* marched up to them,

deposited two glasses and a carafe of water before saluting and presenting arms with a stick.

Unna smiled kindly. 'His name's Ba, one of Farouk's former royal guards ... gone mad.'

'So, that envelope?'

Unna inflated her lungs. 'The Suez Mercantile Bank went bankrupt this afternoon and those papers must *not* be destroyed.'

'Why?'

'They prove embezzlement by the bank's chiefs, in collusion with two high-level politicians.'

'The collapse was orchestrated?'

'Quite.'

'Who was the man with you ... in the Buick?'

'Gerry J. Dawkins, chief cashier and the brains behind the Baltimore-Egyptian Reversible Bonds.'

'Complicit?'

'Absolutely, but they want to dress him up as the sole offender.'

'The crooked temples of high finance? Perhaps socialism *does* have a point?'

'Nasser's lot *are* socialists.'

'As was Hitler.'

Other diners were being ushered in. *Sofraci* in white jackets and black trousers, uttered compliments flattering and deferential, though wholly insincere.

Egon viewed two Americans in rakish Panamas with their *filles de joie*. Some native businessmen in spivish suits joined a *louche*-looking government official.

More picturesque was the Bey Abdul Osman with wife number three swathed in avocado-green muslin, a sylph-like mistress displaying abundant bright jewellery and a futah-wearing 'cup-bearer' or body-guard.

Unna whispered, 'He's a major arms dealer. The title "Bey" is bogus.'

Egon sensed her warm breath on his cheek.

She wore an uneven gold ring on her left middle finger, a flared dusky-blue linen skirt and a thin white blouse.

'I had hoped to be posted to Norway in the war, but no one asks for your preferences ... so it was Italy.'

'Brighter skies, at least ... although Scandinavian summers are quite warm.'

Ba padded up more softly, this time with champagne and mini-blancmanges.

'*Shókran*,' said Unna.

'I don't speak a word Arabic,' confessed the German.

She pointed to the water. '*Myah*.'

'*Myah*,' he repeated.

She indicated herself. '*Al bint*. That's "the girl".'

'*Al bint*.'

'So, now you know *two* words.'

Egon tapped Unna's knee, as two oily-looking specimens headed their way.

She turned, stood up and smiled politely.

'*Signorina*.'

'*Mon chevetaine*. May I introduce Herr Baus ... Professor of Ancient History at Leipzig?'

Egon rose.

Unna continued. 'Professore Ottavio Nicolotti ... Mr Hani al-Qalanisi.'

Baus shook hands with restricted grace.

'*Herr Professor. Guten Abend*.' The bronzed and raffish

Italian – who had a pore-pitted nose and a gold tooth – paraded a false smile.

Al-Qalanisi, short-sighted, slightly stooped and bent forward like a chemist over his retorts, also focused on the immediate, forcing a smile.

A harp twanged with a slow arpeggio and a Klieg light lit up the stage.

The foursome sat down and watched.

Flanked by a wooden palm tree and a paper moon, the *compère*, in an orange wig and brown robe, coughed. 'Revered friends, welcome. This evening, to open our feast of entertainment, is the renowned and ever-devious Mushir Pasha, Order of the Ludicrous Turban … '

The conjuror strode on and bowed, waving a large green kerchief in a circular motion.

' … and the large green kerchief.'

Mushir gave it a flick and it changed to yellow.

A ripple of applause spread across the audience.

Nicolotti leant over. 'Here is a letter of introduction to "The Head of Antiquities at Cyrene". It will lend verisimilitude to your journey if you are interrogated.'

Baus slipped the purple 'Brandywine' envelope into an inside pocket.

'Are you *au fait* with the Libyan excavation sites?'

'No.'

'The fertile coastal belt runs from Derna to Benghazi, backed by the Jebel Akhdar … the "Green Mountains". Ancient Cyrene is sited in a well-watered and verdant cleft. Its seaport, Apollonia, has graves … '

Two waiters brought the food; bowls of 'harisa' – pieces of lamb rolled in flour and herbs – a basket of coarse bread called *hubz*, a platter of dried sherbet-sprinkled lote fruit and a bottle of Cypriot wine.

A fakir in baggy pantaloons and a capacious shirt warbled on a wooden flute, whilst a Circassian peasant girl – in gauze negligees and gold bangles – performed a modified Dervish dance, with extraordinary acrobatic agility.

Everyone clapped in spontaneous admiration.

Nicolotti breathed, 'So agile, so willowy ... awesome.'

Hani leered. 'Or "whore-some".'

Baus saw that Unna disliked this.

Next a duo played on a native harp and a sistrum, exhibiting an extremely limited repertoire.

A large fellow strolled up to the Bey's table. 'Hi, Abdul.'

'Ah Bernie, my friend ... the card game went well?'

'No. The other guy had the runs.'

Egon wondered what diarrhoea had to do with a card game?

Bernie, with a scar on his cheek and looking as if he had shaved with a cheese-grater, sat down unbidden.

Hani spoke in a hush. 'Americans here are either rough and brash – like McGowan there – or ultra-smooth, but both species are despised.'

'And the British?' asked Egon.

'They had great prestige once ... but it's declined.'

'What do you know about El Adem?'

'Hmm ... it is primarily an airfield, though it *has* been used to test rockets. A friend saw three buckled red and green Vickers prototype wire-guided anti-tank missiles there ... and scorch marks on the concrete. They had been fired at the hulks of old Italian tanks.'

McGowan had brazenly taken a fork and dug into the

shared plate of pilaff.

'Are you a Texan?' queried the Bey's wife. 'Texans eat with forks.'

'Nevada.' The guest burped. 'Abdul, I've sixty overhauled Cromwell tanks with spares and ammunition, forged shipment documents ... '

'Shhh!' hissed the Bey sharply. The hairs in his ears stiffened.

'Oh ... sorry.'

'Not here. Some other topic.'

'Er ... yes. All right. How's the clap?'

'The clap?'

'Al-Qubba'a said you'd caught it?'

The sylph inserted a tinkling laugh.

'Huh. So much for confidentiality.'

His wife laughed too, touched his hand and added, 'Still dear, at least they were discreet about the psychiatric problems.'

The theatrical mix of English and French with snippets of Arabic, gave the performance a cosmopolitan air.

The *compère* introduced Justine. '*Voici une belle chanteuse.*'

'*Je viens de Tombouctou.*'

'*Je le sais bien.*'

She sang in lilting French of a mouldering ancient manuscript which told of an heroic medieval outlaw in a voice vibrant, yet touched with melancholy.

During this, Hani gave Egon a railway ticket for Mersa Matruh. 'The train leaves from the Maritime Station at ten past eight tomorrow. At Mersa a blue taxi will be waiting for you. Its driver is called Qutb.'

Baus repeated the name to fix it in his mind.

'The missiles arrived today from Avonmouth Docks. They were unshipped in Tobruk ... '

'Avonmouth?'

'A port somewhere in England ... but if they test them there in the desert ... how will you observe it? It's in the middle of nowhere.'

Unna beckoned to Ba and ordered four coffees.

Baus avoided the question. 'Is "*qahwa*" your word for "coffee"?'

Hani smiled. 'Yes. Ordinary coffee. "*Caffè alla turca*" is now "*espresso*". We still remember the Turkish period for its cruelty. The local governor or "*effendi*" always returned home hideously rich at the end of his period in office.'

Almost as a memento of that Turkish era, a belly-dancer took to the floor. Her orbit took her out between the tables, where she writhed python-like, whilst her indigo-lined eyes flashed with bold conceit.

Her tethered bouffant hair bore *faux* diamonds and her *brassière* and the thin linen triangle knotted around her pelvis – which held the long see-through skirt – were fringed with jingling silver coins.

'She likes minerals,' Hani noted. 'As do most women.'

Nicolotti pointed to a bottle of fizzy water. 'But not this variety?'

After finishing their coffees, Unna asked, 'Home time?'

'And no Buick, Unna?' Egon stated. 'Can I be your escort?'

'So fabulous,' sighed Hani.

'The Buick or Unna?'

'What do *you* think?'

Egon leant his bristle-haired noddle forwards. 'Well, I know what I think, but tastes differ.'

They arose and left in pairs.

CHAPTER EIGHT

Her Edmondson railway ticket read: 'Single. Dover to London Cannon Street.'

None the less, Ulrica alighted at Chatham and after a short bus ride out of the town and another back in, found a quiet guest house with a 'Vacancies' sign and booked in for one night. She gave a Norwegian name, Grete Eiden.

She took a bath in the communal bathroom, taking with her her sturdy tan-coloured handbag with its long wide shoulder strap. In it were numerous false papers and her short-barrelled if rather heavy pistol.

Dozing in her bedroom's armchair, she remembered the young blacksmith. The world had moved on, brightened for many by rhapsodical new suns, but not for her who had never reaped the harvest of that youthful passion.

Love is a woman's weakness. Her need is to love. Without it she is unlovely and then how easily commonplace follies pop up and degrade?

Walther she also recalled, adrift in Egypt, a hopeless misfit.

Like him, she had been brought up in a castle – *Schloss Tannfels* – a sturdy squat tower with a courtyard and ramparts, similar to many a Scottish tower house. Born in 1919, she had had when a toddler, a panicky English nanny called Miss Nunn.

The name Ulrica might once have conjured up a noble or Arthurian aura, but the hardships and disturbances of between-the-wars Germany had snuffed out any such romantic or fairy-tale allusions.

Her father – an Arabic scholar – had been appointed consul-general in Damascus in 1935. In their quaint old *qasr* or palace, they had dined under a modest stone colonnade, next to a fountain which cascaded softly into a small pool in the high-walled garden. A servant had waited on them. For her family then, lyrical Croesan delights; whilst at home, many – still feeling bitter and battered – were being drawn to Fascism.

Largesse, in the form of gold coins, had been distributed between 1898 and 1918 by German consuls and their agents to keep Islamic Levantine clerics on side, but when that ceased, so did German influence.

Syria and Palestine were engagingly awash with antique artefacts. When digging near the Haifa to Tiberias railway, the consulate's clerk had unearthed a huge dump of Roman pottery and coins which were usually abundant too around all old ruins, though invariably of poor quality.

In Jerusalem the Latin Patriarch's chaplain had taken her around the misnamed 'Tower of David' which had once been the headquarters of the Crusader Kingdom of Jerusalem. It was actually the Hippicus Tower, a remnant of the city's ancient Herodian citadel. There she had had sex for the first time – aged eighteen – in a deep quiet dungeon.

With the outbreak of war, her fluent English, French and Arabic led to her being trained in wireless telegraphy and despatched *au Maroc*, to the German Legation in Tangier – then designated a free international zone – to encode and decode both cablegram and radio traffic.

Downstairs the dinner gong sounded.

*　　*　　*　　*

'I'll walk back with you to retrieve that envelope,' Unna Engström said.

Lamps and cafés glowed on the corniche and they could hear the sea lapping the beach.

Baus spotted an army patrol ahead.

Unna dragged him behind a parked bus, but she was not quick enough. Two grubby-looking soldiers strolled up to them and demanded to see their papers.

She fumbled in her bag and handed them some money. They nodded wordlessly and left.

'We'll take this side-alley,' she said.

'Were they looking for you?'

'I don't know,' she admitted.

'They were easily bribed.'

'This is Egypt. Besides, the army here consists of upper-class officers – who serve long commissions – and conscripts from the lowest levels ... and each despises the other.'

'But both are open to bribes?'

'Naturally.'

They entered the Hotel Ptolemy via a service entrance at the rear.

Outside his room, Egon knelt down and felt carefully round the door, but the tumbler had gone. When Unna turned on the light, he noted the dull maroon stain on the carpet.

She peeped behind the wardrobe. 'Phew! It's still there.'

'Unna?'

'Yes?'

'Spend the night with me?'

'No! I thought I'd made that clear.' She hissed crossly. Surveying the wardrobe again, she struggled to tilt and swivel it.

'*Could* you help me?'

Her paucity of carnal or dissolute mannerisms increased her appeal.

His mind puckered darkly ... and it shone in his psychotically distorted face.

In a sombre contralto – steadied by fear – she said, 'Touch me and I'll scream.'

His two hands leapt to her slender neck and locked tightly round it, his thumbs pressing with insane force on her windpipe.

Unable to produce a sound, she clawed ineffectively at his tensely-sinewed forearms; she kicked his shins ... but to no avail. She grew dizzy, turned a delicate violet and slowly crumpled onto the floor.

He eyed her small but well-shaped paps, her strictured waist. She had denied him, as pretty girls always did. In less artificial societies this one-sided game of 'entice then renege' would not be tolerated.

With his antipathetical lust, he dragged her body onto the large rug before pushing up her skirt and under-skirt and pulling off her panties.

'You trail your loveliness like a red rag ... then refuse ... then, with amused confidence, boast to your friends.'

His savagery and knots of self-idolatry would have exceeded her understanding. After all, her rural upbringing had been quiet and even-tempered.

He throbbed with a pugnacity too long thwarted. A

polemic of envy, inauspicious but exciting, had prowled in his psyche like a hungry leopard. Time to lance the boil.

In neither her dress nor her poise had she sought elegance or *haute couture*. She just *knew* she was fair and winsome.

Opening her blouse, he slid upwards the horizontal white baldric of her *brassière* before letting his cheek rest against the smooth pale skin of her left breast. Her face, somewhat pinched, was perhaps her least good feature. He kissed her. 'Do you want to be shagged?' Her lifeless head rolled slightly to the right.

Her still malleable form allowed him a grim relief, an admixture of base ore and gold.

Ejaculate flooded out of him, before vague clouds of unwanted guilt gathered.

He blotted them out. Her linen skirt and starched under-skirt crackled as he reconnected again for a second frenzied bout of copulation. 'I'll shag you to Venus and back.'

He stood up, drank some water, sat down in the armchair and lit a cigarette.

Her blue neat's-leather handbag contained a welcome wad of money – which he pocketed – and her sister's address; Idunnsgatan in Mariefred.

He retrieved the envelope.

It described an 'Operation Zeus', an anagram of 'Suez' he noted. Baus gleaned that the chairman and vice chairman of The Suez Mercantile Bank, knowing that their bank was in trouble, had made generous loans to themselves but also to several government ministers to ensure protection from any recall being ordered by the courts. Here were the original signed letters, agreeing to the loans and giving the details of the foreign bank accounts into which they were to be paid.

This affair though, had no link to his task in Libya.

Unna's elastic face had become drawn and patchily blue. 'Impregnable fortress? No, I knew your weak point … you "unsolvable" mystery.'

He opened a bottle of juice and remembered the phrase, 'the banality of evil', but felt that on the contrary, evil is often uniquely captivating.

But tomorrow … tomorrow he had to be up early. He must spur himself to sort things out.

Baus rolled Unna's stiffening corpse in the rug – like Cleopatra being readied to be carried into Caesar – before opening the louvred French windows. He peered into the dark night sky and then down at the lights on the corniche before placing his cumbersome load on a wide ledge beside the narrow balcony. The rug's reverse was a deep grey and so with luck, no one would notice it for a time. And with the banking scandal, it might be expediently deduced that the Egyptian Secret Police had killed her?

Egon lit a second cigarette.

Hani had said, 'At Sollum – on the Libyan border – Qutb will sell you a cheap car for five pounds. He should have filled it with petrol, but make sure … taxi drivers are all crooks.

You'll be met in Tobruk.'

A slip with the address of a safe-house in Benghazi, he had also handed over. 'In case things go wrong. Memorise it, then destroy it.'

Egon knew the drill.

His travel clock read one o'clock.

He threw his belongings and Unna's shoulder-bag into his scuffed suitcase.

He took a last look from the balcony. Two army lorries growled past, a beggar slept in the doorway of a tobacconist's kiosk – *La Nicotiana* – and the night watchman at the *Sainte-Monique Collège de jeunes filles* stood outside, taking occasional swigs from a bottle.

All seemed quiet.

CHAPTER NINE

At dawn a muezzin wailed the *Adhan*.

The city's early noises swelled, seeping through the slats of the shutters.

In the breakfast room, Coburg consumed two croissants with jam, some decent coffee and a glass of juice.

He walked to the Maritime Railway Station, whose brick façade contained ornate onion-shaped openings edged with accurately-cut wedge-shaped stone blocks.

At the heavy wrought-iron gates a plump Alexandrine woman decked in a scruffy uniform jacket, a patterned headscarf and silvery bracelets, checked his ticket. He strolled onto Platform 2, to await the 0810 to Mersa Matruh as instructed.

He studied some signs and watched some natives and sensed a slight quickening of that fascination with the Orient, over which European Arabists had enthused for two centuries or more.

A soot-caked engine drew in amid a cloud of steam, vapourised oil droplets and coal-dust, with a grime-covered shunter riding on its red buffer-beam.

Coburg climbed into an antiquated carriage with wooden seats and after the engine had run round the train and recoupled, a whistle blew and they moved jerkily off.

Cinders and smoke wafted past the window, but as this cleared and they left the city, he took in the thin golden sunrise and the glistening dew which clung to the weeds alongside the track.

A moss-green lake appeared, a rye field with a hazy

low sun peeping across it, then hump-backed cows, a gamoose and a field of sugar cane. They swung inland, but would regain the coast farther west.

As they swayed and rocked, a Sudanese lad – wiry-haired, ebony-faced and bright-eyed and the only other occupant of the compartment – offered a few pleasantries. He told – in passable English – of a robbery in his village and how a mystic in Cairo had named the thief as Ahmed the Grinder, someone whom he had suspected but whom this clairvoyant could not possibly know. Such seers were banned from the Islamic faith, for – as with Christianity – Islam forbids dabbling in the occult.

The honey-coloured terrain, cracked and dotted with twisted scrub-like bushes, rolled by under a cerulean sky.

Salim, the Sudanese boy, told how his family grew henna a few miles from the White Nile. The British had sunk an artesian well for them.

Walther managed a clenched smile. Salim said that the English called teeth so displayed, 'park railings'.

From behind a plantation of dark-leafed cork trees the sparkling blue and chrome of the Mediterranean reappeared.

The boy then sold him a small wallet made out of black-stippled buff cobra skin before alighting at a halt named El Dab'a, a place which seemed to be no more than a whitewashed water-tower and a siding.

Had Salim's friendliness all been a softening exercise to sell the wallet? Oh well, the price of education.

Eventually Mersa appeared – the end of the line – a cluster of whitish box-shaped houses and fig groves set in shallow depressions.

He climbed down.

A harsh noon-day white-yellow sun blazed down. The mercury would be sky-high.

Men rolled oil-drums onto a railway wagon, whilst a water-carrier – as always a woman in a black gown with a pitcher on her head – walked erectly along the rusty pressed-steel sleepers to a well.

He strolled to the beach. Waves surged lazily against a promontory beyond a lagoon and some fishing boats lay tilted over on the shingle.

Then he spotted Qutb, leaning on his old blue Chevrolet. He waved.

Hired to take Baus to the Libyan border, he checked gruffly, 'Professor Egon, *Sayed*?'

'Yes.'

'Hot today?' A stunning understatement.

Qutb slung Egon's suitcase in the boot, then helped his charge buy a tasty lamb kebab, a ripe tomato and four bottles of a dubious bronze-coloured fizzy concoction. 'Cola,' he explained.

'How long to the Libyan border?'

'Three hours?'

A crudely daubed slogan on a wall read, 'Cil the jues.'

'The Jews gave the British a tough time in Palestine,' said Egon.

Qutb formed a bent smile. 'It is good when your enemies fight one another.'

They climbed in and the Chevrolet nudged its way through a flock of brown sheep.

'I fought the British in Italy. Have you fought anyone?'

'No. At the Defence Ministry in Cairo, I bribed a smallpox-pitted clerk to fix an interview for me with a junior defence minister. The minister asked what I wanted. I said, to dodge my military service. "Two hundred pounds." An envelope crossed the table and I received my exemption.'

'In Egypt, anything is possible with money?'

'Certainly.'

They drove westwards along the littoral. The taxi's soft American suspension resembled the gentle pitching of a boat. They crossed dry wadis on former British Army Bailey bridges.

The remnants of a railway could be seen in places parallel to the coast road. Qutb waved a hand, 'An abandoned *prolongement*.'

Various stock subjects cropped up, none of any practical use.

'Crocodiles eat one big meal every few months ... perhaps the odd snack in between. They digest a goat say slowly and then vomit out a stony calcified oval ball, the reformed residue of its bones. And they don't like fresh meat ... they bury it in the mud at the bottom of the river to mature.'

'Connoisseurs?'

Qutb laughed.

'They like it falling off the bone?'

'Their mouths have strong closing muscles and weak opening ones. Cobras are similar.'

Just before Sollum, Qutb swerved onto a bumpy dirt track and halted beside a derelict fort.

'In 1915 Senussi tribesmen – bribed with German gold – fought here against a troop of Australian light horse, a company of turbaned Sikhs, a Rolls Royce armoured car and a single aeroplane.'

'And lost?'

'Naturally.'

All was silent apart from the soft buzz of insects.

Qutb led the way to a battered Fiat.

'Does it go?'

With the choke out, at the third tug of the starter knob, it burst into life.

The petrol gauge read 'three-quarters' but Egon undid the filler-cap and poked a stick into the tank before handing Qutb twenty U.S. dollars.

'Not enough. More.'

'Five pounds was the deal. That's the equivalent.'

Qutb yielded with ill-grace, then favoured the departing car with an obscene gesture.

Initially the German drove cautiously, as if transporting a Ming vase.

Beyond an extensive citrus orchard came the border.

The Libyan guards raised the red and yellow boom and simply waved him through. Someone must have squared them in advance.

The coast road had been built by the Italians. It had signs in Italian, Arabic and English and was the only proper road here. The vast arid desert of the Cyrenaic Hinterland had only the occasional remnant of an old Roman road or an odd caravan track.

As dusk gathered, after two tedious hours, plots of date-palm, olives and barley started to border the road; happy precursors to a large sign-board which read 'Tobruk', his resting place for the night.

He drew up in the long shadows of the square and climbed stiffly out. All seemed still. Three palm trees and the one-storey buildings stood as mere black laminae. Just three lights glimmered dimly; in the Italian priest's house, the telephone exchange and the Lebanese school-mistress's house.

A soft-footed urchin emerged from a gloomy alleyway, then scampered off toward the non-tidal port.

Makkawi and Tariq were bent over a backgammon board on a small sail-boat – a *zarug* – which had its sails furled.

They clambered up onto the mole. Tariq – with an old sabre hidden under his robe – stumbled languorously along, mouthing nonsense induced by poppy-seed juice.

Makkawi in a *sirwal* – baggy trousers – a loose black top and a keffiyeh, snapped at the German with a quixotic abruptness, tantamount to impudence. His flattish face had censuring deep-set eyes and his nose and mouth seemed squashed together.

He led ' Herr Baus' to a squalid upstairs room in a hovel which he flattered with the title of 'fondouk' or 'hotel'.

On a bench stood a plate of oily fish, a coarse loaf and a jug of cloudy water. A well-dented bucket and three grubby so-called *jaafas* or leathern sacks to sleep on were the sum total of the amenities. There were mercifully no flies.

Makkawi left.

Egon leant on the gnarled wooden balcony rail. Only the ceaseless rhythm of waves breaking on unseen rocks could be heard.

Above the charcoal-grey flat roofs, the last traces of a sunset of radiant scarlet and violet faded, surrendering to an eerie darkness in which a rising pale green moon made love to a matt black minaret.

His 'hosts' were clearly not mules in the Bolshevik cause. Their motive might be to score hits on the British or else just dirty lucre, but it was not the dissemination of communism. Treachery lurked everywhere.

Grogginess seized him and he fell onto the fusty camel-hide *jaafas* as they were a trampoline and went out like a light.

* * * *

In Montpelier Square, Ulrica sat on a bench under the trees with their yellow and orange autumnal leaves.

Her watch said ten-twenty. Time to go.

She walked down the street under a balmy sun, a show of modest confidence masking a hint of trepidation as she entered Bonham's and asked for Mr Roland Dampier.

In the elegant foyer a stylish receptionist offered her a seat. A copy of *Antiques Quarterly* had on its cover a misty scene outside a Wren church. She thumbed through a copy of *Punch*, produced it said in Bouverie Street.

Mr Dampier appeared, gaunt though courteous; 'Vampier-Dampier' his underlings called him.

In a recess they sat at a table of cream travertine stone, where he opened a thin folder.

'Miss Steyr, I bring good news. The Tate's forensic specialist has established the authenticity of *A Green Moon with Oranges*.'

'Good.' Ulrica nodded gravely.

'And so we are willing to place it in our auction catalogue for November – Lot 33.'

'Good,' she repeated.

'Shall we sign the necessary papers?'

'Of course.'

She took out her false passport whilst Dampier took the top off his fountain pen.

A hefty fellow wearing a jacket with a fur collar entered. He thumbed through a brochure and then eyed a bust of William Pitt the Younger. Through the windows, she saw a delivery van draw up.

'My brother shot down a Heinkel 115 in 1942,' Dampier said, 'piloted by someone named Steyr.'

Ulrica smiled. 'No relation.' She signed the forms.

'Igor Ohotnikoff,' she muttered inwardly. Suddenly she understood.

She shook hands with Dampier and stood up. Glancing round, the K.G.B. man had left.

She asked the receptionist if they had a ladies' room?

The girl stood up, opened a door which led onto a less glamorous corridor and said, 'Second on the left.'

The corridor led straight through to the back of the building and then out into a cobbled yard which served the backs of a number of tall houses, but – after a hundred yards – came to a dead end.

She entered a back-yard and ran up three steps into someone's spacious Victorian kitchen, through its half-open door. Her heart thumped. Voices could be heard upstairs. Tip-toeing along the passage-way to the front door, she let herself out.

Walking briskly along a side-street, she came to a busy thoroughfare with offices and shops and as a red London bus growled past, grating its cogs in a rough gear-change, she hopped onto its platform.

Holding onto the pole and looking back, no one seemed to have noticed her, so she climbed the stairs, sat on a front seat with her handbag and small suitcase and heaved a deep sigh.

Once, at a high-ranking cocktail party, Uwe Engel had introduced her to the President of the German Democratic Republic, Wilhelm Pieck. 'Ulrica has been very successful in posting agents to northern Europe. Their counter-espionage set-ups seem unable to second-guess her tactics ... a bonus perhaps of her not knowing them herself.'

Pieck had laughed, sipped his wine and replied, 'Unpredictability is a useful asset.'

Engel's quip though had been unnervingly close to the truth.

But ... her and Engel's thefts had now been rumbled.

The clippy appeared. She said, whilst fumbling in her purse, 'The terminus, please.'

The puzzle began to solve itself.

In Amsterdam, she had offered a diamond dealer a thirty-three carat stone, with a certificate attesting its purchase from 'Windhoek Mines Consolidated' in 1938.

The dealer had frowned, before pointing out that that Namibian company had folded thirty years before.

Ulrica had swallowed. The result this of careless homework. 'Namibia was once German South-West Africa ... perhaps an old receipt?'

She had given her name as Monika Steyr, but fortunately no other details.

In a coffee-house on the Heren Gracht, she had taken a window-seat as an older man left, before ordering coffee and a Napoleon layer-cake. She then picked up a pocket-sized fold-up timetable and slipped it into her pocket.

After thus collecting three micro-dots, she had walked to the Centraal Station.

In the high echoing concourse, a blonde woman of about her own age was having a spat with four uniformed Dutch policemen.

In the shadow of a bronze sculpture, they were handing her passport back. 'We're terribly sorry, Miss. It's a case of mistaken identity.'

'Well that's wonderful isn't it? You've dragged me off my train and now it's gone. The next one isn't for almost four hours … so I shall miss my interview in Heidelberg.'

'I can only repeat Miss, we are very sorry for the inconvenience … '

In the distance a ruffian, lolling against a cast-iron column, had thrown away the stub of his thick Turkish cigarette and scurried off.

The penny now dropped.

Their Muscovite masters would give her no credit for past success. Her irregularly acting as a mere courier or a tip-off from the diamond dealer must have alerted them.

She dared not turn herself in to the British. They were so deeply penetrated.

The bus ended its run at Chalk Farm and here, from a Barclay's Bank branch, she withdrew two hundred pounds, the rough equivalent of six months' wages for an ordinary person.

A large van stood nearby with its engine running. On its side in bold letters, it read; 'Cuthbert's Removals – Coventry.'

'Are you going to Coventry?'

The driver replied, 'I am.'

'Could I hitch a lift for ... ten shillings?'

Her clear blue eyes and fair brow made it hard to doubt the agreeableness and sincerity of her disposition.

At a transport café on the A5 they ate egg and chips.

'Are you English?'

'Irish. Clare.' She thought to herself, 'Clare Voyant ... not.'

'Oleg. White Russian ... from Minsk. I was on a destroyer in the Baltic, but in forty-three she was torpedoed. Four of us on a raft paddled to the Swedish coast ... and sought asylum.'

She sympathised.

'I thought once to visit my old home ... and the Russian embassy issued me with a travel visa, but ... I daredn't risk it.'

In a guest house in Coventry, she finally allowed relief to flood her senses, but ... what next?

She thought of Uwe Engel, he who had proposed their smuggling stolen artefacts to the West with a view to later escaping there. Was he lying black and blue in some rat-ridden hole ... or was he already dead?

And thinking of Uwe, her thoughts went back in time to North Africa.

Tangier had been a fuzz of milky-white dust, with Arabic illusions and separatist zeal lurking in its maze of alleyways and hovels. European literati, Sodomites and reactionaries though – who were known as 'Tangerinos' – still inhabited much of the old walled Medina.

The heyday of *Tanger la Blanche* – trips into the countryside with picnics and easels – were of a bygone era. By 1940 many natives had become sullen and unfriendly.

The Head of the German Legation, Graf Johann von Steuben, had on occasion asked Ulrica – as they both spoke French – to accompany him to the home of the Chief-of-Police for a game of cards.

Geoffrey Laneuville told of an agent of Göring's who had asked about 'borrowing' a tenth-century wooden diptych from a local friary. 'The world is full of scoundrels,' he sighed. 'Wisdom is about how you react.'

Von Steuben had given him an understanding though non-committal smile.

Isabelle, Laneuville's wife, beat Ulrica's king unexpectedly with the jack of trumps. 'Aha! As today in politics, the knave beats the king.'

'The earth is a mystery to be wondered at,' continued Geoffrey in a long-suffering monotone, 'not an entity to be understood.'

'Another rubber?'

'Why not? And more champagne.'

Ulrica dreamt she were ambling again between white-washed dwellings with the omnipresent purple bougainvillaea tumbling over walls and the *cherqi* – an abrasive local wind – blowing, as she went to meet Philip Dark-Coombs in his white suit and his loosely-knotted, blue-patterned, silk Charvet tie.

Rain rattled at the window.

*   *   *   *

Next morning, Tariq appeared.

A tousled Baus ate two bites of hard bread and mouldy goats' cheese, then sipped the abysmal filth which his host termed 'coffee'. Even the wasp buzzing round his cup seemed unsure whether to risk it.

Outside a pulley squeaked as a bucket came up out of a well.

Hani had used the Arabic word *'bayt'* – or 'house' – for this slum. The word *'casa'* had been one of the first Italian words he had learnt, when a girl in Marina di Massa had pointed to her house; *'La mia casa.'* So what? Only later had he twigged; she was a prostitute.

As his innards gurgled, Egon threw away his suit and pulled on knee-length shorts and a loose shirt.

For two pins he would bail out of this lunacy now. Deserting to the West and settling down in some modest job, sounded good; incredibly good.

He had been 'given' to Moscow, who intended that he fall into this English 'trap'. But did he know enough about this *Bloodhound* missile malarkey to sound convincing?

Unsure if he might vomit, he went onto the balcony.

A British Army three-tonner went by, cornering with a rasp of cogs.

Tariq joined him.

'That lousy coffee.'

'Ah, *Sayed*, the English refuse to drink the local water. They have a deep bore-hole at El Adem … crystal clear they say.'

Egon vomited.

A fellow pumping up a brass blow-lamp across the street looked up. Whilst distracted, his blow-lamp set fire to the curtain hung over the door of his workshop. His wife in a loose kirtle came out and shrieked at him.

Tariq gave a skirling laugh. 'Westerners think Arab women are submissive, but inside the house they are the boss.'

The sun, like a fire-breathing steed with pale yellow locks fluttering, rose abruptly over a bar of grey satin-like mist.

'I had someone guard your car overnight.'

'Good. Time to be off.'

The rough stony road to the south – metalled in patches – led to El Adem. After three miles, a ridge of loose sand which had drifted across it, caused the Fiat to stick fast.

'N'importe.' Using the shovel and the two sheet-metal sand-channels – fortunately provided – though sweating profusely, he extricated it.

He opened his bowels and felt easier, then drank his last bottle of 'cola' and lit a cigarette.

The air quivered with the rising heat.

Life behind the Iron Curtain might be conspiratorial, but in your own country you knew the tricks. This adventure was so pitted with invisible hazards as to be insane.

He set off again along this undulating desert road, bordered by stretches of creviced ochre-coloured limestone and expanses of featureless sand.

A jumble of angular strata-lined rocks loomed, on top of which was a triangulation point on a concrete block.

Here he sat to await a 'chance encounter'.

It happened. A golden hyaena gazed at him. He jumped out of his skin. After a lengthy staring match, the hyaena grew bored and loped off.

An hour went by. A faint dust-cloud appeared to the north. A Scammell recovery tractor pulling an R.A.F. fuel bowser and a Leyland Hippo artillery tractor towing a tank transporter trailer, drew up.

'Eyes on target, Sir?'

'Er, I think you mean, "Some fellow in a spot of bother," Sergeant?'

'Sir.'

The Italian priest's housemaid – who also worked shifts in the telephone exchange – had called the airfield yesterday evening.

Major Dardry and Sergeant Hogg jumped down.

'Is this going to be funny, Sir?'

'Hilarious, but he doesn't know that.'

The Fiat whinnied twice, then a rugged sun-hatted Coburg climbed out with the crank-handle, which he inserted and jerked round savagely. Its metallic scraping noises were likewise ineffective.

'Good morning. A spot of bother?'

'Good morning to you too ... I am pleased to see you.'

'Oh?'

'I was nearly eaten by a wolf.'

'A wolf? Where?'

'Where?'

'Here?'

'Perhaps it was a "where-wolf", Sir.' Sergeant Hogg subdued a grin.

'I stopped to look for an ancient cistern ... supposedly below this outcrop ... but now I'm stranded.'

Dardry seemed puzzled. 'No cistern here.'

'On an old map it's labelled *"Dar al-maa'a"*.'

'Place of water? But ... '

'I must have misread the co-ordinates.' He tried to look sheepish.

What a corker this was. 'Old maps here are notoriously unreliable.'

'It was Turkish … early this century … '

'Drawn for your Asien-Korps? All part of the Kaiser's intended pan-Islamic uprising?'

Coburg reddened a little. 'Exaggeration and rumour, Major.'

'So desperate to conquer, he betrayed his country's Christian beliefs?' Dardry – following this provocative remark – saw the fire blaze in the German's eyes. 'And you are?'

'Egon Baus. Archaeologist.'

'There's a water-hole farther south, owned by the Zuwayya tribe.'

'Oh well, that explains it.'

'Travellers may use it, but not sell it on. They will sometimes give away ancient artefacts too … if they like you. They're not yet wholly commercialised.'

'Very charitable, but I know almost no Arabic.'

'Anyway,' Dardry waved at the vehicles behind him, 'we can tow you back onto the road, if you're stuck?'

'They have winches?'

'Well, they do, but they could just use a rope.'

The German eyed these sand-coloured giants. They had high ground clearance, tyres of a thickness and quality unknown in Germany and regimental squares painted on their mudguards which were divided diagonally into blue and yellow triangles.

'Do they have differential locks too to prevent wheel-spin?'

'They do.'

'However, I'm not stuck. My decrepit car simply refuses to start.'

The Major hailed one Corporal Stokes and a R.E.M.E. squaddie.

'Let these chaps take a look. If they grumble and mutter, "We'll see what we can do," then they'll do an excellent job. If they say they can't fix it here ... well, that's that.'

'That is most kind.'

'The British Army ... always willing to assist.' Dardry again glimpsed Baus's repressed fury and smiled.

The German considered Dardry's rank. A 'major' – as shown by the crowns on his epaulettes – would carry much authority in a backwater like this.

The British Army's dispersal around the world meant too that it did not have that Prussian barrack-block square-bashing war-only mentality.

Sergeant Hogg strolled over to the R.E.M.E. lads and told them to say they could not trace the fault.

Using a few stock nuggets about the classical Greek North African 'Pentapolis', Dardry cheerily unpicked the intruder's bogus status. He knew not that 'Berenice' was the modern Benghazi nor that the Romans used sulphur in viniculture here, to arrest mildew.

Walther, still feeling drained by yesterday's long journey, unavoidably yawned.

'You slept badly?'

'Some leather sacks for a bed ... or "corium" which stank of animal urine.'

'Up early too? "Before the Devil has tied his shoe-laces," as my Grandfather used to say?'

Corporal Stokes approached. 'We can't repair it here, Sir.'

'Oh dear. Bit of a how-d'ye-do, eh?' Dardry rubbed his chin, before offering to take Baus's stranded vehicle with them to El Adem and give him a billet for the night.

'That is most generous, Major.' Baus was surprised that the Russian plan was succeeding so effortlessly ... or did they know? Was this a double-bluff or a treble-bluff?

'Right, chaps,' Dardry pointed and gave a wink to one side.

With his diminutive vehicle on the tank transporter trailer and himself high up in the cab of the recovery tractor, they set off deeper into the hot noon-day Sahara.

CHAPTER TEN

David Fairweather strolled to the corner shop to buy bread, Stilton and a quarter pound of liquorice toffees.

Tight-fisted old Hollyoak placed a four-ounce brass weight on one side of the scales, then shook the toffees warily from a large glass sweet bottle into a paper bag on the other, until it tipped.

'Ah, bumping weight!' he growled.

The scales had to tip. He could not actually give less.

David's old Squadron Leader, Jonathan Thurling, had rung earlier. Visiting his sister nearby, he asked if he could drop in?

David greeted him cheerily, then set about making tea.

'Still no maid, then?'

'No. No "Polly" to put the kettle on.'

'We once thought we were entitled to a touch of ego, but it seems not.'

'The chap across the road took on this chancer ... allegedly "cognisant with the skills of a butler". Quite an exaggeration it turned out. Then some money disappeared so Tom kicked him out.'

'I came up on the Birch Brothers' coach from King's Cross. It ended its run at that unusual art deco bus garage in Rushden.'

'And you manage a bus company in Dorset?'

The kettle whistled on its gas-ring.

'I did. My "Yellow Brick Road" though has taken a livelier twist ... teaching mathematics. A fellow at White's Club fixed it up.'

They settled down with tea, cheese and biscuits.

The A.V.M. showed his guest a description of the Elliott 402 computer which the R.A.F. had ordered for use at West Byfleet.

Jonathan read: 'Linear programming reduces complex functions to linear ones. For example: Maximise c^Tx subject to $Ax \leq b$ and $x \geq 0$, where c and b are vectors of known coefficients ... ' He laid it down. 'This is way above me.'

'My only talent was good aeronautical decision-taking.'

'And leadership.'

'True. At Repton the need for "character" was drilled into us.'

'Caesar translations indoors ... improvising palisades with stakes and wire outdoors?'

'Where do you teach?'

'At a top-notch girls' school.'

'Ah, that explains the "livelier twist".'

'Well ... pretty girls ... ' Thurling dabbed the cover of a mail-order catalogue of Marion's, where a lissom blonde posed in a neat skirt and jumper. 'She's quite a cracker.' He opened it at random. 'Oh, here she is again ... in a coat.'

'I expect the same girl models everything.'

'Yes ... where's the swimwear page?'

David chuckled. 'A game of chess?'

'Why not? Like old times ... waiting to take off.'

David fetched a box. 'These very irregular chess-men were hand-turned – or hand-carved – half in this dark purple nyankom wood and half in ivory. They're supposedly fifteenth-century, from Timbuctoo ... Tug bought them in a suq in Dakar.'

David was nearing his target topic.

'Tug's a member of White's too, isn't he?'

'He is.'

The host decanted some brandy. 'What do you make of him lately?'

'How do you mean?'

'Stability … trustworthiness?'

Jonathan frowned. 'Why do you ask?'

'Oh … just a throw-away remark made by an army colonel.'

'Well … people can change.'

David sipped his cognac. 'A while back, he called on a young lass to fix up a date … at least that's how he put it to me. He had told Ellinor that he was off to the Co-op to buy a few items. When he returned, she asked why it had taken so long? He said that the Co-op was shut and so he had had to go somewhere else. So she asked, "Then why is this butter wrapper stamped 'Co-op'?"'

Thurling laughed.

'By itself, it's not much … but so many of his exploits lately just don't add up.'

'Hmm.'

'We sent some bogus signals six weeks ago … using an A.G. cipher … about despatching *Bloodhounds* to El Adem for trials … with the intent of narrowing the field on whoever is betraying our communications. The enemy though seemed to know in advance that it was a ruse.'

'Well,' Jonathan shook his head, 'the word "amateurish" springs to mind.'

'We didn't know what else to try,' said David simply.

The visitor grew more thoughtful.

'We sent Squiffy to inform Colonel Goodman and our Station Commandant at El Adem … and a further cohort of ground crew were despatched in September as window-dressing.'

'That low-grade cipher would look odd for a start.'

David exhaled slowly. 'Oh well, "Queen's gambit declined." Something might pop up?'

'The Russians are masters at chess … especially in the field of "pawn sacrifice".'

'The O.C. at El Adem – this Colonel Goodman – and his outfit, are pretty clued-up on local villains … which is one good card in our hand.'

'I suppose the enemy can't really infiltrate somewhere like that?'

'Unless they're Tuaregs?'

Jonathan surveyed the chess-board. 'Chess pieces are loyal. No traitors. A straight bat.'

David squirted some soda gingerly into his brandy. 'In the last century there was a pretty clear consensus about society needing to stick together, but now "it all depends on where you're coming from" … i.e. you can make up whatever harmful pseudo-moral nonsense takes your fancy.'

'Check.

I've heard two rumours about Tug. One is that he frequents a house of ill-repute in Marylebone, where his favourites are Katya Holowka and Anna Glinka.'

'Hmm.'

'And – *en passant* – the Czech air attaché also enjoys their favours.'

Sir David prinked his eyelids. 'Such a plant is surely *too* obvious?'

'Is the attaché a false link ... sent to complete an imaginary chain? If so, all is then ready to be "uncovered" when the time is ripe?'

'It's an old trick.'

'But it works ... especially with "friends" in the press. And rigged "leaks" divert suspicion from the real villains, whilst also blackening others who are perhaps loyal.'

'Two birds with one stone?'

'Your turn.'

'Consistent conduct, though advantageous, is not the ultimate virtue. All good men have done something silly at some time.'

'Like moving that bishop?'

'Oh ... the knight was a decoy? Drat.' David sighed. 'Tug says he's trying to dispose of his current albatross, not accumulate another.'

'Which doesn't tally with the Co-op story?'

'If it *was* to see a young lass? And rumour number two?'

'He's bought a flat in Gibraltar.'

Fairweather stared at his old C.O.

'I've a cottage near Aberdovey ... if you feel at risk?'

*　　*　　*　　*

An R.A.F. sergeant in shirt and shorts with a blancoed belt and a white-topped cap watched the two-vehicle convoy enter the main gate at El Adem.

The station's motto board read; *Nec aspera terrent.* Lieutenant Bagnall had unpicked this as, 'We fear not trouble.'

Dardry and his 'guest' jumped down, the latter trying to

look self-assured in difficult circumstances.

'Our C.O. is Colonel Goodman. I'll introduce you later, Professor Herr Doktor.' The Major was enjoying himself.

'And you're his deputy?'

'Yes. The "2 I.C." Where did you stay last night?'

'The mullah at the mosque in Tobruk put me up.'

'Very kind of him … the saintly murderer.'

'He claims that in paradise there are springs flowing with the fermented juices of the grape. They will eat jujube fruit served by houris and any warrior who dies facing the enemy, they will allow to delight himself with sexual climaxes lasting not less than a thousand years.'

'Sounds a bit monotonous.'

'He doesn't like the British.'

'I wouldn't be too sure he likes you.'

They passed through the shadow of the octagonal control tower. A small R.A.F. band stood lined up in an open hangar.

'They play for an hour each lunch-time.'

A closing refrain of a Sousa march made Baus shudder. 'I quote, "A village bandmaster who's heard some Wagner."'

'Music isn't my forte.'

Next came a lively French marching song, with an unusual rhythm.

'Some legionnaires visited recently. A *caporal-chef* sang that and Flying Officer Young jotted it down and scored it.'

'You co-operate with the French?'

'Unofficially. René Coty would go crazy if he knew.'

As they rounded a Fleet Air Arm *Sea Venom*, Egon saw two mechanics pushing his Fiat into a workshop, alongside an R.A.F. pressure refueller.

'Anyway, here are the wash-rooms,' Dardry pointed. 'Tidy yourself up, then come to the mess for a spot of lunch.'

Unexpectedly, the agent glimpsed some way ahead, the four large trailers with their tarpaulins and sentries. He saw too how impossible it would be to discover their secrets.

As he splashed soap and water about his face and upper body, both dismay and a capricious fury seized him. He loathed the British Army. He had last seen it – through field-glasses – in 1944 in Italy.

Freshened-up outwardly, but darkened inwardly, he emerged into the sunlight.

R.A.F. electricians were playing some tank crews at football. Their pseudo-jollity infuriated him too. 'Spiffing shot Jones!' 'Ripping stuff!' 'Lashings of ginger beer.'

The crew of a Saladin armoured car returning from a tour of the periphery were clambering down. Its commander gave him a studied look. Why? Was his defective humanity so starkly evident?

These bastards had shot him up, high in the Apennines.

*　　*　　*　　*

Barry Haines dug up and discarded four cabbages, which consisted mostly of leafless ribs. 'Slugs,' he cursed.

Resting on his spade-handle, he spotted amid the weeds of the neighbouring allotment, a mildewed boot.

This off-duty policeman studied it. It was a woman's, black, knee-length and size six. In his little hut, he wrapped it in newspaper, put his coat on and set off for the police station.

An hour later, he was back with Detective Inspector Golding.

They viewed the ill-kept patch.

'Who rents it?'

'Howard Tait did until he died.'

'Hmm.'

'He liked red-currants, but its clayey here and wet, so his bushes didn't thrive.'

'Someone's dug over the middle bit quite heavily.'

'Yes. The rest's just prolific briars.'

'I do have eyes, Haines.'

This plot lay beside a broad track, on the other side of which a brook gurgled.

'An orange excavator was here a couple of months back. It cleared out that ditch.'

'Who sent it?'

'The council I suppose.'

Later, at the District Council Offices, Inspector Golding discovered the ill-tended allotment holder's name and address and that he had paid his rent on cue and in cash.

From Gainsborough he rang his colleagues in Doncaster, who an hour later rang back to say that the given address did not exist.

By mid-afternoon, four policemen in Wellingtons and with sleeves rolled up, were digging a trench. The earth was loose in places and two feet down, they hit a large metal box.

Oblong, three feet by four and two deep, made of heavy three-sixteenth-inch steel plate, it had an access hatch sealed with some thick wax-like material.

Beside it lay the decomposing bodies of a young woman and a dog.

The patrol sergeant – in charge of the force's new black Riley motor car – and a more senior detective, arrived.

A constable was posted to guard the scene and next day the ditch-deepening was investigated. One council employee Martin O'Hara had authorised it. He was brought in and the D.C.I. interrogated him.

The Scouser though remembered his training; 'Deny everything, admit nothing.' Yet the forms sanctioning the excavator's hire, bore his signature.

CHAPTER ELEVEN

In the deserted and not unduly hot Officers' Mess, Major Keith Dardry – the camp's adjutant – stood at the bar whilst Mr Pinkney poured two large tonic waters and set out a few of yesterday's left-over crab-paste or cream-cheese rolls.

The severe and lean figure of the German ambled cagily in, wearing green shorts and a T-shirt with broad vertical stripes such as might be used upholster a deck-chair.

'Professor, come. Sample a Stone Age bun.'

'Thank you … or should I say, "Rather!"'

'Either will do, gratitude being the sign of a noble soul.'

They exchanged arch-smiles.

'Trowel on some more paste if you wish … sieve on some salt? Carbon date it.'

His guest ignored these frivolities.

'Brotherton says one of his chaps is dealing with your old banger.'

'My car?'

'Yes … not your sausage, although we know Germans like sausages.'

Dardry indicated a faded tin plaque. It depicted an art deco six-litre Bentley with the caption, *'La conquerante aux 24 heures du Mans'*.

'Left by your former Italian allies.'

'Our utterly *inept* allies,' came the scathing reply.

'Brotherton's the M.T. Sergeant … smokes like hell, grumbles constantly and yet adores his vehicles. Don't ask him anything mechanical unless you've plenty of time to spare.

He has a one-lorry transport business at home … says it used to be lorry first and wife second, but when he gets back, it'll be the other way round … if she's still there. Salt of the earth.'

He led the way to some padded chairs and a small table.

'So, dialogue? In which stratum shall we sift?'

Baus looked sulky, testy, even Neolithic.

'Your friend the Mullah, did he throw you any crumbs?'

'He thinks you have an informant in Tobruk.'

'Does he?'

'He said they knifed one last year.'

'He did?'

'Yes, he *did*.'

'That fellow had had himself kicked out of the Syrian army,' Dardry observed, 'and that's no mean feat, I can tell you.'

'For something immoral?'

The Adjutant was almost speechless. 'That would be the least of their worries.'

Mr Pinkney – the civilian quartermaster who kept the stores and the officers' bar – brought over more tonic water and the platter of stale buns.

'The locals are a miserable bunch … not a trace of humour … unhelpful … '

'Yet still you employ them?'

'The Army's not responsible for everyone's integrity … we just have to do our best with what's available.'

'Even perverts?'

Dardry gave another half-laugh. 'In North Africa everybody it seems has some sort of "tendency".'

The stranger bit into the white fluffy English-style bread. 'And you need to gather intelligence … to keep law and order?'

'Quite.'

Egon stammered, 'So, a bit of rough justice?'

'Yes, when it's expedient.'

'Germans believe in rules and philosophy.'

'Yes. We know all about that.'

'And what does *that* mean?'

'The fantasy of metamorphosis. Caterpillars become butterflies, so German stock can become Atlases and Amazons?' The Major leant back. 'Luckily, mother nature usually thwarts such delusions.'

Coburg croaked hoarsely, 'Britain's days are numbered.'

The Major permitted himself a sphinx-like grin, sipped his tonic water and said, 'But moving from the general to the specific, Baus – or whatever your name is – I'll tell you a story … a spy story in fact.'

The German listened.

'In March, a French D.S.T. brigadier stopped over. He told us of an East German agent – a Dane called Sören Theill-Rige – who had defected in Bordeaux.'

Coburg's falcon-like expression froze.

'Now, the question arises in such cases, "Is he bogus, sent deliberately to sow disinformation?"'

The chewer coughed and a few shards of bread and crab paste flew across the table.

'If Rige *was* a fake … *un contrebandier* sent to give the Frogs some "flapdoodle" as the Yanks call it … how might you make him *appear* authentic?'

The captive's hand shook despite his trying to control it.

'You *could* have him killed ... to lend *credibility* to his seeming betrayal ... and incidentally ensuring that he doesn't let the real cat out of the bag?'

In the background Captain Stanton strolled into the mess.

'And ... that's *exactly* what happened.'

The Major moistened his tongue with another swig. 'Rige lay hidden in Saint-Thibault, a village in Picardy, with a poor woman who still cooked in a black-leaded oven heated by the fire and where the postman was her lover.

But something frightened him and one night, he fled ...

Archie, come and join us.'

Stanton put his cap down on a table and came across. 'Good afternoon, Sir.'

He greeted Baus with a nod, but – as when dismounting from the Saladin – experienced a double-take. The missing lower front tooth ... the longish face?

Dardry asked, 'You know Berlin, Professor?'

Coburg shrugged. 'Naturally.'

'You were in Berlin, weren't you Archie?'

'Yes Sir, for three years.'

Mr Pinkney brought a jug of lemon juice with spherical ice-cubes in it and a third glass.

'A libation to the forces of reincarnation,' Stanton proposed inscrutably as he raised his glass, sipped it and sat down.

'Where was I?' Dardry inquired of himself. 'Rige was seen fording a stream, stumbling over a log and wading through a sward of knee-deep cow-parsley near a sun-dappled copse.

Next day some loggers found his body in a gully between a rusting tractor and a ruined croft where probably he had cowered to evade his killer.'

The listener – outwardly attentive to his bun – had covertly alerted his numbed senses. 'Your point, Major?'

'Well, *you* might be next?'

'Me? Why?'

Dardry eyed him. 'Very well. Act your part. Hold out for a bit.' He stood up. 'Archie, find Sergeant Hay and ask him to fix this doughty intruder with quarters for the night.'

'Sir.'

'Oh, Professor, dinner is at seven. And ties are worn in the mess after six.'

As Sergeant Hay – wearing a Glengarry with a chequered band – led Walther past the tall steel radar tower with its rotating scanner, he eyed the Kraut's flushed, anxious face.

'I dinna ken wha' kind o' trouble you're in pal, but I wouldn'a think o' tryin' to run.' The sandy heat-distorted horizon quivered.

In a rickety building, they passed through a disused games room where a snooker table had been laid out with a wooden map of Libya, with coloured pegs to represent towns, oases, airfields and military bases.

Hay opened the door on a dreary box of a room with a low bed and a metal cupboard.

'There's a ball of soap, a razor and a new razor-blade.'

The soap looked hard and the wax-paper-wrapping on the blade read '7 o'clock'.

'*Shókran*,' said Baus.

The Glaswegian glared. 'I'm no damned Arab, laddie.'

Baus tried to glare back.

'You just watch it, son.'

The door closed with a bang and Baus kicked the bed violently.

*   *   *   *

Elizabeth Blanchard eyed the gallery's two new acquisitions.

Red-hot Charcoal with Four Logs she thought a good investment. Contemporary and 'effective', its four tortuous glowing lumps of wood hit you in the eye without stirring any finer emotions.

Someone had said, 'Quartered drawn and hung.'

Next to it hung *A Green Moon with Oranges*.

'Dove, did you say this is on loan?'

'Er ... yes. From Bonham's. They're auctioning it in November.'

'Hmm.'

'It was painted in 1902 by Isaac Steiner ... *floreat* 1900 to 1930. It has been authenticated.'

'But Galland – or someone – said it had hung in Göring's dining-room at Carinhall.'

Roderick Dove blushed. 'Steiner sold it to a Rabbi in Mainz named Benjamin Amos. In November last year, Amos's son – the owner of a small art studio in Tzfat – sold it to one Erwin Bachmann, whose daughter now intends to sell it at this coming auction.'

Blanchard knew that corruption in the art world was endemic. 'The daughter's name?'

'Monika Steyr. Also West German.'

145

'Bank accreditation?'

Roland Dampier says they have British bank accounts ... Carlisle I think?'

'They?'

'She and her father. They are to share the proceeds.'

Blanchard sat on a wooden bench and looked at it. 'Ask Terence Lucas to look into it.'

Lucas was a private investigator specialising in art fraud.

'If someone harbours suspicions, why not let them look into it ... or just pass our doubts on to Bonham's?'

'No. We have to act properly ... and its history gives grounds for suspicion.'

*   *   *   *

Nina wore black boots and a black coat with a white woollen scarf round her neck. Her peroxide-blonde hair hung in an uncombed cascade down her back and she had carelessly applied black eyebrow pencil, blue eye-shadow and purple lipstick and clipped on large circular silvery earrings. She looked brassy and tart-like and liked it so.

Most would steer clear of such a blatant apostate, but that was why Nina had chosen it; to shock, to dare, to defy ... and to taunt society's hypocritical values.

Off Belgrave Square – in a small tea-shop – she drank coffee and read a copy of The Red Nonagon, printed by The Quorum Press.

'Nasser is throwing out the Jews,' said an article. 'Only one Alexandrian family refuse to go.' They claimed to have lived there for eight hundred years.

She murmured through her cheese-bun–stuffed but *fausse maigre* face, 'Sod the Jews.'

This flub, penned by one 'Hadrian', was skewed to be anti-Israeli.

In Devonshire Street, under light grey scarves of cloud, she etched a chalk triangle on an elm tree. Next she spent an hour in a news cinema before walking to Saint Luke's Gardens.

That evening she discovered that on the morrow she had to go by train from London Saint Pancras to Elstree and Borehamwood, where in a wood, a sad old Trojan donkey – 'horse' was too noble an animal – was to be shot.

CHAPTER TWELVE

The officers stood as Colonel Goodman entered the mess. He bid them a good evening, then bade them sit.

Over pre-dinner drinks, Major Dardry introduced the 'famous archaeologist' to his devout and unpretentious C.O.

'So, Herr Baus, it might be an enterprising start, if we knew your real name?' The Colonel as always, exercised restraint, resisting witticisms or the stating of unnecessary facts.

Coburg took a deep breath. 'Coburg. Walther Coburg.'

The bronze dinner gong boomed softly.

Goodman sat at the head of the long table with Dardry to his right and Walther to his left. A colour photograph of the Queen – wearing a silver tiara and a blue sash – hung on the wall behind him.

Goodman asked Walther about his home and listened to a description of Schloss Lynfels, a fortified tower sited on a low crag.

'I was in Germany briefly in forty-five. I recall re-railing a tram in Hamburg ... and a stockpile of shells – made from inferior lead-like end-of-the-war steel – which we detonated.'

Coburg knitted his brows. An ox stuck in the furrow.

The stubby candles positioned down the centre of the table, flickered. The soup was being served.

The R.E.M.E. officer – Lieutenant Adamson – to Coburg's left said, 'Your Fiat ... the spark-plug leads were loose. Rodman – the chap who fixed it – says that is not something likely to happen as a matter of course ... and especially not on all four plugs?'

To change the subject, Coburg asked the Colonel why the British were in Libya?

'Stability,' came the simple reply.

'But the locals do not like you.'

Goodman smiled graciously. 'They don't like anyone ... Italians, Turks, French ... at least they have their own leader now.'

'They don't like him either. So why *are* you here?'

Dardry said pointedly, 'The rules of conversation here Coburg, are that any query or assertion should be either original or humorous and dispensed with *savoir-faire*. Gaffes will be ignored.'

'However,' Goodman continued, 'to elucidate for the benefit of our guest, on Christmas Eve 1951 Libya became independent under Sidi Muhammad Idris al-Mahdi as-Sanusi – known now as King Idris I – and an advisory council of tribal leaders and feudatories.'

'How would you like your steak, Sir?' asked the mess waiter.

'Britain, by treaty, maintains army and air force bases here, both to support the monarchy and to protect the country.'

'Idris is pro-British?'

'Yes.'

'The world though is changing, Colonel. Duty is in decline ... revolution on the up.'

Dardry replied. 'Dissidents and opportunists have always been around, but good sense usually prevails.'

The Colonel narrowed the field. 'I think we can take your prepared false interest in *Bloodhound* and its radar

Yellow Mist as history? Yes?'

The soup plates were being removed.

Dardry proceeded. 'Coburg, you see that young officer at the far end of the table with the wavy hair? That's Captain Stanton whom you met earlier. Do you recognise him from 1952?'

The prisoner frowned. 'In 1952, I was behind the Iron Curtain.'

'You came to West Berlin, to Charlottenburg Station in the British Sector and there you boarded a train to Bruxelles ... from which you alighted in Liège?'

This was a quite unforeseen sleight of hand.

'A prostitute was murdered in Liège on that July evening ... and the Belgian police will still wish to talk to the man with the missing lower tooth.'

Would they extradite him?

Coburg folded. 'I will tell you the whole story.'

Goodman repressed any display of pity. 'Failure is never as bad as it seems. Churchill said success was failure followed by failure but without a loss of enthusiasm.'

Walther conceded, 'I can boast neither true success nor true enthusiasm and that surely counts as failure?'

Dardry nodded.

'And my abject profession is seemingly obvious?' He looked embarrassed.

'In Syracuse in classical times, only prostitutes could wear ornaments in public – mostly red and blue beads – to advertise what they were.'

'And what are my tell-tale signs?'

Goodman smiled.

'In Egypt,' Dardry bluffed, 'a Maltese fellow at *The Blue*

Ibis – a half-Jewish fellow with black curly hair – noted your contacts.'

'Unna Engström?' Coburg blurted out.

Dardry hid his satisfaction. A *Blue Ibis* paper napkin had been found in the German's suitcase.

Dessert was being served, treacle pudding and custard.

'Coburg, your fate is very much in our hands, but … if you tell us all, we could release you … and then probably it would be sensible for you to contact the Americans.'

He had no real cards to play. 'Why not? My colours were never really nailed to the East German mast.'

Crusted port was being passed to the left ready for the loyal toast.

'Very good, Coburg. We'll debrief you tomorrow.'

All stood. 'The Queen. God bless her.'

'The Queen.'

In the background mess games were being prepared.

Dardry dabbed his lips with his napkin. 'We'll put you in the cooler for the night.'

'Cooler?'

'Army-speak for a prison.'

Adamson and Maynard led the craven German away, settling him on a stack of pressed-metal green ammo boxes in a cramped masonry cell.

'No bed?'

'There's a square of carpet here you can lie on. Don't worry, it's not Whitehall standard.'

'Whitehall standard?'

'Well, it's not so thick that you might asphyxiate in it.'

At the bar Goodman lit his pipe whilst the Major explained that Moscow's Near-Eastern operations were usually run from Beirut, from a second-floor apartment near the flower market. 'Coburg though is likely to be a "special".'

Behind the bar, beside the spirit bottles, hung a slap-dash but colourful painting of a P. & O. steamer in the Suez Canal.

Mr Pinkney – now in bow-tie and waistcoat – served them with two glasses of a cloudy whitish-coloured wine.

The Colonel raised his glass. 'To tomorrow's revelations.'

In his padlocked cell, Walther saw that his stage-managed defection had taken an unanticipated turn. Colonel Zaharoff had not reckoned with the threat of a long sentence in a Belgian gaol. Still, if he spilt all his beans – and why not – he should soon be free.

*   *   *   *

Mrs O'Hara called upstairs to her son. 'Martin? Your dinner's on the table.'

He seemed oddly quiet.

Even before reaching the top of the stairs she smelt gas. Tense with unease, she drew back the bundle of blankets beneath which lay her limp ashen-faced thirty-year-old son, still clutching a hissing unlit gas-poker.

After shaking him violently to no avail, she turned off the gas-tap, opened the windows and collapsed in tears.

The discovery of Stephanie Chalk's body had been reported in the press, although not the steel box.

It contained a weapons cache – two radios with frequency plugs allowing six predetermined settings, six rifles with ammunition and sixty pounds of explosives with an assortment of time-delay and plunger-controlled fuses – all of Soviet manufacture, though with instructions in English and sealed in heavy polythene.

Expecting imminent arrest for plotting acts of treason and also a possible murder charge, O'Hara feared betraying the name of his underground lover, one 'Evelyn Vickers'. This border-line female courier would link 'Action Group N' to 'The Red Sky'.

His colleague, a social worker called David Fraser, would often spread malicious rumours to blacken anyone who criticised their misuse of their offices, but this murder jam exceeded even his evil and nasty talents.

When a councillor had recently queried their helping some in need, but not others – whom they seemed to wish to hurt – Fraser spread the rumour that he had sent death threats to a doctor and spied on a young girl. When the victim by chance heard of this and tried to have it investigated, the whole department stuck together and flatly denied that any such gossip had ever been circulated by Fraser. Rotten boroughs, indeed.

At autopsy, thirty-eight per cent of O'Hara's haemoglobin was estimated to be bound to carbon monoxide, forming carboxyhaemoglobin. Coal gas consisted of methane, hydrogen and approximately thirteen per cent carbon monoxide.

*   *   *   *

The tele-printer clattered. Paper with punched holes along both edges and horizontal perforations every twelve inches, lurched in small steps out into a metal receiving tray.

The print-out read: 'ElAdX4C to HiWyE5R Stop : Bow-wow hoax yield Stop : Catalogued item 2 bagged Stop : Status confirmed Stop : End of message '.

Flight Lieutenant Wynn Todd-Hines left it to see if 'suspect one' would blanch when she saw it.

If she were 'Cog One', she might lead them to 'Cog Two', who in turn might sign-post a higher and more misty terrain. Boy Scout stuff which exercised their detective coterie.

Eiddwen Dovey – a W.R.A.F. cipher clerk – glimpsed the print-out.

Todd-Hines approached quietly. He had an easy and natural dignity.

Looking puzzled, he tore off the print-out and frowned. 'What on earth does this mean?'

'It's from El Adem, Sir.'

'I can see that. But "Bow-wow hoax yield"?'

'I think they've arrested a spy.'

'Oh ... but that's odd isn't it?'

Dovey threw the young Flight Lieutenant a sorrowful glance. 'Everyone knew that the missiles were a ruse, Sir. My brother's a panel-beater in the vehicle sheds and he'd heard.'

'Goodness,' sighed Todd-Hines, 'It seems I'm the one in the dark.'

'Crystal ball malfunction, Sir?' said the gracile Welsh Dragon with a tiny hint of mockery.

'Indeed. I'll return it ... and demand a refund.

Yet if everyone knew of this ruse, why should the Red Foe send a spy?'

'I don't know, but Aline Sayer told me that only scrap metal was sent.'

In her repressed hubris, she had made a slip. She had given him a name.

Also, did she hope that her apparent openness would dispel any ripples of suspicion?

'But Corporal, why should you interpret "Bow-wow hoax yield" as meaning that a spy has been caught?'

A telephone rang and she excused herself to answer it.

The Flight Lieutenant let it rest there, retreating to his desk in front of the glass-fronted cabinets with the data logger and its rows of twinkling dekatron valves which served as the volatile memory store. The information they held was transferred intermittently via a rapidly clicking punch onto paper tape.

Off duty at six, Eiddwen left the deep underground operations bunker, passed through the security gates at the end of the tree-hidden path, walked past a cycle-rack and over to the lay-by near the tennis courts where an R.A.F. bus left at a quarter past the hour for the railway station in High Wycombe.

There she would meet Aline. They would go together, firstly to her flat and then to a local dance hall, because this evening they needed alibis.

*   *   *   *

A bugle sounded reveille.

Coburg awoke.

The horse-hair carpet was prickly and the sun fell in strips through the barred window. Despite the coolness of the night, the heat of the day was starting to rise.

Standing on tip-toe, he could see a Thornycroft fire

engine with its hosery laid out to dry and hear the barks of an instructor as an unseen squad did P.T.

At their headquarters on the Gross-Berliner Damm, Coburg had learnt that Moscow required an East German defector. Fräulein zu Lauenburg, his controller, had put him forward.

He was to spy clumsily, be caught, defect, recite some well-rehearsed falsehoods and then he would be free; free to settle in the West.

Whether Sören Theill-Rige had been the real McCoy or a fake defector, he did not know, but given the whereabouts of his hidey-hole by Ulrica, he had flown into Orly Aerodrome, hired a car, tracked him and killed him.

A rattle of keys heralded the arrival of a native civilian – Useless Youssef – who worked at the barracks.

'*Sabah il kheer*,' announced the old man.

'Ah, breakfast ... good.' He peered at the tray. 'What is "milk" in Arabic?'

'*Laban*.'

'And "corned beef"?'

'Corned beef.'

'Thanks ... I mean *Shókran*. Your name?'

'Youssef Bibawy.'

'Any tit-bits of news?'

The oval of sagging wrinkles smiled slyly. A hand appeared.

Baus gave him an American one-dollar bill.

'A Russian bomber – no doubt from Egypt – tried to make a reconnaissance flight here late last night.'

'And?'

The hand appeared again.

'I said "and", not "hand".'

The bony hand stayed.

A second buck appeared.

'They scrambled two fighters to chase it off.' His Adam's apple bobbed up and down.

'*Shókran*,' Coburg said sourly and waved the man out.

'*Ma'a as-salama*.'

He must be straight about this present task – and tell it in a persuasive manner – in exchange for not being dumped in Belgium. His sexual peccadilloes he would try to conceal. He was utterly alone. His malign masters would not lift a finger. He was expendable.

Some dot-sized flies joined him for breakfast.

Maynard appeared, bright and cheerful. 'Morning, Professor.'

'Good morning.'

'A penny for your thoughts?'

'I was philosophising about pain.' A touch of sarcasm.

'That sounds heavy ... even for a German.'

'Is it real or is it just in the mind?'

'Of course it's real.'

'If I punched you on the nose, would it hurt?'

'I wouldn't try it.'

'But is it a physical sensation ... or just a distressing thought process?'

'Enough of this rubbish. We're to photograph you and then the C.O. will debrief you.'

'You English lack depth.'

'Well ... perhaps shallowness is more fun?'

'You're arrogant too.'

'So, we have something in common?'

Coburg went a dusky red.

Outside, his eyes adjusted to the sun. A troop of Centurion tanks stirred up a dust-storm as they rumbled along making quite a din.

Colonel Goodman sat eating breakfast with his wife and their middle daughter on the terrace outside his house.

It had been built by the Italians and was referred to as *Casabianca* because its walls were white. It had large keyhole-shaped windows with decorative fretwork surrounds and a main door carved from dark sidr wood from Arabia.

The Goodmans were having difficulty marrying off their daughters. Rowena – tall, with a graceful gait and elongated eye-slits – had joined them for a week from her consulate post in Switzerland, having just rejected another suitor.

'But Mummy, I have to *feel* something ... I can't just marry anybody.'

Her mother dimpled her cheeks.

'And besides, he's not very bright. The address on my birthday card had "*appartement*" spelt with a single "p".'

'Well, you can provide the brains, dear,' said her mother.

Her father smiled. 'And remember, no one loves a Smart-Alec ... except us.'

'Daddy ... ' She decided not to bother.

Some remote thuds conveniently ended this boyfriend discussion.

'A two-inch mortar,' Goodman observed. 'The old three-inch one gave a deeper note.'

A few ladies in the camp added a touch of civilisation, just as a few men in a woman's world can add a touch of sobriety and calm.

Dardry in his pre-fabricated wooden office opened a letter from an old school-friend who worked in the city making piles of money by pushing bits of paper around and now – it appeared – was showering all sorts of exotic rubbish on his directionless and spoilt kids.

Dardry wondered, 'Has he not the wit to see that with his bent toy train and a few wooden bricks he had had a happier boyhood than these brats with all their expensive junk? Oh well, the coming world order.'

He heard boots.

'Left, left, left-right-left. Squaaa...d, halt!'

Two Red-caps brought in the prisoner, handcuffed him to the wooden chair, handed the keys to the Major, then saluted and left.

'Good morning.'

'Good morning, Major.'

'*Haben Sie gut geschlafen?*'

'*Danke aber nein, ich habe nicht gut geschlafen.*'

The interrogator smiled gravely. 'Anyway ... are you ready with your exposition?'

The Colonel entered.

Dardry stood up and greeted him.

They sat down.

Dardry opened a note pad, placed it on the trestle-table and took up a pencil. 'So, begin. "The speaking oak"? As on the prow of the Argo?'

'I underrated you,' said Coburg.

'Easily done. The classics ... unromantic perhaps, but a

good antidote to modern fads.'

'We have a common legacy.'

'So if you're the sprat, what was the mackerel? If your Russian bosses knew that the missiles despatched here for trials were only scrap – old Meteor fuselages in fact – why send you?'

'To be caught, defect and feed you some gourmet-class hogwash.'

'We suspected that,' said Goodman.

Dardry pursued his thread. 'As to *Bloodhound*, we assume that the Russians have "eyes and ears" in the Air Ministry and in Bristol's Cardiff works ... and so know everything about it?'

'I would imagine so. The G.R.U. has a very poor opinion of British security.'

'Sadly, we Anglo-Saxons are often no longer well-represented.'

'The Soviets are brutal, but not deluded.'

'Anyway, time to parley,' Goodman stated. 'Tell us all and we will put you on a Greek freighter due to tie up in Benghazi on Saturday. It's sailing on to Beirut where you can contact the Americans and they – I've no doubt – will look after you.'

'I accept. Thank you.'

'The Americans are noted for their generosity.'

Coburg felt a surge of relief. 'I am relieved – and grateful – that you are prepared not to "play by the rules".'

'The Army has a command "break step" for when troops are crossing Bailey bridges ... to prevent any amplification of oscillations, should resonance occur.'

Coburg smiled austerely. 'You are eccentric. In England

last year, I discovered that railway carriages are either first or third class.'

'They did away with second class.'

Coburg spoke at length and without inhibition. He included much detail. The Major made notes.

He omitted though, his killing of a Belgian policewoman in fifty-four, but wondered how to portray the murder in Liège?

'I have shown you my picture-cards, but what about the chicanery in Liège?'

Dardry looked puzzled. 'Liège?'

Entente.

'So after reading philosophy in Freiburg and writing a thesis on "angst", you then went to Moscow to test it?'

'I've not been to Moscow.'

'Apparently it's awful ... yet the Russians are so proud of it.'

'Strange, to be proud of something so awful?

What if London were to order my "repatriation" to East Germany?'

The Colonel gave a shadow of a smile. 'We have ways of side-stepping such things.'

At the shrill whine of a jet engine, Goodman stood up and walked to the window. A De Havilland *Venom* was being serviced outside a hangar. Mechanics in shorts on airframe-specific steel platforms, were replacing machmeters, oil pumps and perhaps those low-creep nickel-titanium alloy turbine components he had heard about.

'Actually,' Goodman admitted, turning round, 'we have received a signal from London ... they know you're here.'

'But you will let me "slip through your fingers"?'

'All your feathers, then we won't wring your neck. You have my word.'

CHAPTER THIRTEEN

In London, Hayley Ellyard walked from her part-time job as a dental receptionist to her flat in Cadogan Gardens on this, the wet afternoon of Saturday the eighth of October.

Someone had said, '"Nice" girls live here.' That meant, 'girls from well-to-do families'. She had savoured the ambiguity for she was unruly, a girl merely posing as being decent and of the 'right type'.

She bought a bottle of milk, bread and a 'Punch' caramel bar from a newsagent's. Outside, against the enamelled advertisements for Raleigh Cycles and Saxa Salt, sat a beggar. She tossed him her change, a farthing – the smallest coin then in circulation – before kicking over a *News Chronicle* A-stand. It read, 'Work-shy thugs cosseted by unions.'

She waited for a gap in the traffic – a British Railways lorry pursued by a convoy of red buses – before crossing over to a row of tall and once grandiose four-storey Edwardian mansions, built in that unattractive smooth-faced red brick.

Having climbed the communal stairs and shaken her umbrella, she unlocked her solid front door. Two men appeared, inside the hallway. They wore white shirts and plain ties and their trousers were held up with braces.

'Who the hell are you?' she stammered, taken aback and turning a lobster-like pink.

The older man with an air of thoughtful authority, pulled a wallet out of his pocket and displayed a warrant-card. 'Police,' he replied. 'Inspector Gosney. And we have a search warrant.'

Hayley knew herself to be scrupulous. The return railway ticket from London St. Pancras to Elstree and Borehamwood she had torn in two and dropped in a bin, as also the pencilled receipt for tea and a Welsh rarebit at The Dutch Oven, a small café in the road beside the station at Elstree.

She threw off her sage-green coat and faced this dross, wearing a chequered blouse with the cuffs rolled up a few inches and a plain black skirt.

They moved into the spacious high-ceilinged main room with its wide bay window, blurred by trickling rain-drops.

Her desk's drawers had been removed and placed on the floor.

'Sit down, please, Miss Ellyard.'

'Oh, thank you.' She had recovered enough to risk a touch of sarcasm. After a sigh and a short hiatus, they all seated themselves. A copy of 'Teach Yourself Russian' lay on the coffee-table with an exercise book.

The senior officer looked at her with gauged circumspection. Did a peculiar emptiness inhabit her?

A photograph of her in gown and mortar-board stood on the desk.

'At which university did you receive your degree?'

'My *two* degrees! That's my masters, from Hull.'

He puckered his brow. 'Where?'

She stuck out her tongue and blew a raspberry.

'Hayley, where were you two evenings ago? On Thursday?'

'Um, I stayed in ... and read Turgenev.'

Gosney eyed her. 'Allow me to jog your memory. In Devonshire Street you etched a chalk triangle on an elm tree?'

'Is that illegal?'

'Well ... that depends.'

'On what?'

'On what you're up to.'

'And?'

'Well, if we suspect criminal activity, it's our duty to investigate.'

'Duty!' she scoffed. 'Every value here is just a travesty. You're just brain-washed.'

'I saw your article in that open magazine there; "How to Discombobulate English Snobs."'

She smiled sweetly.

'Anyway, our concern is with crime ... not ideology.'

'Aren't they linked?'

'In your case, very likely.'

Sinclair joined in. 'Next you spent forty minutes in The Albany News Cinema.'

'More lies.'

'We have your ticket.'

'You're just bluffing.' She *always* threw tickets away.

'There's a hole in the pocket of your black coat. The ticket was inside the lining.'

She gulped, rallied and shrugged.

'Then you took a walk ... to Saint Luke's Gardens.'

'Is there another ticket ... to prove *that*?'

'Saint Luke's Gardens ... the pied yellow and russet of autumn leaves? You collected something from a gap between two coping stones on the top of an old brick wall.'

'Did I?'

'Don't be so coy. An oblong tobacco tin, "Bulwark Cut Plug"? Not a common brand.'

'Perhaps Pyramus and Thisbe liked it?'

'I doubt Babylonians smoked "Bulwark Cut Plug",' stated Sinclair, producing the empty tin.

She pressed her lips together. 'You're talking drivel ... a row of beans.' She waved Turgenev at them; *Sketches from a Hunter's Album*.

'What was in it?'

'Tobacco perhaps? A love letter?'

'In Russian? Did it come from a man who is supposedly one of the Soviet "Trade Mission" here?'

'My curtains are red too. Is that a political offence?'

Gosney grinned modestly. 'I think to test that hypothesis, we would need to wash them first?'

'We're right, even if – like Cassandra – not believed. You're blinkered ... like the adherents of the Bourbons ... propping up the fading beacons of a crooked order.'

Sinclair said, 'We've been here all morning ... we waited for you to leave at eight o'clock ... a cup of tea *would* be nice, Miss.'

She frowned but then went into the kitchen, shadowed by the Sergeant.

With tea and buttered toast laid out on the coffee-table, they resumed their sparring.

'Do you reply with a single-use pad?'

Hayley stared at them blankly. She experienced no difficulty in being difficult; no awkwardness in being awkward.

Gosney, ignoring her unwavering steely stare, brought out a sheaf of bank statements. There were neat headings in capitals underlined with two lines of red crayon and lesser annotations underlined in orange.

'You write tidily.'

No response.

He pondered his slice of toast. 'You receive a monthly income – twenty-six pounds, three shillings and thre'pence – from the dental practice. Twenty pounds too a month from a C. Ellyard ... an allowance from your father? Also though – some months ago – you paid in a cheque for £300 from a bank in Luxembourg.'

'An older dentist – with a Bentley, a pad at Bandol on the Riviera and a wife he is fed up with – gave it to me.'

'Oh?'

'He was a locum ... flirtatious, a dryish wit ... and a good private practice.'

'And he paid you for ... ?'

She sighed heavily. 'Shall we say, "personal services"?'

Gosney stared at her.

'Do you possess any imagination, Inspector?'

'You must be very good to be worth £300?'

Hayley blushed, batted her eyelids and looked down into her lap. 'Perhaps I am?'

Sinclair laughed lightly. 'We will require a name and an address.'

'Your fur-hatted friends are mean with money *and* they do not make traceable payments. So ... blackmail?'

'Who?'

'You tell us.'

She poured more tea for herself, feeling that things were generally going her way. These clumsy fools were clutching at straws.

'I believe that within the "peace campaign" fraternity, you call yourself "Nina Hyman"?'

'"Nina" is a Russian name ... I like it more than "Hayley". I'm a communist and I go on marches ... I'm seeking a more *humane* dimension to life.'

Gosney peered depreciatively at his hostess, whilst Sinclair entered her bedroom and came out with a navy leather handbag, somewhat worn but of quite good quality. He opened it. 'Inside the flap here, someone has with an ink smudge, tried to blot out the original owner's initials ... "S.E.C."'

Hayley blanched. 'I bought it second-hand at a stall in the King's Road.'

'You're wearing a low-cut blouse, Miss Ellyard ... and in your jugular notch I can see the pulsations from one of your main arteries. Your heart rate has just risen.'

Gosney cocked his right eyebrow. 'Back in August, a girl with those initials was murdered in Lincolnshire. One suspect was seen together with a young woman – her description is rather non-specific – who wore a duffle-coat.'

'So?'

'A lilacky-coloured duffle-coat ... which is unusual. In your wardrobe there hangs such an item.'

Hayley's face reddened beneath her peroxide-blonde tied-back hair and her pose stiffened. 'Still, I cannot be the only girl in England with a lilac duffle-coat?'

'We *could* arrest you on suspicion of murder.'

'Support the "pukkah" and the "wasters" ... all so well served by the class system.'

'Have you thought to ask, what put us on to you?'

Whilst Hayley eyed the large Moorcroft table-lamp on a side-table, Gosney lit his pipe and a full half-minute passed.

'All right, what led you here?'

'A list of names and addresses found in O'Hara's room. Combing through his books, the local C.I.D. chap found it tucked into an encyclopaedia.'

Her fraught face betrayed a repressed anger. 'That was careless.'

'It ties you in with him.'

She produced a theatrical yawn and there followed a period of silence.

'You never yawn at what you yourself say?'

'I can't speak and yawn at the same time,' she explained drily.

'*Touché.*'

'Anyway, the Chalk murder can be dumped wholly onto O'Hara's posthumous shoulders.'

'Let us hope his ghost does not object?'

'It won't. Anyway, I don't believe in those superstitious tricks.'

'Ghosts can be vexatious,' Gosney reproached her.

'He might take my side? That would be fun. So beware-e-e!' She attempted a deep tremolo.

'But there's a second murder, isn't there "Nina"?'

She froze.

'A wing commander ... found in undergrowth beside a track leading to Haycomb Farm ... in woods near Elstree?

He was duped into going there, we think ... allegedly to meet his controller.'

She said inwardly, 'Damn all deference to these

169

puppets. The workers are poised to seize power and then I shall be rescued.'

'The girl serving in The Dutch Oven – a New Zealand girl, solid colonial stock with brown plaits – remembers a peroxide-blonde calling and ... '

Eyeing the debris from her emptied drawers and cupboards, she saw an old *brassière*. 'Oh, an old bra!' she interrupted. 'I've given up on bras. You can each have a half of it if you want ... as awards or "cups" ... for being the world's biggest pair of tits?'

The detectives sipped tea and said nothing for a time.

'So then, have you finished?' asked Hayley.

No one moved.

'Your file is ... not the blackest black, but ... "entertaining" shall we say?' Sergeant Sinclair spoke as if in earnest, but his purpose was subtly to tease or annoy. 'The newspaper headline, "Collared", made us smile. The press boys around Cuckfield had a field-day.'

Gosney recalled, '"Priestess of 'The Idaho Immersionary Tabernacle'"? A face of beguiling remorse on the front page ... in a too-large dog-collar?

So cute ... and inventive? A pity it back-fired.'

'And,' chipped in Sinclair, whilst his chief tamped more tobacco into his pipe, 'when your father drove you to court, the duty policeman said, "Thou shalt not park here," and the magistrate addressed you as "Reverend" ... they all had a good day.

Then the fake press cards you had had printed to gain entry into free buffets, *premières*, V.I.P. conferences ... '

'I'm pleased that you're managing to amuse yourselves,' said Hayley in an ominous rather than a humorous tone.

Did the detectives fail to see – or only pretend not to see – that her eye had again rested on the Moorcroft table-lamp?

'You were too – by the way – already on our list of "potentials" … spotted at that East Berlin initiation *séance* in fifty-three.'

Hayley muttered an oath.

Gosney had bluffed, gambling on an imperfect description, in order – via Hayley – to spread unease amongst the traitors. She matched though – they had realised – the physique and the accent of one 'Hayley' as reported by a Lancashire girl who had been at that gathering.

This lass had blabbed to everyone about how she wanted to be a spy and so – of course – had *not* been chosen. Feeling slighted and piqued, she had later marched into Scotland Yard and blown the whole episode to a very amiable counter-terrorism sergeant.

Suddenly, with a jaguar-like bound, Hayley grabbed the lamp, turned it upside-down and from its base, took out the hidden and silencer-fitted Makarov pistol.

Her left hand pulled the slide back and released it so that the top round in the magazine was pushed into the breech, then her right thumb pushed the safety-catch off.

In an amateurish stance, she pointed it at them. As pipe-smoke floated upwards, the targets seemed surprised but not unduly perturbed.

'Lie on the floor, you thick bastards!' When they failed to move, she closed her eyes and pulled the trigger which resulted in a rather feeble metallic clunk. Her forehead wrinkled.

'Hayley, when you made the tea and toast, did you not notice traces of a dark grey powder in the sink? I forgot to swill it away.'

With that, she hurled herself at them with claws outstretched and feet kicking and a ruckus of all-in-wrestling ensued.

The plain-clothes policemen bundled her – trussed up and purple-faced – into their Humber Snipe.

She did manage one short victory though. In the car they had sat her down on the car keys and unable to discover them, only when they took her out again after five minutes of searching, did they come to light.

She laughed hysterically at this huge success.

As the starter motor whinnied, Sinclair asked, 'We established from your neighbour, that you do not use a milkman, so does your milk-bottle-request disc somehow indicate when you are free to exchange tobacco tins?'

'I'll wager a pint on it, Sergeant,' replied Gosney.

'You're on, Sir ... beer or milk?'

*　　*　　*　　*

The following day, Dardry was still debriefing Coburg.

'My life, on the whole, has been a disappointment,' the German acknowledged. 'Yet I have to function – even given a duff script – so to have told you the whole plot rather than the proposed Stalinesque contortions, was no personal sacrifice. I am not breaking faith with my true self.'

'Very Hegelian.

Out of curiosity, what was your motive for killing girls?'

Dardry inquired, lighting his second cigarette of the day.

'Ah, motive? The idol of the self-pitying. Do we need motives?'

'You do if you write crime novels.'

'If whores can sin with impunity ... '

'Impunity?'

'You are right. That a momentary frenzy might be richer than love ... is a sad delusion.'

The Major gave him a cigarette and lit it for him.

'Thanks.'

'You were in the military in the war?'

'Initially I was a navigator on an iron-ore carrier in the Baltic.'

'Charts, brass dividers, sextants?'

'We passed the *Bismarck* in forty-one.'

'An R.A.F. chappie here took part in mine-laying sorties off the Dutch coast ... to obstruct those ore convoys as they neared the mouth of the Rhine.'

'Then I was called up, eventually being drafted to the 26th. Panzer Division ... so Italy mostly.'

'I was in Italy too.'

'Which unit, Major?'

'Derbyshire Yeomanry.' He pointed to a framed photograph of a Daimler armoured car with its crew – commander, gunner and driver all perched on the turret – and on the side its name, *Erechtheus*.

Coburg eyed it; the jerry cans, fire extinguishers and other paraphernalia hung on its sides and its type 19 radio aerial and Bren gun atop.

'Heady days?'

'Originally we were a part of the Cairo Cavalry Brigade.

In 1945, in northern Italy, our recce troop drove over a low ridge one morning and there below us in a broad valley of white stone farms and sloping fields, we saw a long row of retreating German tanks and guns ... all being pulled by oxen, mules and horses ... '

'Because they had no fuel?'

'Yes.'

'That was probably the 26th. ... or what was left of it. I had been invalided out by then.

After the war I joined a Danish shipping line ... '

Walther closed his eyes. He had strangled a pretty stewardess after docking in Esbjerg. Why?

Dardry noted his sudden inertia.

'Then ... back behind the Iron Curtain?'

'Yes, perforce ... '

'To jollity unbounded?'

'To communists, only "the cause" matters. Human life counts for nothing.'

'Doesn't that sap morale?'

'There is no morale; only fear.'

The enamel army-issue clock on the wall read twenty past twelve.

'Time for some lunch.'

As they walked to the mess, Coburg asked, 'Why are there both a ring of green and a ring of red nuts on the wheels of your vehicles?'

'The red nuts hold the two halves of the wheel together. They must not be undone until the tyre's been deflated.'

'Have I now screwed up some "red nuts"?'

Dardry looked ahead and smiled. 'Let's hope so.'

CHAPTER FOURTEEN

Terence Lucas grinned through his myriad wrinkles. 'Rod old chap, I have found some ill-fitting pieces in your jigsaw.'

Dove inhaled. 'So, Blanchard was right? Drat.'

'I've been to Mainz and the retired surveyor who lives next door to the Amoses' old house remembered the family. They emigrated to the States in thirty-five. He has also heard a rumour that after the war, they moved to Israel and – to start with at least – ran a falafel bar in Tel Aviv.'

'So ownership until 1935 is possible but not definite?'

'Quite. I next went to Bonn to inspect the inventories of items found in Göring's hunting lodge.

The information officer there was pleasant enough, but said that the archivists were just sick of oddballs probing the Nazi era and would simply block such an enquiry.

When Jews left the Third Reich, they were allowed to take very little with them ... and it seems hardly likely that such a painting could have been taken in a suitcase.'

'So it's an open verdict ... just?'

'The owner of the "small art studio" in the Old City in Tzfat in Upper Galilee – one Aaron Amos – was blown to pieces by an anti-personnel mine almost two years ago and his business closed.'

'So ... it sounds like a dead-end?'

'Nothing is ever a dead-end.

First off, who is this Erwin Bachmann, whose daughter plans to sell it via the auction at Bonham's? We need to pin-point this pair.'

'Bachmann and this Monika Steyr might be crooks?'

'Or ... he is a crook and she just a sure-footed beast of burden ... the ass bearing the gold?'

'Hmm ... From Dampier's description, I would say that the ass knew what it was doing.'

Dove and Lucas went to a tea-shop near the British Museum where tea-cups and a plate of éclairs duly appeared.

'I've been to Tzfat and in a steep cobble-stoned alley – with a step up every half metre and a view of the ruined Crusader castle high above – I found Amos's former bric-à-brac shop. Like the castle, the rows of shops and dwellings there were also built of large well-weathered old ashlars.

Above the thick blue-painted stone door-lintel, a wrought-iron sign hung at right angles to the wall: *Café Dido*. The proprietor was cordial and still had a few second-hand books, prints and bits of decorative porcelain which had come from Amos's business and which were still for sale.'

'And what could he say about Aaron Amos and *A Green Moon with Oranges*?'

'Only really that he has a surviving daughter – she who had sold the premises on – who now lives in South Carolina and is called Judith Herzog.'

'And?'

There was a pause. 'I'm unable to trace a telephone number for her ... so ... will you stand me a trip?'

Dove grinned awkwardly. 'Well, Miss Blanchard thinks we have to solve this ... so I suppose so.'

'In *Schloss Karnzow* in East Germany old masters lay hidden in a huge iron safe ... to protect them from the bombing in the cities. It was blown by the advancing Red Army in forty-five ... Prints from the *Bremen Kunsthalle* were found dumped in a local forest ... a Van Gogh was found in a puddle ... '

'Obviously a water-colour?'

'Some Dürer sketches were seen too, two Titians ... boot-prints on one of them. Most though have disappeared ... probably to Russia.'

'And may now be being smuggled out by those in positions of power?'

'Two have turned up in Italy. And lesser works naturally, arouse less scrutiny.'

'Your detective work involves a lot of travel,' Dove observed.

Lucas smiled. 'I paddled in the River Jordan on this last jaunt. It was shallow and pale green ... between drooping willow-like trees. And I went up to Belvoir Castle above the Jordan Valley ... superb masonry.'

The listener took a second éclair. 'Geographical pleasures?'

'And such travel tonics – for me at least – equal happiness.'

'Or mix an elixir to mask sorrow?'

'That's a bit depressive, old chap.'

'Still, I envy you your cure.'

*　　*　　*　　*

Walther Coburg had arrived in Beirut, still then known as 'The Paris of the Near East'.

On board a red and white tram, he wound his way

through busy streets, tinged with the exoticism and frenzy of the Levantine world.

Lebanese women appeared fat and jolly, fed on sweetmeats and scented fats, laughing animatedly with one another and festooned in colourful scarves and gold jewellery.

The men were leaner, more dour and with neat white evenly-spaced teeth, yellowy-green limbs and wary, slightly feminine smiles.

At the faculty of *Lettres Orientales* at the Université St. Joseph, the fugitive met up with Bernard Emmitt, a globe-trotting New Englander who wore a voluminous orange shirt with ruff-edged-cuffs and a silk cravat. Goodman's daughter had some link with him.

They drove downhill in Emmitt's *coupé* under a jagged noon-day sun, the glittering blue sea ahead framed by a knotted oak and a crumbling tower.

'I saw Rowena's telegram, saying that you were coming.'

Walther outlined non-specifically what he had to offer.

'I can put you in touch with someone in the U.S. Embassy.'

At the *Club Esclairmonde*, a waiter in a green sleeveless *abaya* over a white shirt showed them to a table with a red table-cloth laid diagonally on top of an orange one and padded cane chairs. He recommended the kleftico.

'Kleftico?' Coburg asked, '*Qu'est-ce à dire?*'

The waiter explained that this dish took its name from the Greek 'clepto' meaning 'to steal', because Greek brigands would steal a sheep, take it to the mountains and roast it very slowly in a pot with garlic rosemary and tomatoes so that no tell-tale smoke should reveal their hide-out to their Turkish overlords.

'I see. A sort of mutton *en daube*?'

Emmitt waved to two American girls passing in the street. 'My students. The taller one is quite wealthy. She had her handbag stolen last week.'

Out of the blue, a squad of police – led by a lance-sergeant – charged onto the terrace and ringed the two swarthy men eating at the far end.

'*Mon Capitaine*, what is this?'

A briefcase was emptied containing six green cotton bags, each jingling with counterfeit Lebanese fifty-piastre coins.

The forgers tried to bolt by vaulting over the balustrade, but were seized, hurled to the ground, beaten fiercely with wooden batons and handcuffed.

'In the Lebanon,' explained the Bostonian, 'there are two difficulties. If you have no money, it is making it. If you have it, it is keeping it.'

The pretty serving girl who had come with the lamb dishes, smiled wryly. 'If I may poke my nose in Sir, that remark – though very philosophical – is of little practical use.'

Emmitt opened his arms. 'I yield ... but I tip well.'

She blushed.

Emmitt then asked Coburg if he were a 'rounder'?

'A "rounder"?' queried Coburg, perplexed.

'As in one who "does the rounds"?'

'If I understand you correctly, no. I was cornered by the Brits, but their army intelligence officer suggested I contact your "Deputy Head of Mission" here in Beirut.'

Emmitt accepted this. 'The C.I.A. guy here is Algy Burrows. He's "chunky" but quietly astute ... in his fifties.'

'Chunky' was an American 'in' word at the time, used to describe everything from marmalade to pullovers.

One telephone call later from the bar and Emmitt told Coburg to call at the U.S. Embassy next morning.

'*Au point du jour*?'

'First thing? God no. It's an embassy.'

'I thought Americans were hard working, up-early guys?'

'I repeat, it's an embassy. Ten at the earliest.'

'The British gave me forty dollars, so I could stretch to ten for a neat casual jacket.'

'Here, ten dollars will buy you the Rolls Royce of casual jackets.'

The next day over a leisurely hotel breakfast, Coburg read *Le Monde* whilst dreaming of '*le beau monde*'.

A sallow self-preening Levantine lass refilled his coffee cup. If you had money, these hotel lasses were available for a small extra charge, he had heard ... unlike the Scandinavian Unna-types. Those girls only seemed to fall in love in corny Burbank movies.

At half past ten, he presented himself at the U.S. Embassy and was shown into its well-watered garden.

'Welcome to "The Stockade", Walther.'

His host was a calm, softly spoken fellow possessed of an understated but well-informed grasp of the world stage.

After a firm hand-clasp, they sat down on outdoor sofas.

Walther sketched briefly his childhood, his schooling, his time in the German merchant navy and his war years.

'So, Walther, spring 1945 ... I take it you weren't too pleased to see the Red Army on the horizon?'

'Bizarrely, I owe my life to them.

I was invalided home from Italy in January forty-five and then in March found myself in charge of a *Volkssturm* troop in East Prussia.

By a wood we knelt in some heather, behind these angular-shaped rocks ... myself, four old men, three boys of about ten and two teenage girls, armed with First World War rifles on which the youngsters had been given about ten minutes of instruction.'

'Mauser 1871s?'

'Yes. Bolt-action. There were no 98Ks available ... and uniforms were just yellow arm-bands with "VS" stamped on them.'

'I've seen them.'

'As midnight approached the stillness grew eerie. The sour-smell of the ferns and bracken tinged the air and a hazy white moon sank slowly below the tops of the deep-blue pines.

Suddenly we heard tanks clattering and grinding somewhere on the bleak moorland nearby ... and we guessed they would be Russian. No one spoke, but sweat trickled down our spines.

We peered into the gloom, expecting to see Red Army infantry advancing through the undergrowth.

Shooting started, but from where? Then a shell exploded and a great clod of earth hit me. I came to sometime later, alone.

Picking up my rifle, I crept back along a track and after a while ran into two lugubrious *Feldpolizei* N.C.O.s ... well-fed thugs in warm black uniform coats and riding boots.'

Burrows listened keenly.

'I told my story, but these bastards simply exhibited

knowing smiles. "Ah! Only *you* survived? How fortunate." The *Feldgendarmerie* sergeant exuded mockery. "Where did you hide?" I put my hands up. The corporal drew his revolver, but ... as I awaited my end, a sudden burst from an unseen Russian machine-gun cut the brutes down.'

Burrows could see the scene. 'A lucky escape.'

'They "saved my bacon", I believe is the expression?'

'Yes. Life is never pure black and white.'

Walther described life in East Germany, how say on Party days you turned out and waved your little Red flag. If you refused you ended up at the end of the queue for everything. Silence was not acceptable.

Good coffee and 'cookies' arrived and for two hours the American sifted through Coburg's story.

'My first task was in late fifty-three, but my greatest *coup* – or so I thought – was in fifty-four. I seduced an artist in Dinkelsbühl, whose father was a West German envoy connecting Bonn and various foreign capitals, into photographing some of his communiqués.'

'Seduced you say? With money, your manliness or with threats?'

'Well, initially the second, then the first and lastly the third ... She was attractive ... until she unwisely told another boyfriend. Lying in a flat-bottomed boat one echoless summer's day, moored on a canal spur by some long grass, eating tangy wild berries and watching dragonflies flit over the green water, she let it slip after "linking up".'

'I heard about it. Actually, she *was* suspected and the second "boyfriend" was an undercover B.N.D. guy.

They asked her why she had become so obsessed? She

answered rather pathetically, "I suppose because I wanted it."'

'An honest answer.'

It was the American's turn to open up.

'In the Near East, it's a bit different.

Money always counts of course, but the Arabs have a hard clear-cut faith. No sympathy with other views, no half-tones, but a dogma which despises doubt and lives in terror of Allah. Their religion is one of extremes and superlatives, with an inert incurious intellect and imaginations vivid but not creative. They have no art, no organisation, no idea of great industry, no mythology.

Deserts create – it seems for the Arab – a strange unintelligible yearning, a creed of world-worthlessness, barrenness, rejection.

He may enjoy a few luxuries – good coffee, fresh water, pretty women – but he is not attracted to material ties.

His god is intangible, not anthropomorphic, unethical ... yet alone and great. The Arab is within god, not god within him and this sterile deity robs him of compassion and kindness. Pain and cruelty are a delight; abnegation a pleasure.'

'Very fluent. You should write a book on it.'

'I did.'

Over more coffee, juice and sandwiches, Burrows gave his guest an open offer of American citizenship, protection in the future if required and a generous wad of two thousand dollars in exchange for a detailed debriefing – names, dates, places et cetera – on his time in East Germany.

Walther thanked him sincerely.

'You're a survivor buster. You deserve a bit of luck.'

* * * *

Two quietly bristling civil servants in bowler hats and charcoal overcoats were ushered into a capacious and walnut-panelled lift at the Air Ministry by a smart R.A.F. warrant officer.

In a spacious second-floor corridor, with its relief-patterned ivory Cole wall-paper and paintings of early biplanes, he knocked on a door marked 'Air Vice-Marshal Fairweather'.

A young secretary in civilian dress, called, 'Come in.'

Behind her desk, she enquired of the visitors, 'Mr Torrance and Mr Manley?'

'The same.'

She hung up their coats and hats before knocking and leading them through an inner door.

A uniformed Sir David rose from behind a broad desk and waved them to two studded leather chairs.

In their Anderson and Sheppard Savile Row suits, the callers acquiesced.

Rain rattled on the windows.

'Fortunately you people always carry brollies?'

'But we don't open them, Sir David. If it rains, we hail a cab.'

'Oh.'

Torrance's moustache twitched. 'Do you know why we're here?'

The host smiled without humour. 'No.'

'Would the name "El Adem" provide a clue?'

'Ah ... to commend us on our capture of an East German spy?'

'"To discuss" would be a more apt infinitive.'

'No medals then?'

'It seems that a number of officers – including yourself – set up a deception?'

Sir David feigned surprise. 'Many of our communiqués are being intercepted. And a few toads have popped out from under their stones.'

Manley managed a smile. 'Sir David, let us not jump to rash – or indeed wrong – conclusions.'

The A.V.M. leant back in his chair. 'Have we inadvertently put spokes in *your* wheels?'

'Quite so. Perhaps intending to play for the home team … but in fact queering the pitch.'

'Given the facts, could such a hypothesis hold water?'

'Most Army and Air Force officers are – forgive me – not the brightest.'

'Though knowledge won laboriously, sticks.'

'Before we analyse this Libyan fracas, there is a related topic. The spy-mistress, who ran your prey at El Adem, is hiding somewhere in Britain.'

'Oh?'

'Ulrica zu Lauenburg … though she uses a number of aliases when abroad. Has Coburg mentioned her?'

'Not that I am aware.'

'If she could be persuaded to defect, that would be a major *coup*.'

Sir David shook his head. 'You are crediting me with more than I know.'

Torrance's shrug seemed to say, 'Oh well, it was worth a try.' After a slight huff, he continued, 'The death of Wing Commander Orr-Ellis? What led to that do you think?'

'His lack of discretion, I imagine.'

'So?'

'Well, to belabour the obvious, he was becoming a danger to your friends.'

A stunned pause, then, 'Are you suggesting that *we* played some part in his death?'

Sir David was not to be bowed. 'Not directly, but I daresay you were complicit.'

Manley inhaled sharply. 'This is an outrage, Air Vice-Marshal ... I can only suppose that you are suffering from paranoia?'

'Would it were so, but the day before he was shot, he told me of his recruitment in Vienna, by someone whose real name – gleaned from a hotel desk register – he thought was "Coombs".'

'Even if this story were true, such a name would always be an alias.'

'Contact was by a five-number-group code using a book titled, *The Seventh Turco-Venetian War*.'

Torrance shrugged as if clueless.

'There was a Coombs in the Civil Service, accused in 1951 of spying. Does that ring a bell?'

'Oh, Sir Philip Dark-Coombs? Yes. The Foreign Office investigated him and cleared him on all counts.'

'A coven of top lawyers defended him, which to a cynic, might actually suggest guilt?'

'I do remember the case and that London law firm is one of the most respected within the profession.'

'Ah yes, the legal profession ... renowned for its high principles?'

Torrance stood up and crossed the room.

On a bookcase stood a model of a ponderous 1920's Garrett steam lorry. Sir David had spent many hours in his shed, making it.

Torrance picked it up and – with a hint of condescension – admired it. 'Neatly soldered ... a clockwork motor, split pins, helical gears ... '

'Bevel gears. Helical gears lose too much energy ... the friction of their teeth sliding past one another.'

'Hmm, you may soon have more time for hobbies ... during your retirement ... and without a pension if dismissed for "improper conduct".'

'In the British Library's newspaper archives, I read that in Coombs's barrister's summing-up, he misquoted a prosecution witness. If a witness lies, that is perjury. If a lawyer lies ... well ... perfectly all right.'

Manley gave this senior R.A.F. officer a wooden and unflinching stare. 'Our decrypting your coded messages into plaintext sporadically, is purely to check your security levels.'

'In theory.'

'Also, security abroad is an M.I.6. domain.'

'Security is everyone's concern, surely?'

'Passively, yes, but not actively.'

Sir David smiled. 'Still, nothing ventured, nothing gained.'

Manley also stood up and eyed a large splash-it-on-style painting of a sulphur-yellow Fokker with black Iron Crosses on its wings, diving from soap-sud-like clouds through a powder-blue sky towards a white cauliflower cumulus and a dark grey Avro 504.

'We raised our suspicions with you repeatedly,' Fairweather continued, 'but nothing changed. We might as well be sending our signals *en clair*.'

'Where is Coburg now?'

'With the Americans if he has any sense.'

'Has a rendezvous been arranged?'

'Wouldn't you like to know?'

'And *why* the Americans?'

'The "safer" option, I imagine.

Oh, have you read today's papers? The police believe that Orr-Ellis was murdered by a non-embassy Russian agent.'

Silence.

'They've arrested a suspect and her pistol is being forensically examined.'

'Clearly we are wasting our time.'

'So, off to re-group?'

'Good day to you.'

'Oh, by the way, Coburg has spilt some *real* beans.'

Irritated yet necessarily curious, the two faces turned. 'What beans?'

'Not Heinz, but a good brand. He was outmanoeuvred by unexpected evidence ... snared by past crimes ... so he came clean and exposed as chaff all the lies he was meant to sow.'

The ice crystals could grow no larger. Manley's urbanity cracked. 'Some military officers are just too big for their boots ... far too big.'

The door closed.

The following day in Wellingborough, Sir David went into a red telephone box and dialled the barracks at Aberporth. Coins in: dial: wait for the peeps: press button

'A': a clatter of metallic discs falling: connection and the voice of an army switchboard operator.

'Good morning. This is Air Vice-Marshal Fairweather. Is it possible to speak with Colonel Trewick?'

After some clicks, interruptions and silences, he heard, 'Trewick here.'

'Colonel, David Fairweather.'

'Sir David!' A note of surprise. 'How are you?'

'Very well, thank you Colonel. Is it possible that we could meet up in the next day or two?'

Trewick understood that this was not a social call. 'The Army and Navy Club, tomorrow evening?'

CHAPTER FIFTEEN

The 15.22 puffed out of St. Pancras Station, heading for St. Alban's.

Roland Dampier, in a first-class corner seat, lit a small cigar and re-opened his P.G. Wodehouse book.

The door of the compartment slid open and beneath his lowered eyelids he saw two black-stockinged female legs enter. They sat opposite him and crossed themselves.

After a minute or two, their owner coughed, touched his knee and asked with a hint of brightness, 'Mr Roland Dampier?'

'Er ... yes?' He closed his Wodehouse.

'Susan Harwood ... we're both art specialists, I believe?'

'Oh? I've not heard the name.' A trace of unease crept into his voice, but her feminine appeal ignited his interest.

He gauged her to be late twenties. She displayed a bob of cinnamon-hued hair, eye-catching contours and a decided forwardness in her manner. A handbag and a paperback lay beside her. 'Neither of us though are reading books on art.' She held up her book, *Nuclear Physics for the Uninterested*. 'Perhaps we just *pretend* to like art?'

He puffed his cigar.

'I was in Bonham's last week, looking at the toy auction catalogue ... my father has two unusual early tin-plate aeroplanes. He salvaged them from his parents' home after it was shelled in the war.'

'Indeed.' His eyes gradually explored her once more. They rose from her plain black leather shoes, up past her thighs, her rounded pelvis, her soft magnetic breasts, arriving lastly at her face.

A house in Britain might have been bombed, but not shelled.

She forced a stereotypical smile onto her harsh features. 'As you have guessed perhaps ... I am about to ask you something?'

He gave her a puzzled look.

'I understand that Bonham's had intended to auction a painting by an Isaac Steiner in November ... but it has been withdrawn?'

'Er ... yes.'

'Might I ask you about the girl who brought it to Bonham's?'

'Miss Harwood ... I cannot discuss our clients.'

'Forgive me. I am really a private detective.' She sat forward, her knees pressed together.

'That does not alter my position.'

'Suppose I start the ball rolling?' Her mint-scented breath wafted across to him. 'Uwe Engel was executed two days ago in Magdeburg.'

Dampier snuffed out his tobacco leaf and felt his penis stiffen. 'I'm sorry ... "Uwe Engel"?'

'He *was* East Germany's Foreign Minister.'

'Was?'

'He has stolen many *objets d'art* from the state archives ... including *A Green Moon with Oranges*.'

'I see.' He smiled faintly. 'So socialists do – deep down – have bourgeois values?'

She hid her irritation and rested some fingers deftly on his left knee. 'Would you have his name down as "Erwin Bachmann"?'

'Possibly.' He placed a hand lightly on top of hers.

'And Monika Steyr is his co-crook.'

'Not his daughter?'

'Unlikely. His torture wounds became infected ... fodder for some bugs ... and they were treated with a flame-thrower ... '

'Burnt to death?' Dampier looked aghast. 'Could you call in to Bonham's and inform us officially?'

'No, because I would like you to tell me something confidentially.'

Dampier kept his breathing steady.

'Ignore the rules and rescripts. No one will know. I can come back with you to your flat.'

He gave her a restrained smile.

'Ah ... just as I had you down as a church mouse.'

Though middle-aged and outwardly non-descript, he was more astute than at first appeared. He guessed that 'Susie' was some sort of Red ghost. 'You wish to trace this "Monika Steyr"?'

Susie nodded deeply. 'Good. We understand one another.'

He sensed perilous waters. 'We have an address in Monaco ... but I expect that'll lead nowhere?'

'Or be someone she trusts. The name and branch of her bank will probably be the best lead.'

The train clicketty-clacked and smoke drifted past the window, but it was gradually slowing.

'What are you offering?'

'Twenty-five pounds?'

He was thinking hard. 'That's a bit stingy?'

'Stay the night with you? If you wish?'

'Ah, *les beautés du diable.*'

She winked and smiled at the same time.

'We *do* have her bank details. And she will have given them a genuine address when first registering.'

'Yes.'

'Unless it was something temporary ... until the confirmatory documents and a cheque book had arrived?'

Miss Harwood squeezed his thin hand and smiled artfully.

'But there must be *someone* at that address. Also, the staff at her bank could pin-point withdrawals, cheques et cetera ... if you can persuade them to divulge such things?'

Again came the sly smile. 'We should recruit you into our agency.'

Her English was near perfect, though the 'oo' in her 'good' had been too drawn out.

Brakes squealed.

'This is Hendon. Return to Bonham's ... pretend you've forgotten something ... ?'

'Er ... that's easily done.'

'And meet me in the station tea-room at St. Alban's, say ... seven-thirty?'

'All right.' He spoke decisively.

Four hours later, Roland Dampier and his shapely new companion sauntered together down Beresford Road. They went through a side-gate then up a flight of steps to his top-floor flat in a house which had a wide crack down one wall, the result of a land-mine dropped by the *Luftwaffe* in 1941.

He put on the lights and the kettle and asked her if she wanted some toast with grated cheese or perhaps tomato soup?

Susie said soup would be nice, then with Roland in the kitchen, kicked off her shoes and tip-toed softly to the outer door to unlock it. It was though not locked. She seated herself elegantly on the sofa.

He placed the supper items on the long coffee-table and sat down beside his guest. As he leant forwards to butter his bread, their thighs touched and she sustained the contact.

After a spoonful of soup, she took from her bag her book on elementary nuclear physics.

'Did you know that when Russia exploded its first atom bomb in forty-nine, that it was a hoax?'

'A hoax?'

'It was half a million tons of dynamite with a sprinkling of uranium 235 on top. It worked. No one here guessed for three years and by then the U.S.S.R. had the real thing.'

'Oh.'

He put his hand on her thigh and she gave him a peck on the cheek before picking up the physics book and opening it at random, at a diagram in blue and yellow.

'I can just understand this,' she said. 'A uranium 235 nucleus when hit by a neutron, becomes a uranium 236 which then breaks into a barium atom, a krypton atom and three single neutrons and if there are enough uranium 235 nuclei around for one or more of those three neutrons to collide with, then that will trigger a chain reaction.'

'I think I follow.'

'Good.' Unabashed, she cuddled up to him and read the caption aloud. 'Slower neutrons have a greater chance of splitting a uranium nucleus, so heavy water or graphite are used to slow them down and ... '

A narrow but tough cord fell before Dampier's eyes and then tightened on his scrawny throat. He tried in vain to loosen it, but rapidly turned purple.

The two agents emptied his briefcase, but found no notes on *A Green Moon with Oranges* or on Monika Steyr.

They ransacked his pockets. They combed painstakingly again through the briefcase's contents. She swore. Grigory smashed a vase.

The wall-clock chimed.

'The bastard!'

The girl hissed, 'Calm down.' She had three hours to get back to the World Athletics' arena.

After savage angry sex on the rug, she pulled on a pair of gloves and wiped everything she had touched with a soapy flannel before she and her ruffian assistant left.

They locked the door and threw the key into a lush bed of irises, before descending the steel steps quietly, then crossing the garden and leaving via the side-gate.

Ten minutes later, a squad car pulled up and four plain-clothes officers jumped out.

'The lights are on,' noted the inspector.

When no one answered the door, a hefty sergeant shouldered it open.

'We're too late.'

Behind the sofa lay an open book. 'In uranium ore only 0.7% of the uranium atoms have an atomic weight of 235 whilst ... ' Inside the front cover was written its owner's name; 'E. Zielonka'.

*　　*　　*　　*

The next morning, Coburg met Burrows again. Two of his 'green-ink' intelligence colleagues were present.

'So, you've led an exciting life, Walther?' remarked Larry, a walrus-like old-timer.

'I'm not sure if "exciting" is the word.'

'My history master said, "If it's not exciting, it's not real." Give us heroes and villains ... none of this balanced-approach crap.'

The office was high-ceilinged, comfortable and attractively furnished.

These were the days of Eisenhower and of an America at the peak of her wealth and power. This trio though – whilst direct and open-handed – were under the surface, little different to businessmen. Their money, though welcome, conjured only a dependent and thus artificial connection. It forged no ideological bond.

'Have you gotten a fire-arm?' asked the rather prim Rebecca Naish.

'Er ... no.'

'I'll speak to stores.'

'Thanks.'

'Cowboys and Indians,' noted Larry. 'And these Indians have had their feathers badly ruffled.'

A serving girl brought in coffee and rolls.

Rebecca – brought up in an affluent and modish pre-war New York – had a pleasant if airy manner. 'So Walther, you are our new Pied Piper, who will lead the rats to the river?'

'I'll do my best.'

The triumvirs smiled.

Coburg knew from Ulrica, that French counter-espionage had traced some financial skulduggery here to a Lebanese minister and linked it to a bribe whereby the McDonnell Aircraft Corporation had secured an order in preference to the French company, Sud-Est. This crew were not wholly white.

'Soviet infiltration is our current number-one enemy,' Algy stated. 'It saps confidence, undermines trust.'

'That's their method. My old home – *Schloss Lynfels* – is some sort of training camp for secret subversion ... *and* it's gone to rack and ruin.'

'I understood that German aristocratic names were prefixed with *von* or *zu*?' queried Rebecca.

'In the south of Germany, but not usually in the north ... though there are exceptions, for instance Cecilia von Kleve.'

She reflected, 'Your former boss, Ulrica zu Lauenburg, is thought to have gone to ground somewhere in Britain.'

'Oh?'

'To have fled the brutal and thought-denying utopia of collectivism?'

The over-weight Larry asked, 'Any idea where she might be?'

Coburg thought for some seconds. 'I never grasped the whys or wherefores of all her foreign trips.'

After a further two-hour debrief, he was shown out by Rebecca, who after handing him some money and a Luger in a small box, squinted into his cold eyes with their juvenilia-level of humanity. 'Be careful.'

Back in the small Hôtel Etap and after a nap, he felt the need for a girl.

He popped out to buy a pair of white flannels, a dark-blue blazer and a pair of sun-glasses, before combing his greasy hair and trimming off a few aberrant tufts; after which, the scissors were well-oiled. He pocketed the pistol in an inside pocket and – after eyeing himself in the mirror and adjusting the sun-glasses – left.

In the foyer, the receptionist returned his passport. It had been required for registration. 'Thank you, Herr Baus.'

He sauntered down to a quiet open-air bistro beside the harbour, where in the gathering greyness of dusk, a string of red lights were reflected in the dark wavelets lapping the mole.

He sat on a bar-stool, leant his elbows on the brightly-lit bar-top and ordered an Americano.

A slim sharp-featured blonde appeared. 'Make that two.'

She perched herself, cross-legged, on another stool two feet away from Coburg and glanced at him with cool affection. Her skewed and acne-pocked face resembled perhaps a mask from a Greek tragedy, but she had a good figure. She wore a black leather skirt, a lacy-edged white bodice and a pink angora cardigan.

'Hi, I'm Circé.'

'Circé? You're very pretty. You would have caught my eye even if you had not presented yourself so boldly.'

'Am I *so* tempting? Well yes, I can see that.' She gave a coy smile.

'But … I thought girls usually pretended to be indifferent to male curiosity?'

'That's only *after* they've aroused interest.'

The barman served their coffees.

Coburg guessed she were a part of some plot, but he wanted urgently to screw her. He would rely on foiling the trap when it came.

He put a lump of sugar into his cup.

'There was a sugar bowl closer on your right.' Her English had a slight nasal twang.

'Your nearness was a sufficient reward for the detour.' He moved his stool closer to hers and slid a hand onto her right thigh.

Her cheeks dimpled. 'Do you have a name?'

'Er ... Albin.'

She nodded slowly. 'And why are you in the Lebanon, Albin?'

'I'm checking the beaches.'

'For pretty girls?'

'No, for landings ... I'm German.'

'What? Oh, very funny. Still planning to conquer the world?'

He smiled archly. 'May we eat together? I'm here alone.'

She feigned hesitancy. 'Hmm ... you look a bit dodgy.'

'Is that good or bad?'

She smiled cryptically. 'We'll eat in Le Donjon. It's fine here at lunch-time, but now it's growing chilly. One day last August, I melted ... literally.'

'Well ... you've solidified back into a very agreeable shape.'

They walked to the nearby hostelry.

'Are you French?'

'Half-French.'

'And your work?'

'Banking ... the Nile Deposit Bank.'

In an ambience created by a flickering oil-lamp and the aroma of sliced limes, she gazed at him.

'I've seen your picture ... linked to a Swedish girl and

The Suez Mercantile Bank?'

He looked up and shook his head. 'A look-alike perhaps. *You* remind *me* of an Austrian farm lass I once yearned for … with a yoke with two wooden milk pails.'

Circé pulled a face. 'That's *not* what a girl wants to hear … and it sounds a bit like a fantasy.'

'What else should I say? You know you're irresistible … so why repeat it?'

'Because I cannot hear it too often.'

'I will give you a gift instead … a thousand-carat diamond.' He slid the cut-glass salt-cellar towards her.

'Oh, it's beautiful!'

In a graver tone, he added, 'But you would prefer a particular envelope?'

A hand laid on his forearm, signalled that she had understood his inference. She also perceived the coarseness of his psyche.

They ate goulash and sipped a local wine. Her allure was perhaps heightened by the danger. Oh yes, she was bait, but … he would fix his as yet unveiled assassins.

'Come back to my place.'

This all seemed so easy. The ox though knew it was being led to market.

They set off, wending their way past gimcrack bars and a gaggle of raucous party-goers, before turning into the quieter *Rue des Soeurs* under a greeny-yellow moon which floated calmly in a patchy dark-grey sky.

In the deep doorway of a squat Romanesque basilica, they exchanged oozy kisses. Her bust rose and she sensed his prong expanding and pressing itself into her lower belly.

He kept a wary watch over her shoulder. All seemed

quiet. He fingered her leather skirt. 'Does wearing leather make you feel powerful?'

Leaving the twinkling lights of the town behind, they climbed a gorse-edged track.

'My house used to be an artillery bunker. There are still some rusty aerials on the roof. In the last war it was used as a listening post.'

This scary girl revelled secretly in her subversive act.

The former blockhouse stood on a promontory above the bay. It now had ornate wrought-iron railings and a neat garden with apricot trees which gave off a tangy scent. The rasping of the cicadas echoed squeakily.

Circé descended the three stone steps and unlocked the carved teak, vine-surrounded door. It creaked open on its hinges of hammered iron.

'So ... my little nest.' She smiled invitingly.

Coburg nodded earnestly. This was where they would trap him ... but he was ready.

In her low-ceilinged abode, with its three-foot-thick concrete walls, she turned on the light.

Next she twirled round on her heel beside a rough redwood chest and smiled at her quarry to draw his eyes upwards, whilst her hand sought her old-fashioned revolver in her brown leather handbag.

It snagged in the lining and as she fumbled and panicked, a bullet from his Luger hit her in the solar plexus just as her weapon clattered onto the floor-boards.

She buckled and fell backwards – people only fall forwards in films – and groaned.

Coburg quickly retrieved her key and locked the main door before checking the four rooms.

A black cat stared at him.

Circé's body lay supine between a potted palm and a sofa, whose cushions were dark blue, patterned with light blue Parua Bay birds with pink beaks.

His old habitual addiction strangely deserted him. This dying nymph incited no urge for an aberrant sexual release. Compassion for once, though minimal, broke through.

The door handle rattled. There was a furious hammering on it.

Coburg stood to one side of this solid piece of woodwork – in case they should shoot through it – and on its hinge-side to be out of view if they entered.

The windows were narrow and barred.

As he flicked off the light-switch, he received a high-voltage shock. Inept Frog electricians!

'Mademoiselle Beauclerc?' shouted a voice urgently.

Ten seconds of tense silence passed. Sweat gleamed on Coburg's face. Bullets tore into the door around the lock. He mimicked a loud groan. The first burst was insufficient, but a second splintered enough wood to allow the door to be kicked open.

The shadowy obese Arab who entered was hit in the flank by shots from the Luger.

Walther's skin was as cold as ice.

He seized Circé's handbag and stepped cautiously outside. All seemed quiet.

As he set off downhill, towards the hum of the town, he thought, 'Egyptians? I thought the Russians would be first on the scene?'

It was too late to swap hotel.

Drinking strong coffee in his room, he emptied her

handbag. Money; his picture; nothing more.

He checked and reloaded his pistol, in case more of pharaoh's eunuchs with hieroglyphs and machine-guns should appear, then lay down on the bed.

O pretty Adeline! The off-duty Belgian policewoman in Leuze-en-Hainaut had seemed so unaffected and pleasant. Strychnine in her *Marie Brizard* in *Le Café Royal*? In God's name, why?

Belatedly he saw. Had he married and had children – even if not an easy ride – how much more would that have shaped a rounded and proper life?

*   *   *   *

In a quiet hotel in Bayswater, David Fairweather sat on a stool whilst his wife powdered his face with some greyish-pink powder, pulled on a suspect-looking wig and pressed a pair of plain-lensed wiry spectacles backwards onto his head.

'David, is this a good idea?'

'Well, Mrs Worthington … acting was never my strong suit.'

'You look undignified.'

'I suppose that's pretty usual for these punters.'

At a theatrical costumier's she had purchased a shabby serge surcoat and various make-up items.

Marion pursed her lips. 'I have an uneasy feeling … about this.'

'But … it's *all* I can do. Others are willing to join in … but I have to make the opening gambit.'

He put the barest necessities into his inside pockets;

nothing which might identify him; a photograph, an envelope and forty pounds in ones and fives.

'Forty pounds!' Marion exclaimed. 'How much do these tacky call-girls charge?'

'I've absolutely no idea.'

'The last story I sold to *Woman's Own*, earned eleven pounds and five shillings.'

'Clearly dear, you're in the wrong business.'

She cuffed his ear none too playfully, then relented and kissed him.

He stood up. 'So, forward on the foe; smoke these traitors out of the woodwork.'

'Mind that wig doesn't catch on something and come off.'

He took a deep breath and paused, uncertain of the game ahead, though not doubting his purpose.

Marion opened the door. The corridor was empty.

In Cavendish Square – a couple of blocks away – he nervously ascended three stone steps to a bright scarlet-painted door which stood minimally ajar.

He tapped and entered.

In the wide, dimly-lit and flower-pot-adorned hallway, 'Madame' sat wedged behind a small desk. She was bosomy, over-made-up and facially effusive.

Behind this false smile – the hallmark almost of her profession – he could see that she could see that he looked seedy … and that he was a newcomer.

'May I help you?' she enquired encouragingly.

'Er … two of your girls … have been recommended to me … ' His mouth was so dry he could barely speak. This was worse than flying through flak over Germany. 'Umm

'... a Miss Holowka and ... a Miss Glinka?'

Still the concierge smiled fulsomely. 'Miss Holowka is not in today, but Anna is free.'

'Oh ... er ... ?'

'She's fifteen pounds ... for half an hour.'

'Er ... good. Yes, I would like to see her please ... if I may?'

Again Madame's puffy face was wreathed in smiles. 'If you may? Of *course* you may.'

He fumbled in his inner pockets and found three five-pound notes.

'Do you wish to give a name?'

'Er ... Roger?'

'Up the stairs and first on the left then, "Roger".'

He climbed the long flight, holding on to the ornate wrought-iron banister and duly knocked gently on Anna's door.

'Come in,' came the fluting cajoling feminine voice.

The heavy brocade curtains were drawn to and a single table-lamp supplied a pool of subdued lighting which spread across the rug-dotted floor to where its mistress sat on the edge of a three-quarter bed. Outwardly she was leggy, smooth, curvy and dyed-blonde, yet there was an unappealing aura there too – an impure draw which flaunted only the flesh, its cavities and fluids – which inescapably impressed itself on an observer, even if he tried to disregard it.

'Good evening,' Sir David said timidly.

'Good evening,' she said huskily and on a rising pitch. Invitingly she uncrossed and re-crossed her long bare legs.

He too sat down on the edge of the bed, but left a space between them.

'You are Anna?'

'Yes,' she said with fake sweetness as she moved closer and started to caress him.

'Er, sorry ... this must seem a bit strange, but I have come on behalf of my friend.'

She looked confused. 'Friend?'

'Yes. Tug?'

'Tug?'

'Er ... Mr Orr-Ellis.'

She pouted and shook her long face. 'I'm sorry. I do not know these people.'

Her visitor took out the photograph. Fortunately he had foreseen this hurdle.

'Ah, that is Mr Follicle-tickler.' She giggled briefly. 'He is such a funny man.' She smiled, but without conviction.

Fairweather felt like a bridge player playing dummy. Also his scalp was moist and starting to itch under the wig.

'He gave me this,' he produced a small Manilla envelope and held it up in front of her. 'Can you give this to your Czechoslovakian friend?'

'Sorry? Who?'

He stared at her, straight in the eyes. 'Bodan Husak?'

Her eyelids dropped. 'I understand.'

He paused as she slowly took it.

'"Follicle-tickler" said it was *very* important.'

He stood up. She looked at him. He gave her a peck on the forehead and moved towards the door.

'Thank you, Anna.'

He closed the door softly and descended the stairs at a steady, thoughtful pace.

Madame looked surprised, even concerned. 'Was all

well, Monsieur?'

'Yes, thank you, Madame. Very well. See you again soon.'

He re-entered the Bayswater hotel unostentatiously, removed the wig and bathed in a hot soapy bath.

The door was partly open.

'Marion,' he called, 'do you remember when I first tried to woo you … how everything seemed to go wrong? And yet despite that, you know it's right. Obstacles can be sent almost to test your resolve?'

She gave no sign of having heard, but then said, 'Do you really think they'll fall for it?'

'They're bound to be suspicious … but dare they risk passing up on … on the chance of such a meeting? I doubt it.'

CHAPTER SIXTEEN

Ulrica watched the swaying masts on the steamer's black outline as – against the red glare of the sun – it preceded their own ship into Larne Harbour.

Her ticket for the ferry crossing from Stranraer had been bought using a one-pound note.

Puffs of cloud hovered over the bay which was a blurred seascape of wavy pale greens. In the distance flickering surf broke against layered stack rocks.

Leaving the train at Carrickfergus, she booked into a quiet guest-house with a cosy lounge and a warm fire.

The magazines and newspapers arrayed on the window-seat ranged in date from a pre-war copy of *The Strand Magazine* to this Saturday's *Dublin Evening News* in which she studied the 'situations vacant' columns.

Since Third Secretary Ohotnikoff had led his happily unsuccessful snatch squad outside Bonham's, she had travelled to Carlisle via a circuitous route – as female moles are said to dig zig-zag tunnels rather than the straight ones of males – and there, with her Monika Steyr passport, withdrawn all her money from Barclay's.

She would not use that account again as her pursuers might have tellers enlisted or blackmailed into 'the cause'. Any approach to the U.S. Embassy in London too would be risky.

The Eastern Bloc had plenty of killers ready to be despatched, should any circling hawk spot her.

In Leuze-en-Hainaut, the twenty-year-old Adeline Lavallée had been poisoned by Walther for simply – and off her own bat – tracking a low-level informant to a tryst with his contact 'Gisele'. How trifling was that in contrast to her own potential to create havoc?

Eating alone – a high-tea of Manx kippers and potato scones – she saw an advertisement for a private girls' school which sought a French teacher urgently.

Eyeing her forged Swiss driving licence in the name of 'Lina Schniewind', she telephoned Miss Bridget Greystone, the Headmistress.

A quaint red and cream railcar – a spluttering boneshaker with slatted wooden seats – struggled up from the Foyle Estuary and through the Barnesmore Gap, before dipping down into Donegal Town.

A prim scarecrow-like Miss Greystone and a Mr Higgins – the art master – interviewed her.

The questions were basic.

'Which towns in Britain have different names in French?'

'*Londres, Douvres et Edimbourg.*'

They nodded sagely.

'Otherwise they might say "Donay-goll" but they would still spell it as you do.'

Miss Greystone smiled a little less rigidly. She was quite formal but gracious by provincial standards, Higgins a trifle self-important.

He said, 'Your accent is good enough … especially here, out in the sticks.'

'Can you start tomorrow, Lina?'

'I can, Miss Greystone.'

Over tea and biscuits, the disruptive Republicans were touched upon and Ulrica – now Lina – told a story.

'A duke trying to escape Revolutionary France, had clothed himself in peasants' garb. Progress was good until in a tavern he made the mistake of ordering a twelve-egg omelette.'

'*Twelve* eggs?'

'I daresay they were smaller than ours. Quails' eggs maybe.'

'But even so ... and he was rumbled?'

'It was the end of him.'

Miss Greystone laughed with a touch of gaiety.

'But to sustain such *rôle*-playing – for extended periods – must be hard,' Higgins deliberated.

'Indeed,' Lina concurred.

'If we need to fire you, we promise not to chop your head off.'

'Phew! That's a relief.'

'There's a Miss Aoibheann Deas nearby who offers long-term board at a very fair rate.'

A trap-door in the ceiling of her room opened into a dusty and unused attic; but was it too obvious? A board in the bottom of the narrow window-seat box she managed to prise out and beneath it, hid her pistol and the bulk of her money, forced it back and replaced the spare blankets on top of it.

Lying on the bed, she ambled alone into the quiet forests of the mind and liked it.

She floated back to when five. She and the gardener's boy had planned to travel to Africa and marry, with giraffes and palm-trees in the background and smiling natives serving dates and lemonade.

In 1940, a crueller image of Africa in the shape of

wartime Tangier had loomed, where a harsh sun waxed over its milieu of crooks and rogues, from among whom the cynical Philip Dark-Coombs had later emerged, the man in the white linen suit at the *Café de Paris*.

The German Legation had inhabited a modest castellated eighteenth-century palace built of irregular yellowy stone blocks in the Moorish-style. A flight of steps with a carved stone balustrade led to an ornate doorway above which an angled flag-pole carried a large red white and black swastika flag. On the roof were numerous aerials.

Here in a back room on the second-floor, the *ci-devant* Gräfin Ulrica, then of the 'Horchdienst' – the German Intercept Service – had worked. An unglazed, finely-cancellated wooden-screened window looked out onto the sun-bleached town and the diminutive garden below, with its fragrance of orange-blossom. The Legation's cat, Tommy, often sat on the sill.

When off-duty, she would sometimes walk with one or two of her telegraphist colleagues to the *Café Hafa* overlooking the Strait or cycle out through groves of cork oak and broom to Cape Spartel, there to swim out to the rusty ribs of a wrecked cargo boat.

Here in Tangier you could still buy fresh bread, pineapples, jam, chocolate, brandy and even good Ethiopian coffee. 'Proper' coffee they heard had disappeared back in the Fatherland. The French franc was the official currency, though Spanish money was accepted too due to their adjoining Spanish Morocco.

Life then had been pleasant enough ... until the autumn of 1942, when the catastrophes and the uncertainties began.

A saturnine Coburg took a trip to Damascus on the dilapidated railway. He just had time for a cup of muddy coffee outside the ramshackle station, before returning to Beirut.

Back at the Hôtel Etap, he was on the point of inserting his room key into his door's lock, when he heard snoring. This *was* his room? Room 14?

He turned the key quietly and eased the door open. He put the light on and saw Larry Scarffe asleep in the armchair.

Flustered, Larry came to.

'Oh, Walther?' He rubbed his eyes. 'Sorry about this … we need to talk to you.'

'That's all right.'

Now more awake, the caller said, 'Hold on. The bar's still open.'

Walther realised that despite his reservations about Americans, he did basically trust them.

Larry waddled back with some bottles of pale beer and two cheese rolls.

'Walther, the boxer in the Red Corner knows you're in the Lebanon. You need to move on. And quickly. They found out about three o'clock local time, according to Washington.

There's a crack-of-dawn flight to Athens. We doubt they'll be watching that. We can get you on it … then a military plane to Lisbon … and finally a transfer to New York.'

Coburg fingered his glass. 'It sounds like it has to be.'

'But there's something else.' The broad-beamed Yank clasped his hands between his splayed knees. 'A long shot.' He looked at Coburg quizzically.

Walther opened his hands palm-upwards. 'All right … nock the arrow to your string.'

The stiff short hairs in Larry's nostrils quivered. 'The Suez Mercantile Bank … Heard of it?'

'Er … yes.'

'The crux is, do you have a set of missing original contracts?'

'Oh yes … I did have them, but either the British took them at El Adem … or they're lost.'

'Shucks.'

'Are some of your people on the "list of creditors" … meaning they'll never see anything?'

'No. These sacred texts were stolen by an employee named Dawkins at the request of our ambassador in Cairo and it seemed likely to us, that via a Miss Engström – whom no one's seen hide nor hair of since that night – that they might have fallen into your hands.'

'Well deduced.'

Scarffe screwed up his face. 'It's about political leverage, not "rooting for truffles" or "snouts in troughs". Their Finance Minister – Dr "Jingly" al-Hufuf – needs to be given the razz … "Read 'em and weep, buddy."'

Coburg could scarcely imagine it. 'You'll have to ask the British.'

'Also, Na'ob or "Nozz" – a creep with a huge conk and titular head of … '

Walther held up a hand. He had heard a floor-board creak.

A second squeak came from the corridor.

Both men took out their pistols and watched the door with sweat running from every pore.

CHAPTER SEVENTEEN

A coke-burning stove in the old high-ceilinged schoolroom kept the girls warm.

Chalk dust swirled.

Her lessons were colloquial and not overly grammatical. Things were going well enough.

In the staff-room, Ulrica – alias Lina Schniewind – sat down to do some marking. A ten-day-old copy of *The Southern Irish Observer* lay there, discarded and open. A lesser headline caught her eye; 'U.S. Diplomat killed in Beirut hotel shoot-out.'

It was world news only because an American diplomat had been murdered, but in passing, it did mention that one Egon Baus – Professor of Archaeology at Leipzig – had also died in the cross-fire. It claimed that the killers were Mossad operatives who had stayed at La Pensione Corelli in the *Rue Héliopolis*. They had escaped down the back fire-escape.

Ulrica guessed the true scenario.

The free-lance hack, 'Hadrian', who had effeminately wavy hair and had scribbled this article for *The Fleet Street Letter* – which had then syndicated it – was renowned for his anti-U.S. and anti-Jewish squibs.

The news of Walther's end though unnerved her.

On the Saturday morning, whilst walking to Donegal's railway station, she kept a weather eye on a slowly moving car ... until there was a bang and a cloud of smoke from its engine.

In Ballyshannon, as she watched the school's senior hockey team play, was a gnarled old fisherman staring at her? No, he was just leering at the gym-skirted young girls.

In Londonderry, in a bric-à-brac shop facing the old town wall, she spotted a blue plate patterned with a white bowline-knot and 'Emden' in Gothic letters; a relic from a German cruiser. As she emerged, she almost collided with Mr Higgins and his wife. Ulrica jumped.

'Miss Schniewind, good day. Is all well?'

'Oh, Mr Higgins, good day to you.'

He smiled. 'Did Cavan lend you that spare violin?'

'Er, yes. I'm out of practice, but it's coming back.'

'The pieces for this soirée musicale are all very basic ... easy classics, Irish reels … '

'Yes.'

Higgins raised his hat, smiled again and departed.

Her fright or edginess – whether irrational or not – could not have passed unnoticed.

A flight of birds – angular and flying en échelon, passed overhead in the early evening twilight.

In Siobhán's tea-shop she hid her shaking hands and ordered tea and crumpets. She must not despair, but keep her spirits up … but also leave.

After extracting her pistol and her money – all in Sterling – from beneath the loose board in the bottom of the window-seat box, Ulrica packed two bags.

She embarked on the T.S.M.V. Ali Baba, a cargo ship lading at Cork, which had a few passenger cabins and was sailing to Lima via Panama.

Three days out and on a south-westerly course, the weather grew warmer and she took to sitting in an old deck-chair on the upper deck, drinking bitter lemon and reading books found in her cabin. One was entitled Un

Voyage aux Iles de l'Amérique.

One afternoon, two rough-looking and overweight couples in their thirties – whom Ulrica had glimpsed at meals – lined up four deck-chairs nearby, adjusted their reclining angles and lay back, soaking up the sun with their eyes half-closed and their hands folded on their tummies.

After a while, Fred said in some northern regional English accent, 'I think it's time for a beer.'

After two minutes of no response, he said, 'Ali, go and fetch us four iced beers.'

'Aw,' grumbled the hefty lass, 'it's always me. You go.' She began picking her teeth with a tooth-pick.

'Cut the whinging woman. Four beers.'

'It were the same when we was in Rome. Every time you wanted ... '

'Shut it. Just fetch 'em.'

In her floppy white sun-hat and blue-striped frock, Ali pushed back her sunshade and struggled to her feet, returning ten minutes later with four iced beers and some waffles.

Ulrica had hoped for a sign of defiance; just one beer for Ali herself perhaps, or three, one for everyone except her oafish mate? There could have been an entertaining row.

'Thanks Fred,' said the other couple.

'How about, "Thanks Ali"?' said Ali.

'Well I paid for 'em.'

'No you didn't. Lloyd's Bank paid for 'em,' Gail contradicted.

The foursome all laughed. Were they bank robbers?

Fred downed his beer before lying back again in his shorts, sandals and sun-glasses. 'Hey, Ali, rub my tummy with this sun-tan lotion.'

She surveyed Fred's big exposed belly. 'Do you think one bottle will be enough?'

Fred threw her a wounded look whilst she tittered.

'So,' the eavesdropper smiled to herself, 'she has some spirit in her.'

The foursome laughed about an officious bank manager whose family had 'camped' in the garden, paying out an electric cable so they could have a gramophone in the tent and scuttling inside when they wanted a bath.

'Still, it gave us the chance to copy his keys.'

Were they on the run like her? Butch Cassidy and co.?

She drifted into a half-doze.

In Tangier, she had sat in the shade of the rust-coloured awnings outside the *Café de Paris*, waiting for her friend and gazing out over the *Place de France*.

A fellow in a white linen suit at the next table, pinched out his small cigar before leaning sideways and speaking softly. 'Excuse me, but could I borrow your newspaper?'

Recognising him as one of the British Diplomatic Mission – whom they had *de rigueur* to ignore – she lifted her nose in the air and looked to where – under a eucalyptus tree – unceasing Moorish music from the thick wooden flute of a dark-skinned Rif enticed a cobra to writhe up out of its pot.

'Your *Sunday Dispatch* … if you would be so good? For five minutes?'

Wordlessly she handed him her paper.

Her companion emerged from the colourful tangle of

the many races who criss-crossed the square. They ordered lamb with prunes and cheese and a sweet red wine.

An artist, with a contrived ennui and a beret, painted at an easel. He daubed at a scene near the *Bab al Babar*, watched briefly by passers-by.

Bright sunshine suffused a swarthy toothless Mauritanian pimp, who called out, 'Twenty francs for young clean girl and cup of nice mint tea.'

Their food and drink descended onto the orange table-cloth and the girls raised their glasses. 'Out of sweetness cometh strength.'

The Englishman handed Ulrica's paper back to her and departed. '*Danke schön.*'

The tedious wail from the cross-legged snake-charmer's flute rose incessantly.

The *Ali Baba* must have hit a big wave, for suddenly a weighty shower of spray, half a bucketful of salt water in large droplets, doused her and she woke up with a jolt.

Before going below to dry and change, she went to the rail and surveyed the endless ocean. Were her pursuers stumped, struggling with dud leads? Had anyone – Mr Higgins for instance – even laid false trails on her behalf?

The radio operator had received a message. They were to divert to Trinidad to lade eighteen tipper trucks as deck cargo. If she went ashore there, it would foil anyone waiting for her at Colón or Panama.

*   *   *   *

The old dark-brick drill hall in Northumberland Road had once been used for training cavalry horses. Now though, at seven o'clock, on this chilly Tuesday morning, three officer cadets stood in the 'at ease' position in its now wooden-floored spacious main hall.

Major Edmund Trewick – the Training Major – eyed them. He headed the nucleus of permanent staff posted to this Territorial contingent in Newcastle.

'Right chaps. The Commissions Board is in a five weeks' time.'

'Sir.'

'Today is the "escape and evasion exercise". I trust you all had a good breakfast?'

'Sir.' Faint smiles.

They wore battle-dress trousers with puttees and 'ammo' boots, green pullovers, blue and red stable belts and berets pulled down to the right with Saint Cuthbert Cross cap badges.

'You will each have your great-coat and a pair of woollen gloves. Q has prepared a haversack each with a sharp knife, a pair of spare socks, a waterproof poncho, mess tins, a box of matches and a bottle of pop. Also between you, one live chicken.'

The cadets smiled weakly.

'You may take cigarettes if you wish but no money.

There is a map in a sealed envelope. The use of it implies surrender to the enemy.

You will be dropped off just below the Cheviot at zero eight-hundred hours and you are to make your way to the Reed Shiel Hotel by nineteen-thirty hours. That counts as successfully making contact with your own side.

Per crow it is thirteen miles.

You may stick together or you may split up.

The clocks have now gone back so it will be dark by six.

There will be enemy patrols out looking for you.

As you know, the country there is pretty barren – an odd Forestry Commission plantation, some rocky ravines, a sprinkling of stone sheep pens – so give thought to camouflage and avoid open ground or vehicular tracks.

Understood?'

'Sir.'

This robustly delivered 'Sir' implied that everything was perfectly clear and could not possibly be improved upon.

'Questions?'

'No compasses, Sir?'

'No compasses. No binoculars.'

'We may keep our watches, Sir?'

'You may.

Right, a quick cuppa in the mess and then Sergeant Swindell will take you in a three-tonner to the drop-off point.

Squad! Left turn! Dismiss!'

Outside it was raining horizontally as the threesome climbed over the tail-board and into the Bedford, under its canvas awning.

Swindell believed that their lorries were under-used and so unreliable. 'This bugger gave trouble starting this morning.' It was certainly producing copious exhaust fumes, much of which was sucked back in under the canvas.

For a while the trio just stared out the back of the wagon at the lashing rain and the receding asphalt, but as they neared Ponteland, Appleyard – still clutching the live chicken – said, 'We might as well wring this thing's neck and pluck it.'

Suddenly the lorry lurched and skidded to an abrupt halt. They all fell off the wooden side-seats and the chicken flapped its wings and disappeared over the tail-board and down the street.

Bayram jumped down and went to see what had happened. 'Sorry Sir,' Swindell said, holding up his cigarette and looking down from the cab, 'I dropped it down my shirt.'

Climbing slowly towards Otterburn, the rain slackened, but with the higher ground came a cold thin wintry mist, half-obscuring the odd stark wooded knoll. Beside the road were reedy marshes and sheep huddling up to stone walls.

They rumbled through a picturesque if isolated settlement with the Reed Shiel Hotel on their right.

On a narrow undulating road which crossed the lightly-frosted artillery ranges some way north of Otterburn, the lorry stopped and they climbed down.

Swindell handed them each a chocolate bar. 'I expect a pint out of each of you for those,' he said slyly.

They grinned uneasily.

The wagon's rear-lights vanished and standing on a spur of scree, they surveyed the shallow treeless valley.

Bayram said, 'We're east of the A68 which runs north-west to south-east – Galashiels to Corbridge – so if we set off due south, we should hit it.'

Gunn indicated the barely discernible, fog-shrouded sun. 'That'll be south-east now, so if we proceed with it at forty-five degrees to our left, that should give us a roughly due-south line.'

They squelched across a miry stream – jumping from one mossy tussock to another – before setting off, aiming for a distinctively greyish crag a mile or two distant. They marched steadily over rime-whitened undulating hillocks where sheep grazed small islets of grass. Gunn, who came from a farm in the Lammermoor Hills, said, 'Where sheep can go, men can go.'

Appleyard said, 'They could spot us crossing that ridge,'

'The "enemy",' Bayram remarked, 'will be too busy tucking into hearty breakfasts for the first hour. Let's just risk it.'

After descending a heathery hill, they came to a gravelled track which crossed a stream on a small hump-backed bridge, guarded by a 'road narrows' sign whose reflector-studded red triangle surmounted a white oblong cast-iron plate with two converging black lines on it.

Here Appleyard and Gunn split from Bayram, whose view differed on the direction of some overhead power lines.

The twosome passed a low cairn and then strode on downwards, beside a beck where a diminutive torrent cascaded and frothed.

'Vehicles.' Gunn pointed to the right. 'That has to be the A68.'

Appleyard nodded. 'We're pretty exposed still.' He waved at a roofless shepherd's hut at the bottom of the shieling. 'Let's pause there, then head for those fields. There we can stick to ditches and hedges.'

A fine sleet-like drizzle was sweeping in from the west. 'This weather should help,' added Gunn.

At the derelict croft, they sat on a collapsed wall of rough stones and rubbed their gloved but cold hands. They drank some pop and shared a chocolate bar, whilst their breath condensed in small cloudlets in the bleak hostile air.

The grey-white part-shadowed hills they had crossed were disappearing as the sleet thickened. A huge frost-topped spherical boulder seemed strangely prescient.

'A Christmas pudding with rum sauce on … '

'Hands up!'

Major Trewick sprang out from behind said rock, brandishing a revolver.

*   *   *   *

Evening meal was served at the Captain's table.

Its long cloth was of stiff white damask.

There were present, the Captain, the Third Officer, the Chief Engineer and unusually all ten passengers. The latter consisted of the four lolloping sun-bathers and six, if not top-drawer specimens, at least tolerable imitations.

'I don't think this tie suits me,' said Fred.

'You mean it's stylish?' queried Gail.

'Ali,' asked the Third Officer, 'are you the girl who spots comets? Or is that Halley?'

'It's me … when I'm not fetching beer for Fred.'

This won a ripple of laughter.

'Perhaps you should complain to the Astronomer Royal?' offered the older Canadian.

The Irish steward circumnavigated the table softly, serving the lamb and the vegetables. He had the matured wisdom of the old rather than the latent insolence of the young.

'Anyway, as well as beer,' said Fred in self-defence, 'I'm also reading a book.'

'You're reading a *book*?!' spluttered Gail, with incredulity.

'It's called *Casino Royale* ... and it's a spy story,' he elaborated, whilst still chewing.

Ulrica – who was now Emma Nagel – passed the silver-plated mint-sauce boat to her right and thought, 'I could tell you stuff a sight closer to reality.'

'And is it gripping?' asked the Frenchman.

'Yes!' Fred affirmed enthusiastically. 'The hero's just about to have his scrotal rash burnt off.'

Ali turned a delicate pink and the plump American actress dipped her brows.

By unspoken consensus, a shift in the topic of conversation occurred.

The Captain mentioned an upper-class English fellow who had sailed with them on the previous run. Hilary de Grey – of that archetypal floppy-wrist coterie – had allegedly spied for some foreign bunch in the Sudan. 'Very full of himself.' He chewed briefly. 'I suppose humility is – in part at least – a willingness to admit that your own convictions may not be right ... or what the Lord wishes?'

'That Aussie squatter made up a Limerick about him,' muttered the Chief Engineer.

All paused expectantly.

'Come on, Angus. You can't whet our appetites and then stall.'

'A puff who lived in Khartoum,
Took a Lesbian up to his room;
And when they got there,
Said, "Now let's get this clear,
Who does what and with which and to whom?"'

Everyone grinned good-naturedly, but more at the Chief's face which had reddened like the proverbial 'exploding tomato'.

The over-the-hill American, in her patterned silk shawl, guffawed belatedly.

'A weird bunch, this spy lot,' remarked the Captain.

'And the world seems to be awash with them ... perhaps a statement on the human condition?' contributed Emma.

The grey-haired Third Officer, named one Philip Coombs – also a plum-in-the-mouth homosexual involved in spying – who had fled to Moscow in July on their sister ship, *Egeria*.

'He jumped ship in Stockholm, vanished, was hit in the chest by a bullet in some arctic-circle town, but somehow made it across the Iron Curtain.

By the time he reached Moscow, his chest was half-full of pus.'

'He died?' Emma queried, as if only half-curious.

The Frenchman, Alain, took up the story.

'The professor of thoracic surgery there said, "Well Comrade, we've examined and x-rayed you and we agree that your chest needs to be opened and this empyema drained. Anatoly here, my new assistant, has done six and they all died. He's free. Vassily has done thirty and twenty died ... he's forty roubles and I've done a thousand or so and I'm four hundred roubles. Let us know what you want to do."'

'Communism in action?'

'So he lived?' queried Emma.

'No, he died.'

They called for a bottle of *Drambuie* to share with the *crème brûlée* deserts. Glenn the steward decanted it into small dram-sized glasses.

Emma proposed a toast. 'To poor spies, twisted and unfortunate.'

Glasses were raised.

The young Estonian mentioned a military pilot from his own country, who had defected to Sweden by simply flying his plane there. 'He too suffered lung injury ... shot by his navigator as they were landing. They tried postural drainage and chest beatings to make him cough up plugs of mucus ... garlic in his socks, strong hot lemon drinks ... '

'Those Swedish nurses ... I bet they were a stimulus to staying alive,' put in Fred.

'Did he live?' asked the Canadian.

'He did. It's me.'

That evening, in her cabin, Emma found it hard to sleep.

The *Ali Baba* ploughed on steadily, her colossal marine diesels humming relentlessly and evenly.

Tangier came back to her yet again.

She had not attached any significance to her encounter with the Englishman and the *Sunday Dispatch* until, when back in the girls' attic dormitory at the Legation, a note fell out of it. 'Join the Comintern. On Tuesday afternoons I take tea at the *Café Sirius* in the Emsallah Gardens.'

Like any *Junker*, she scorned both communists and National Socialists.

In her Prussian blue skirt and white blouse – its small

collar flashes embroidered with anchors – she had gone on duty that evening with a Thuringian lass named Sibylla in the second-floor room, where with their receiver sets they listened to wireless messages.

Here they picked up both their own ships' signals and encoded Royal Navy signals from Gibraltar and the Western Mediterranean.

During daylight hours the only German shore station which was loud and clear, was Tripoli, but with darkness and the lowering of the ionosphere – from which radio waves are apparently reflected – remoter stations became audible.

They had to line up their receivers 'dead centre' onto the various transmitters. A transmitting station would repeat its call-sign at intervals to assist others to tune in. Adjusting the tuning dial, when no hissing in the ear-phones could be heard with the Morse key down, you were 'on'. If it drifted off, you had to retune.

They could select different frequency bands by changing the set's coil. The transmissible ranges reached seven and a half megacycles per second.

It seemed extraordinary to remember such details.

The duty officer, Leutnant Sonnabend, had popped in. 'Ah, the two slender girls on tonight, not the fat one? Tell me, is your rota based on weight?'

Sibylla had said, 'Flattery will get you everywhere, Sir.'

'I want you to encode and send this message. It is to a fictitious Japanese freighter, the *Satsuma Asumi*, heading out of the Gironde.'

'And see if the enemy reacts?'

'Quite. See if they fancy some rice and pickled fish instead of bully-beef?'

A month before, a French yacht – two days out from Casablanca, with a German agent on board for Freetown – had been unexpectedly hove-to by the sloop *H.M.S. Bridgewater*. Using a second intercept from their Canaries station – sited aboard a salvage tug moored in Las Palmas – they had plotted the position of this brush by so-called HF / DF fixing. Reinhard Ekstein – their agent – had been captured and the *Niobe*, the French yacht, sunk.

A week ago, a signal beginning 'KFEA', which signified 'enemy contact' had been picked up from the *Esso Elsass*, a refuelling tanker sailing under a false flag. She had left Saint-Nazaire eight days before and this, her last signal, stated that a *County* class cruiser was closing on her.

Ulrica had an odd feeling.

When *Marinehelferin* – woman's naval auxiliary – Clara Mann relieved her at dawn, she knocked on the antique wooden door of Corvette-Captain Zutt.

'Enter.'

She saluted, then stood to attention with her thumbs by the seams of her skirt.

'*Guten Morgen, Marineführerin?*'

She told him of the contact made by Dark-Coombs and showed the note.

Zutt finished his cup of coffee. 'Hmm ... an unsavoury and Byzantine world Ulrica ... without honour or decorum.'

A blue and yellow braided lanyard denoted her rank.

He summoned their head of security.

Otto Habe appeared in civvies, looking sleepy and with sagging toad-like eyelids.

Now 'at ease' but still quite prim, Ulrica repeated her story.

'So, what ought we to do?' Zutt asked.

Habe cleared his throat. 'We could disregard it ... or Ulrica could pretend to be lured?'

The Corvette-Captain excused them bluntly. 'Well it's your call. I have operational matters to attend to.' He shooed them out.

In his own office Habe lit a cigarette and bade Ulrica sit down. He leant back in his well-padded chair and focused on her breasts.

'No point in purposeless over-activity,' he remarked, 'but ... '

'Why *do* these English public-school types imagine they share some common objective with Slav peasants or Tartars?'

'Baffling ... but I daresay it's linked to sexual deviancies.'

Ulrica looked perplexed. 'What does that mean?'

'Oh, don't ask. Their manifestations are bad enough. As to their sources, I doubt any theory can give a satisfactory answer ... but it seems to make them hate their own origins ... their own country.'

A retarded Tyrolean lass brought in filter coffee and apple tarts.

'*Could* you fake communist sympathies? Trot out some studied hogwash?'

'Would it lead anywhere? I assume they want to gather information, not give it?'

The Gestapo officer poured the coffee.

'Whatever your basic stance, there are always counter-weights. My brother was an ardent nationalist, until he almost froze to death at "The Gates of Moscow". Scant food, no shelter, woefully inadequate clothing, frost-bitten and near to death … national prestige suddenly became meaningless.'

'We are after all, flesh and blood.'

Habe bit into a tart. 'Still, if you're willing, go to this *Café Sirius* and see what transpires.'

'They'll know that I might be double-crossing them.'

'Of course. The barathea-blazer set know all about that.

Don't let them lure you away to any quiet place. A year ago, a girl named Emilia Goggia from the Italian Consulate, was found dead down a well in a village up in the Atlas foothills. Her body had been rolled up in an old tent with some flags and Inglefield clips. No one knows who did it.

As you know, we have to watch the locals we employ here too. In *le Petit Socco* grubby little urchins swap information via notes hidden in their trays of brushes and shoe-shine and try to sell them on to agents of the various combatants or "jumping-jacks" who take coffee at the plusher cafés.'

Later, she knew instinctively, that there was a traitor in the Legation … but who?

CHAPTER EIGHTEEN.

Major Trewick, a pair of binoculars strung round his neck, leapt over an ice-whitened stile.

'A fig for your field-craft. I've been tracking you for close on twenty minutes.'

'Escape involves taking risks, Sir,' said Gunn.

Trewick smiled wryly as if to say, 'Nice try.' He replaced his revolver in its holster.

'What's that purply silver foil? Chocolate! Did bloody Swindell stop at a shop?'

'No, Sir. Our own initiative ... as one would if planning an escape.'

'Huh! Anyway, the exercise is scrubbed. Something else is happening.'

'No duff, Sir?'

'No.'

The Training Major walked them briskly along a stony track to where his short-wheelbase Land Rover lay hidden in a dip. 'Firstly, an "O Group" at the Reed Shiel Hotel.'

With cups of tea and cheese and pickle rolls, they sat near the log fire in the hotel's lounge.

'Now, attention.

Events are likely to unfold here, which are to be *inconspicuously* observed.'

The cadets looked bewildered.

'Some foreign ne'er-do-wells are expected to roll up at around seven-thirty ... or possibly earlier, to check the lie of the land. They plan to abduct an East German woman, who however, will *not* be here.'

'This sounds a bit intricate, Sir.'

'Do you remember the A.A. Milne story, *Where the Woozle Wasn't?*'

'I do, Sir.'

'"Foreign ne'er-do-wells" Sir, is that reverse hyperbole for Eastern Bloc numbskulls?'

The Major nodded. 'Good, Gunn. You're thinking.'

'So Sir, if the magic lamp is elsewhere, Abanazar is on a fool's errand?'

'Correct. The unknown though, is the number of evil spirits he will bring along.'

'Seven Dwarfs, but no Snow White?'

'Evil spirits in pantomimes Sir, are usually green.'

'Black with red minds in this one ... and with an *ad lib* or very haphazard plot.'

'And where do we fit in, Sir?'

'Let's finish our lunch first.'

Outside the sleet had stopped, but a thin mist had reduced vision to a few hundred yards. The quarter-tonner turned northwards onto the A68.

Trewick said, 'If you arrive by car, there's the hotel car park. However, to remain undetected the most obvious choice is here.'

He swung right – after only a quarter of a mile – onto a poorly-maintained single-track road which led to the M.O.D. ranges. After two hundred yards, came a wide, uneven, roughly-gravelled area – slushy in patches – which the artillery often used as an assembly point.

They stopped and climbed out.

Beyond lay a boggy track, passable only by military vehicles.

'This, I anticipate, is where our troupe of artistes will hide their motor transport.'

'No one would normally come here, Sir … especially after dark.'

'Quite. Follow me.'

The Major led the cadet officers up a steep slope to a tumble-down sheep-fold.

'This is your hide-out.

Now get this straight, conflict with these bandits could be dangerous … even lethal. Confrontation must *not* occur.' He eyed his audience sternly. 'Besides, we want to see what they do.'

Gunn swallowed. 'But if they do come, what is our task?'

'Right. If they leave their vehicles unattended, you are to discreetly sabotage them. A delay to their stage exit might create more photo-shoot opportunities.'

'A whiff of embarrassment for them, Sir?'

'We can live with that.'

Back at the Land Rover, he handed Appleyard a Browning nine-millimetre pistol. 'This has ten rounds in it.'

'Not thirteen?'

'Ten. For use only *in extremis*.'

'Sir.'

'These desperados might well be armed.'

He gave them a thin notebook and a pencil, some sandwiches, a thermos flask of tomato soup, some bottles of Tizer and a torch.

Trewick eyed his watch. 'Probably a three hour wait … or more. Gunn, take my binoculars.'

'Sir.'

And with that, the Training Major climbed into his quarter-tonner and drove off.

The two cadets, aware now that something extraordinary was going on, felt sobered.

'Dick, Trewick's older brother's chairing our Commissions Board next month. We'd better not balls this up.'

The Reed Shiel Hotel was a large stone Jacobean farmhouse which had been extended and made into a four-star hostelry and which stood beside the A68.

At twenty past six, a black Ford Anglia pulled up in the celandine and stone-wall-bordered car park of this ivy-clad structure. It disgorged a couple in their fifties and in winter coats, who entered the cosy, fire-warmed lounge, bought drinks and cheese scones and on finding a 'reserved' sign on the table by the front window, settled down in a bow-shaped recess to drink, eat and read magazines.

At six thirty-five, a sprightly Jonathan Thurling arrived, wearing Bertie-Wooster-style casuals. At the bar, he bought a glass of greenishly-tinged wine and some nuts and told the landlord that he was returning home from a salmon-fishing holiday by the River Spey.

Appleyard and Gunn were the first to espy enemy activity.

They had tested one another on the 'section attack' in readiness for their forthcoming exam, then shared the tomato soup and the sandwiches.

'Ah the *longueur*, the tedium.'

'An S.A.S. lieutenant once told me that he had found patience the hardest thing to master.'

'But necessity compels.'

With darkness, an eerie wispy tentacled mist descended, of the sort seen in Victorian murder films.

Then at six-fifty the beams of large round headlights probed the murky darkness, oscillating up and down as a weighty four-door saloon bounced slowly along the track.

It gingerly executed a five-point turn, its lights died, its doors opened, the internal lights came on and footsteps crunched the gravel.

Dim silhouettes could be discerned as a trio pulled on rubber galoshes. The watchers heard muffled snatches of an unidentified tongue through the fog-tinged air.

'One voice is a woman's,' whispered Appleyard.

'Puss in Boots?'

Eventually, as six doubly-shod feet ground softly towards the road, a fitful fuzzy haze of moonlight broke through for perhaps half a minute.

'A youngish couple and an older heavier man?'

After ten minutes the two cadets descended, guided by the glinting glass and chrome window edgings.

Rovers then, were quite a luxury marque.

Appleyard jotted down its registration number, its tax disc details and from a rear window sticker: 'Lowe's Garages; Evesham.'

In the unlocked boot Gunn found a fuel can and a length of red rubber tubing. He emptied its contents into a ditch. Then, removing the filler cap, he inserted one end of the tubing and by sucking on it, started a siphon which drained some of the tank's petrol into the can. He emptied this too, before filling the can with peaty water from a stagnant pool and decanting it into the tank.

Appleyard said, 'I never thought I'ld do this.' He undid his zip and urinated into the tank.

The doors were locked.

'How far should we go?'

Appleyard had tripped over a cricket-ball-sized rock. It seemed like a sign.

They broke a window, opened a door, released the hand-brake and put the gears into neutral, yet were unable to roll the beast into a water-logged depression.

They let some air out of its tyres.

At the hotel, David Fairweather arrived, dressed casually and shepherding his fifteen-year-old daughter Sally.

They asked for a pot of tea and scanned the menu under the wooden ceiling beams in this country-house-style inn.

Sally, wearing a plain black skirt and a blue woolly, had brought her Latin homework and had come because her mother, having been offered a regular column in a magazine, had gone up to London to sign a contract.

In two armchairs with a low circular table between them, they could watch the car park through a small side-window.

'Well, only one actor on stage so far,' David said, nodding minimally towards Thurling.

'Three,' Sally corrected him.

Her father knitted his brows.

'In the recess. That's Mr Holland and his wife. Mummy tipped him off.'

'The crime columnist?'

'Yes. Ken Holland, I think.'

'Hoping for a scoop?'

'Of Russian ice-cream.'

'You're wasted at that school.'

'Don't I know it?' she huffed. 'Mummy knows him through the agony aunt at *Woman*. She says you would approve of his political bearings.'

Bowls of soup and a basket of bread were brought.

With no sign of another vehicle arriving, a young couple entered and took the reserved table in the bay window.

The girl was in her early twenties, with symmetrical swept-back curtains of straight brown hair, a roundish bucolic face, a close-fitting black gauze-like dress and a cardigan. She took a cursory look around.

Her companion, a kelpie-like cadaverous young man with a spotty and runny-paint sort of face, hung his green jacket over the third chair which had its back against the long sash-window. The girl then placed her red raincoat on top of it.

Thurling guessed that the new arrivals might well be the canaries sent down the mine to sniff out the methane. The toughies would be lurking outside.

He picked up a sparkling, pattern-etched glass trophy from the bar. It bore the name of some golf tournament and was filled with candies and trinkets. He approached Fairweather.

'Excuse me, Sir? Might I trouble you to take a photograph of me holding this cut-glass cup?'

'Of course, my dear fellow.' David stood up. 'Actually I think its glass cut.'

In handling it, they nearly dropped it. 'Well it nearly was.'

Sir David took the Hawkeye Brownie Flash camera and angled it to one side of Thurling so that it captured the two newcomers.

The magnesium bulb flared dazzlingly for perhaps half a second.

Thurling murmured under cover of changing the flash bulb, 'If Ulrica had appeared, how were they to tell the heavies?'

'Sally thinks the red coat means, "Nothing doing," and the green will mean, "She's here."'

Jonathan nodded. 'A bright lass. So someone *is* lurking outside?'

Beams of light, showed that a car was pulling in to a slot in the car park.

Sir David glimpsed what he thought were 'C.D.' plates on a dark Hillman. Diplomatic immunity would impose a need for even greater caution.

A smoothly-rounded Polish consular official entered, looking a bit piratical with coppery-to-auburn pigtails, a black and red headscarf and oval platinum earrings. She wore a darkly-patterned coat with a belt whose large metal buckle gleamed.

But the real conundrum was the neat, quiet, erect girl of eleven or perhaps twelve who followed her.

'Who is she?' David mouthed his bemusement to his daughter.

The Pole headed for an old oaken bench close to the large stone Inglenook hearth. She removed her coat and sat her broad round bottom down before pulling the thin shy girl down too.

Sally whispered, 'This Ulrica woman, does she have a daughter?'

'I've no idea.'

'Is *this* her daughter ... brought as coercion?'

'Coercion?'

'Well, as in, "Come quietly or something bad will happen."'

The penny dropped. 'I bet that's it!'

'Blackmail ... heady stuff.'

More unexpected coinage had distorted the plot.

A short-wheelbase army Land Rover drove into the car park and nudged the Hillman. It made an inaudible squeak.

Fairweather was now quite nervous. He would not easily get off the hook if something sparked a shoot-out.

Major Trewick and a mud-spattered Cadet Bayram entered and walked directly over to the Polish woman.

'Excuse me, is that vehicle with the Polish Diplomatic Service disc, yours?'

'Er ... yes. It is.'

'I am so sorry, but I've scraped its wing.'

The threesome went outside to study the damage.

Along the left front wing she examined a thin silver line where the paint had been scratched by the Land Rover's angular bumper.

She rubbed a finger along it and said, 'Well, it's fully insured ... so I suppose it doesn't matter.'

'Well,' the Major stuttered, 'that's very good of you, Miss ... er ... ?'

'Er, Cywinska. Sonia Cywinska.'

'Trewick. Major Edmund Trewick,' he eyed her again. 'Look, the Army will willingly pay?'

'No, really. It doesn't matter,' Sonia repeated dismissively.

'Well, thank you.'

He gave Bayram a wink, before turning to follow Miss Cywinska as she re-entered the hotel through its glass-panelled inner front door.

Over the threshold, he tapped her shoulder and spoke in a low voice; 'Ulrica zu Lauenburg has decided to stay in Kenya.'

The Polish woman stared at him, unsure how to react.

Now Edmund Trewick was much more of a wag than his older brother, the sort of 'it-needs-to-be-fun' species of training major. He wanted the part-timers to be enthusiastic, inventive; not book-worms. Dullness was the unforgivable sin.

During the afternoon it had crossed his mind that amongst the junk in his quarter-tonner, he had a clockwork alarm clock – which he used on exercises when a nap could be snatched – and a dummy Energa grenade round.

An Energa grenade, which looked like a small aerial bomb or bomblet, was an anti-armoured-vehicle weapon, fired from a rifle fitted with a special launching attachment. The practice rounds contained – instead of the high explosive RDX – a luminous green powder, so that if an infantryman on Salisbury Plain fired it from cover at an old rusty hulk say, a puff of green dust would indicate that it had hit a hard surface.

Now Trewick had taped this to the clock, which in turn had two electrical wires fixed, hanging loose. He had also slightly loosened the nose-cone.

Back in the hotel, Trewick stood at the bar having ordered two glasses of tonic water and some crisps, where Bayram now joined him and also gave a wink.

Sonia Cywinska in a state of controlled agitation, turned

to the couple in the bay window and babbling in Russian, told them to leave, to tell 'Ivanov' that the plot was 'blown' and to return to their car and depart. Although the girl tensed, she remained static; either she did not know where 'Ivanov' was or was simply unsure what might be her own wisest course, given this now risky intaglio.

The panic-stricken Cywinska scurried out to her car, but there on its bonnet, lay a home-made 'bomb', with its wires threaded through the radiator grille.

On the opposite side of the A68 were a pair of agricultural workers' cottages. Their gardens were dotted with fruit trees, stacks of logs and rows of bean canes and here 'Ivanov' – the big Bulgarian – stood on a low hummock in the shadow of a holly bush and watched. He watched the red coat in the window and followed any human or vehicular movements around the hotel. He fingered occasionally, in his Mackintosh's right-hand pocket, a heavy pistol.

Appleyard and Gunn had also crossed the road and advanced silently along the inside of a fallow field's hedge until they neared the cottages.

'There might be dogs here,' muttered Gunn.

Then Appleyard nudged him as a small red glow indicated a cigarette being puffed about twenty yards ahead.

Motionlessly they waited until eventually a passing lorry's headlights picked up the dark outline of the long-coated smoker.

The two amateurs knelt in a swathe of undergrowth at the edge of the field from where they could discern the figure dimly through the pig-netting and nettles which bordered the garden.

Neither they nor 'Ivanov' heard the fox creep up to the hen-coop. The sudden eruption of squawking and commotion among the hens as the fox peered at them through the coop's latticed door, surprised both 'Ivanov' and the officer cadets.

Turning to study its source in the gloom behind him – as simultaneously a car drove past – 'Ivanov' glimpsed two shadow-speckled faces and the curve of Appleyard's beret.

Aghast, suddenly he knew. This was a trap.

Slavic swear-words crossed his drying lips as he broke into a silent sweat. Despite their unblackened faces and limited camouflage, he took it that they would be seasoned regulars and not just two green bumbling part-time officer cadets.

The seventeen-stone brute strode across the road to warn his comrades and ran into Cywinska returning from her car.

'Help,' she struggled to keep her voice down. 'There's a bomb fixed to my car!'

'Show me!'

He eyed the 'bomb', saw that there was no detonator and in white capitals, the words 'DRILL ROUND'.

'It's some pissing prank,' he scowled as he grabbed it.

It promptly burst open, coming apart in his hands and a huge whoosh of phosphorescent green dust enveloped both him and the car. Sonia had kept her distance.

Yelling that they needed to scatter, she leapt into the Hillman, yanked the choke out, pulled the starter knob, reversed erratically and roared off.

The fluorescent apparition growled, 'Typical. "I'm-all-right-Jack" diplomats!'

Inside the hotel's lounge, an air of uneasy tension reigned.

The landlord was out the back, washing glasses, when the door flew open under the impact of a bullish lime-green Martian invader, who looked wildly around. He saw two more military fellows near the bar, who like everyone else, simply gaped at him.

'My dear fellow, are you that colour all over?' inquired Trewick.

Ignoring this, he shouted at the pair in the bay window. 'Come!'

As they did not instantly leap up, he grabbed the hesitant girl's forearm and dragged her out like a mail-bag. Her handbag fell to the floor, she tripped and lost a shoe and squealed at him to stop, but he took no heed.

The momentary dazzle of a flash bulb brightened the scene.

The pimply youth tagged on, glancing at the stunned, audience who though not interfering, were paying rapt attention.

Thurling managed – after changing the flash bulb and waiting for the capacitor to recharge – a second snap.

'I'll give you the reel when we're done,' he told Holland.

Holland nodded his thanks. 'This should make quite a spread!' It might also, he hoped, alleviate his currently precarious reputation with his editor.

The contents of the girl's handbag showed her to be Alisa Ohotnikova. Her Students Union pass said that she studied at Durham University, living in St. Mary's College and her Temporary Residence Visa stated that once a week

244

a Russian diplomat would visit her to discuss her previous week's activities.

The college authorities later confirmed that someone in a big black car did come each Thursday evening.

The thin youth was eventually identified as an R.A.F. trainee, based at No. 4 Radio School at Compton Bassett. He was thrown out for: 'Liaisons inconsistent with the security of the service.'

Appleyard and Gunn, with leaves and wet patches on their great-coats, entered the hotel lounge.

'Ah, better late than never. Car fixed?'

'Car fixed, Sir.'

'Good.' Trewick looked at his watch. 'We'll give them five minutes, then walk round and see if they're enjoying themselves.

Are you coming with us, Holland? Thurling?'

They both raised their glasses.

Near the darkened old bench, the young girl stood high and dry; pale, unsure, silent and yet a little bit noble.

David approached her. 'Good evening?'

'Good evening,' she replied a little tremulously.

'May I ask your name?'

'Sabine, Sir.'

'Sabine?'

'Yes, Sir.'

'My name's David. You speak English quite well?'

A tentative smile. 'Moderately, Sir. My mother used to teach me. She said it would be useful one day.'

David nodded seriously. 'And is your mother's name "Ulrica"?'

'It is, Sir.'

'Don't call me "Sir" please. Call me David.'

The A.V.M. already felt a certain affection towards her. 'It seems you've been abandoned?'

'Yes. It does rather look that way.'

He waved Sally over. 'This is my daughter, Sally. She will stay with you. We are spending the night in a hotel in Tynemouth.'

Outside in the darkness, the one-shoed Russian student stumbled along, trying to keep up with 'Ivanov', for when she fell she grazed her knees. Her high-pitched jabber, half-screaming and half-weeping accompanied them.

Seeking their car along the dark track, the three routed figures slithered and slipped in invisible dips of gooey mud; mighty ghosts, suddenly demeaned by their own blind and deluded ingenuity.

They brushed broken glass off the front seats and climbed in.

The ignition lit. The engine fired first time but stalled after twenty seconds. It continued to cough, fire, almost start and then die again.

'Are they with the AA, I wonder?' asked Appleyard as the six advanced along the track.

'I will do the talking, Appleyard,' said Trewick.

Then the horn stuck on. This was the last straw. The Green Titan leapt out and kicked the front wheel, skidded abruptly and fell backwards into some oozy sludge.

Then he heard footsteps; lots of them.

Trewick shone a torch and viewed the slippery reptile. 'Having horn trouble are we?'

The partly liquidy-brown, partly radiant-green monster snarled.

'A lot of phosphorescent algae in that slime,' Thurling observed.

'Perhaps we don't need the torch, Sir?'

'Is it a Christmas tree twinkling? Oh no, it's getting up.'

The camera's flash bulb went off.

Trewick tossed his enraged foe a card. 'There's the number of a twenty-four-hour taxi firm in Jedburgh and there's a telephone-box on the main road outside the hotel.'

'One day, you English snobs will pay ... '

Walking back to the hostelry, Gunn remarked, 'He needs a dumper truck more than a taxi.

Oh, by the way Sir, did we do well?'

'Averaging it all out? Hmm ... maybe.'

Gunn nodded to Bayram, 'Mine's a pint.'

*   *   *   *

A United States Air Force *Constellation* came to a halt beside El Adem's No. 1 Hangar.

Her crew were greeted by their R.A.F. counterparts, whilst Rebecca Naish in a light-weight white cotton skirt and jacket, was met by Major Dardry.

They shook hands, smiled pleasantly and went to the deserted Officers' Mess, where the ever-reliable Mr Pinkney brought them some refreshments.

Crab-paste and cream-cheese rolls were his favourite. There were always plenty available.

After he had opened and poured the champagne, the Major said, 'Your good health Miss Naish.'

They clinked glasses.

'Rebecca, please.'

'This is Pol Roger; Churchill's favourite.'

She smiled kindly. 'If I read between the lines of your last signal correctly, you do have the documents?'

'We do.'

'Politically they could be quite important.'

'I can imagine.'

'Are you willing to hand them over to us?'

'We are, but we would like a small favour in exchange.'

'Of course.' Some cream-cheese dripped onto her blouse, which she removed with a napkin.

'Eric Manley and George Torrance of the British Secret Service, work for Moscow. As always we cannot prove it and – needless to say – they have colleagues who will testify to their dedication and loyalty.'

'This all sounds horribly familiar.'

'Could you send an alert to all embassies, stating that intelligence has identified them as long-standing Russian agents?'

'Certainly we can do that ... but what outcome do you expect?'

'An investigation ... which will naturally conclude that they have no case to answer.'

'But at least distrust will have been sown?'

'Also, it will hopefully protect a senior R.A.F. officer.'

Dardry excused himself to fetch the priceless envelope.

Rebecca refilled her glass.

When the Major returned, she inspected the contents briefly.

Standing up, she said, 'Keith, I am sorry that I cannot stay to dinner, but these are needed urgently. I will ensure that we circulate something about Torrance and Manley.'

They shook hands.

Ten days later, Colonel Goodman handed his adjutant a newspaper. It was four days old, folded at page nine and had an article circled in red crayon.

'New Roads for Egypt. Cairo. Tuesday. In a surprise move, the Egyptian Government has today awarded the contract for the construction of 420 miles of new highways to the American consortium of Cramp and Platt. The Russian ambassador has demanded an interview ... '

*   *   *   *

The *Ali Baba* edged up to the quay at Port of Spain. A line of tipper trucks on the dock showed that their change of course had been a commercial one.

Moored nearby, a battered French tramp steamer, the *Nana*, was about to sail to the exclusive French holiday island of Saint-Barthélemy.

Ulrica agreed a price for her passage with its master and after quickly transferring her bags, they cast off and puffed out across a glittering blue and silver sea.

On the gently rolling deck, she held onto the taffrail and watched from the stern a tiny sail in the distance.

Her unknown future reminded her of visiting a German monk in the grim Malabata Prison in Tangier; a profound faith waiting in the darkness ... for God. She too must be strong.

In the spring of 1942, she had met Coombs at the *Café Sirius*. He had given her a mildly friendly if supercilious welcome as she seated herself.

Her wide-brimmed straw sun-hat had hung on its cord behind her shoulders. Dipping her sun-glasses, she had absorbed with curiosity, his collarless, pink-on-white stippled shirt and his wispy greying hair.

'Philip ... Philip Dark-Coombs.'

'Ulrica.'

'I know.'

'And you speak the local lingo?'

'I read Russian and Arabic at Cambridge.'

His voice seemed thin, pinched; his attitude slightly affected or over-sensitive.

'Does your chief – Sir Leon Bridge-Troughton – know of this encounter?'

He turned over a spare glass and poured some 'Bellapais' for her, a Cypriot rosé.

'Sir Leon is broad-minded ... though he abhors baggy flannels and blithering half-wits discussing cricket.'

'But treason?'

Coombs rocked his head. 'He's an old school chum. Awkward questions are "bad form".'

'Very convenient.'

'However, to our relationship. Germany is fighting a losing battle, *Fräulein*, so it is sensible to think of your future ... and to probe my offer.'

'If I am curious, what might it involve?'

He glanced at her young face, blonde hair and semi-translucent short-sleeved white blouse. 'Initially, just establishing contact.'

'Not rushing our fences?'

'Quite. We don't want you to fall at hedge number one. We're short of pretty young fillies.'

'But not for yourself?'

'Sorry?'

'I understand you prefer stallions?' She felt it essential, not to be the under-dog here.

'I see ... You're well informed.'

'Yes. Out of Kindergarten at last.'

He sighed elaborately. 'O what avails the classic bent?'

'So how do we begin?'

'That Bohemian artist, Ulf Grosz, will act as our intermediary. Just drift into his gallery, a hidden envelope and ... *léger de main.*'

A one-legged Berber brought coffees and sweet buns.

'*Shókran*, Bachir.' Coombs handed him a ten-franc coin.

Bachir bowed and limped away.

'A dog bit his remaining leg last week ... and now it's infected.'

'Poor fellow.'

'I suppose the wooden one looked less appetising.'

Dark-Coombs pictured Ulrica with her head-phones pushed back round her neck. 'Initially, just pass on an odd naval transcript ... to show some commitment. Are you familiar with invisible ink?'

At cipher school in Cuxhaven, they had been shown how the colourless mix of iron sulphate and water could be revealed when dry, by brushing it with washing soda. This was 'steganography' from the Greek verb 'στεγω' meaning 'I conceal'.

He slid her a small bottle, which she dropped into her bag.

'Sign with an ideograph, er ... an inverted anchor?' Her small circular *Kriegsmarine* brooch with its gilded anchor had oddly rotated.

'And yours?'

'Hmm … ? A black five-pointed star.'

'The pentacle? Witchcraft?'

'I left myths behind long ago.' He also despised girls for their – as he judged – irrational instincts.

'Left them with a huff and a puff?'

He suppressed his irritation and downed the last of his coffee.

A Spanish vintner, out for his *paseo*, waved to Ulrica. She waved back. He delivered wine to the Legation. A sweetmeat vendor, juggling skittles, seemed to gaze at her. A double-life would mean constant risk.

Coombs' opalescent skin and smug saltlessness repulsed her. She wanted to say, 'Go to where pepper grows,' a favourite expression of her mother's.

'If all goes smoothly, we'll give you a miniature camera in a few weeks.' He stood up to leave.

Back at the Legation, a cinema news-reel was being shown of the struggle on the Eastern Front; much of it, vehicles bogged down in deep mud.

Otto Habe asked her, 'How did it go?'

'Well, they've taken me on … though we didn't like one another.'

Two days later, the *Nana* tied up in Gustavia. There Ulrica spent her first night at L'Hôtel Américain, before renting a tiny flat above a boats' chandler's near the Saint-Jean beach, which she brightened up with vases, cushions and flowers.

With the start of the tourist season in January, she found employment at the Café 'ti-banane, its name a local abbreviation for *une petite banane*. Their house drink, also *'ti-banane*, consisted of grenadine, rum, pulped banana and shards of ice.

Behind the long arc of fine white sand, in a palm-circled arbour – where red-throated yellow and green macaws squawked – she served wealthy sun-seekers.

A sturdy Swede, after frolicking in the clear blue water, ordered his regular spaghetti carbonara and bottle of Perrier water.

He touched her cobalt-blue skirt. 'Emma, you have not the sunken cheeks so typical of French girls?'

'*What* are you saying?'

'That you are Germanic, perhaps?'

'Or a hamster?'

Axel Lindfors added as she transferred his dish from tray to table, 'Could you call on me this evening?'

'What?'

He re-emphasised, 'Can I see you this evening?'

'You can see me now.' A droll reply, which did not entirely close the door.

'Sorry. What I am saying very clumsily, is that I know someone who would like to meet you.'

Ulrica at thirty-six was still quite attractive and not without flair, but was this about dating and mating or something else? 'Why?'

Axel was the Lutheran pastor as well as the Swedish Consul on the island. He touched his wooden pectoral cross.

'I think it would be in your interest. At the church? Seven o'clock?'

'I thought only sinners needed to go to church?'

'We'll make an exception.'

Emma dimpled her cheeks puckishly.

Violette, who ran the café, called over, 'Emma, the family under the carob tree wish to be served.'

Axel twirled some pasta around his fork.

Emma could separate quite well the trustworthy from the shady and the Consul – though he dissembled proficiently – bordered on the 'shady'.

Yet needs must and so later, she took the winding road across the island to the capital.

Two blue doors, set between fluted white-plastered Ionic pillars, fronted the colonial-style building. Above them hung a Swedish flag on an angled pole.

She rang the bell.

A brass key grated, one door opened and Lindfors ushered her through a darkened chapel and into his study, which held an oaken desk with chairs, two sofas, a tall bookcase and two occasional tables. Colourful Carl Larsson prints adorned the walls.

Emma wore a blue linen dress with a sailor-style collar and a small bow. Her hair was slightly *bouffant*.

The other guest rose, a tall thin man. 'Good evening.'

Lindfors introduced them. 'Emma, this is Lars Svärd, a former director of Bofors.'

They nodded politely to one another like a couple meeting on a first date.

'Sit down, please.' Axel opened a second door and called to his housekeeper Candice to bring coffee and rolls.

Emma sat a little stiffly by herself on a sofa, her knees together and an air of fragile nobility on her face.

The host sat down too. 'Lars owns two estates, one in

Småland and one at Ångermanälven … '

'So heavily taxed – thanks to our socialist government – that I have retired to Barbados … so avoiding at least the levy on my income.'

'Oh, but do you miss Sweden?'

'Swedes are very practical people Emma, but often dull.'

'Not the cinematic image then, where scything the hay is just a prelude to other activities in the hayloft?'

Svärd grinned. 'Sadly real life is more mundane … cutting wood, fishing, mending the roof.'

Emma viewed Axel. 'Do we believe this sob story?'

Candice waddled in with a tray of coffee cups and rusks with slices of cheese.

Lars took a deep breath. 'Emma, I have an offer for you … but not what you are imagining.'

'Do you know what I am imagining?'

Dusk was falling outside. The moon's brightness grew in the long window. The host switched on two table-lamps and drew the curtains.

He put a 78 r.p.m. record onto the revolving turntable of his Pye gramophone, lowered the arm onto the outer edge of the hardened wax disc and there came the crackly strains of *The Eton Boating Song*.

'I believe we have met before?'

Axel fumbled with a tiny tin box of half-tone needles and read its ornately printed lid.

Emma was being more attentive than she appeared.

Lars added, 'In Halle. In fifty-three?'

Emma exercised her knack of looking puzzled. 'I think not.'

'I had come to sign a trade deal between Bofors and the East German armaments industry.'

'Since the war I have only lived in West Germany.'

'A "vice girl" came to my hotel room. I knew you would be filming it, so I pulled a pillow-case over my head before we had sex.'

The record's maroon label stopped rotating.

'As that ruse had fallen flat, an eye-catching Party negotiator offered me a secret cash bribe to lower the price-tag on the deal ... her surname was "zu Lauenburg"?'

Emma shook her head firmly.

'I am sure my own government would be prepared to offer you both money – using up some of those outrageous taxes – and asylum in exchange for information?'

Emma blanched, but held her ground.

'The *S.S. Orestes* has sailed from Lima, having unloaded a shipment of renovated ex-Swedish Army vehicles ... in fact I saw the stevedores loading them at Gothenburg. She's returning to the Baltic via Panama, Cherbourg and Southampton ... She's a freighter, but I could arrange a berth for you?'

Emma flatly denied her true identity. Sweden – she knew – would be a death-trap. She left abruptly.

The two Swedes sighed and poured themselves drinks.

'Stalemate,' muttered Axel. 'Pär won't pay us unless she defects.'

Svärd smiled grimly. 'Someone will.'

'You mean "will pay us"?'

'Yes. And very highly.'

In her tiny flat, Ulrica had packed and by five in the morning was on the government quay in Gustavia.

A two-masted schooner, *L'Esprit Curieux*, was preparing to sail to Cayenne to rendezvous with her owner.

Alex Douglas, its Scottish master refused her entreaty to work her passage, but the housekeeper, Giulia Bononcini, said, 'We've lost Geneviève. She could cook and wash-up?'

Alex eyed the cameo of Emma's elegant head on its slender neck and its finely *coiffured* bun of hair, but still shook his head.

'So you are a "Black Douglas" not a "Red Douglas"?' Emma stated.

This knowledge stunned him. He smiled and relented. 'Climb aboard.'

'Thanks. How long's the trip?'

'Three and a half days.'

Emma carried out her duties conscientiously and also helped with setting the sails. Sometimes she watched the swell of the sea and the flying fish in their wake or listened to the water gurgling along the sides of the hull. The horizon remained free of any frigate or seaplane closing on them.

'Who's your boss?' she asked Giulia.

'Crews on private yachts sign not to reveal their employers' names ... but he's a French industrialist.'

They entered the shallow harbour of Cayenne on the diesel engine and there Emma said farewell to the Master, the New Zealand engineer and the Italian maid.

The town was typically Caribbean, garish but ramshackle. There were squares with tall palms and arcade-fronted shops and streets of two-storey wooden houses which had roofed balconies with ornate wrought-iron railings.

At an open-air café near the old Fort Cépérou, she sat in the mottled shade of a tree whose deeply-creviced bark and sparse foliage emitted a bitter fragrance. A couple caroused coarsely nearby and the sullen waitress fleeced her for her baguette and coffee.

She booked into the Hôtel Les Saintes.

This country – French Guiana – was, like Saint-Barthélemy, another *département d'outre-mer*; officially a part of France proper. It was though, unlike Saint-Barthélemy, poor and unsophisticated.

After a snooze, she opened the shutters of her room and looked out into the languorous tropical evening. A rickety bus chugged past and across the estuary, she could see the tree-tops of the aboriginal forest.

She went out with no real idea of what she might do, but after passing a French missionary school, saw some quite presentable people dining at a restaurant set out on the deck of an old dredger. Here under an awning, copper lamps glowed and beside it, the moon threw its rippling light across the chilly purple surface of the wide primeval river.

She was shown to a table on the *Au Soleil Levant* and the one-eyed waiter brought her a carafe of water. She ordered a plate of the lamb fricassee.

The aroma of coffee grounds reached her nostrils and a battered old steamer, loaded with local timber, throbbed slowly past causing the converted dredger to rock gently for a time.

The waiter brought her food, lowering it carefully onto the chequered tablecloth.

A stout American came up to her. 'Would you mind if I joined you?'

She viewed his severe Roman-emperor-like face, his crew-cut hair and the modest rolls of fat round his neck. He was in his early forties.

Before she could decide on an answer, he had sat down. 'Hi. I'm Alan Doll … the United States Consul here.'

'Oh?' She gave a suck on her 'banana flotsam' through its wide-bore straw.

'Look over my shoulder to the south … some old boats in that creek? Lazare – that local on the jetty – he would take you out for fifty dollars without a scruple. If your old bosses learn that you're here, you're finished.'

Beyond a log-jam, she could vaguely make out the leprosy-ravaged Carib, who was smoking some – probably hallucinogenic – herb and chatting to a circus of his buddies, all of whom seemed to be wearing sadistic smirks.

A large cup of coffee and a Florentine appeared in front of Doll.

With her elbows on the cloth and her face tinged lilac in the light reflected from the water, she surrendered. 'Mr Doll … I think you're my best option.'

'Sensible girl. You've done well to survive this far. I'll get you on a plane tomorrow.'

Without knowing why, she burst into tears. 'How long have you been stationed here?'

'Four years. But it's back to the States in the summer.'

He talked prosaically about this French colony, about the exotically-named rivers; Essequibo, Berbice and Demerara, about its export of hardwoods, especially the dense greenheart.

'A French woman, who upset friend Stalin, came here in fifty-two. Some locals caught her and took her to an uninhabited islet with a ruined Portuguese fort and within its mouldering ramparts they raped her in some long grass and then tortured her by tying her to the half-buried barrel of a corroded cannon and lighting a fire under her legs.

They moved her body into a small caved-in tunnel, covered it with the scooped-out contents of a keg of fine damp black powder of great antiquity – flecked with white grains of some mould – and then lit it with a match and … a flash and a bang later, they all had burnt hands and faces.'

On the plane to Miami next day, she dozed and relived her last days in Morocco in 1942.

On the night of the fifth/sixth of November, they were aware of major Allied shipping movements passing eastwards through the Strait of Gibraltar, but the German intelligence analysts were uncertain of their destination.

Two days later 'Operation Torch' began, the Allied landings in North Africa.

On the morning of the eighth of November, the staff at the German Legation set about burning their papers in a brazier in the garden and hammering their decoding machines into twisted scrap.

Otto Habe – the *en poste* S.D. man – had returned from the harbour and told the Head of Station – Consul-General Graf Johann von Steuben – that there were no boats to take them to Spain.

The forty-year-old Count, in his inner office, had his safe open. The documents had been destroyed but there were two bags of British sovereigns beside bundles of French francs, U.S. dollar bills and counterfeit Reichsmark notes all in narrow paper wrappers.

Habe, a wily Berliner, eyed this Westphalian aristocrat – whom he referred to as 'click-heel Hans' because of his perfectly executed salutes – and suggested that they share the money.

Von Steuben seemed shocked. 'I'm in charge here, Habe.'

'I meant to all the staff … to help them escape.'

When told to get out, Habe drew his pistol and the Count's feature's froze.

Arriving at that instant and sensing something amiss, the young cryptographer, Ulrica, tip-toed over the stone-floor of her boss's outer office and glimpsed the scene ahead with Habe's unsuspecting back facing her. She took the Count's old Husqvarna pistol from his belt's holster which hung on a peg. She intended only to tell Habe to put his hands up, but as she flicked off the safety catch, her index finger's light touch on the delicately-balanced trigger was enough. She accidentally shot the S.D. thug who sank open-mouthed to the floor in a spiral motion.

'Oh no! I didn't mean to,' she gasped.

The Count smiled grimly. 'That Swedish thing fires a slow heavy bullet … but luckily it was enough.'

Bending down he noted that the dying Habe's bow-tie was held in place by elastic. 'A fake … naturally. The clue is its being too perfectly knotted.'

'If its muzzle velocity's sub-sonic, why is there a crack on discharge?'

'Because the gases expand rapidly. It's not the projectile itself. I think silencers work like car exhausts … if you fire through a bottle with holes in either end it will muffle the shock wave.

Anyway, we have to disband … to disperse eastwards.'

'Some of the staff already have, Sir.'

They removed the *Corps Diplomatique* plates from the Legation's official car – a 1936 black Citroën 7A – stocked it with the two remaining petrol cans, some spare clothes and food and then set off, passing warehouses which stored hides and oil, wool and copper. It was a sudden farewell, under a cloudless sky, to this once-renowned tax haven.

In shabby civvies and saying they were *Pieds-Noirs*, they drove along dusty main roads – metalled though in poor repair – passing occasional French army lorries and mule carts, until they reached Mascara the next morning, where they ran out of petrol. At an unused bus garage they tried to bribe an Arab woman with gold coins. 'Are you crazy? There's been no petrol for two years!' Her husband appeared, a petrol pump maintenance engineer, who had hidden away some of this rare commodity. He filled them up for thirty sovereigns. With Saint George slaying the dragon on their reverse, these were sometimes referred to as 'the cavalry of Saint George'. If you could not win by force of arms or by diplomacy, you could try using these as a bribe.

The woman told them that the Allies were already in both Algiers and Oran.

In Algiers they found the time-worn town-house they were looking for. It lay on the Rue Joinville, a third of a kilometre from the water-front. Uwe Engel, the Consul, was unscrewing its oblong brass plaque; 'Das Konsulat des Deutschen Reiches'.

Von Steuben and Ulrica spent the night there with Engel, the doors and windows all shuttered and barred.

Next morning, knotted sheets out of a back window showed that von Steuben had abseiled down into a back alley.

Ulrica though, idly opening his mislaid silver cigarette case, discovered by chance a British Union Jack under the lining. At first taken aback, she then understood.

Ulrica, now with Engel, continued to move eastwards. Progress was slow and often fraught, but by early 1944 they had reached Constantinople. With its parapets, domes, stone porticos, green-turbaned pilgrims, western-suited natives and shawled women, all was astir. Barbaric men lashed mules, iron-bound wheels rattled in alleys, bubbles of anger, clamour, spicy smells, scarlet hyacinths in crevices ... all was mayhem. And here in difficult conditions, she bore a child.

With Germany's surrender, the wanderers took filthy trains northwards into Bulgaria, ending eventually in Weimar, where Ulrica was set to work with a road repair gang.

Then as order replaced disorder, she travelled to the Communist Party headquarters in East Berlin, where she was shown by an hysterically nervous young recruit – a boy unable to distinguish between rank and authority – into a beefy grey-faced unshaven brute.

She explained that she had worked as a Soviet agent in Tangier and was sent almost wordlessly to a thinner shrewder and unnamed superior.

Her childhood – wooden toy figures and bricks in the nursery – and her brother having to drill every morning in the courtyard, made him initially distrust her patrician origins.

'Father kept us on strict diets. We had long hikes, sometimes slept on straw palliasses and we swam in icy rivers.'

'A stoical upbringing,' commented her audience drolly, though her fair hair, her pale head on its long neck, her erect poise and her everyday grace were subtly diverting to his coarser thoughts.

He tested her Arabic, using a few random phrases he had picked up.

He gave her a posting in his espionage set-up, where good fortune and promotions came her way.

Engel meanwhile was a rising politician.

In 1950 he showed her a painting of a lighthouse in a storm. It had been owned pre-war by a well-to-do dentist and in fact the scene reminded her of a broken tooth amid a squall of saliva. He said that the next time she went abroad she could sell it, open bank accounts for them in Britain – not London but a provincial town – and divide the proceeds.

There followed a farm-yard scene in deep snow – bleak, sparing, yet poignant – by Aelbert Cuijp, stolen from a house in Amsterdam in 1942.

Then came the 'modernists'.

She eyed the irregular green and blue squares in a sort of dim underwater fog, whose important feature was not its debatable composition, but its signature; Georg Klee. Next came a purple three-armed dentist pulling a huge tooth out of an unclear and pinkish four-armed maiden.

Suddenly, she awoke.

The plane was bumping along a runway. Through the port-hole she could see two American police cars with deputies stood around them watching the plane land.

Ahead lay America, the C.I.A., perhaps a husband ... and perhaps a family?

EPILOGUE.

One evening in April 1959, David Fairweather, waited at Higham Ferrers station for the last train of the day.

As Marion was not among its four passengers, seen walking out past the yellowish light of a solitary gas lamp, he strolled back home.

Sally sat at the dining-table learning shorthand. She had recently started work as a junior reporter for the local paper, the *Rushden Echo and Argus* and needed shorthand for attending court cases.

'Mummy hasn't rung?'

'No.'

'Perhaps she's missed a connection. It's a long journey from Luxembourg … all in one day.'

Would Sally ever have a scoop like the exposé Ken Holland had had in the nationals when his 'Otterburn Abduction Fiasco' had made such a big splash?

He made some tea and picked up a military aircraft magazine. A *Vulcan* had landed at El Adem, proving that it did indeed have a solid and long runway; nine thousand feet as Tug had said.

At ten-twenty the door opened and in came a travel-weary Marion.

She had been to Holland, Belgium and northern France for a week with the features editor of her magazine, gathering material for a new series.

She sank into an armchair whilst David made a fresh pot of tea and toasted some muffins.

'The London train was late in to Wellingborough so the

push-pull to Higham had gone. The station-master said that usually no one from the London train wanted it. "Oh well," he said, "it'll have to run again … if the crew are willing." And they were, so I had the train to myself.'

'That's service. And how was Europe?'

'Hmm. I was about to say "interesting" … but that's a pretty non-informative word, isn't it? It's nice to be back home. You do feel that there is still quite a lot of trust and innocence here. Over there, a vague aura of suspicion and corruption seems to taint everything … a bit like that book, *The Third Man*.'

The following day was a Saturday. It was bright and sunny and David in his dungarees was amassing bricks from a nearby demolished cottage.

He saw his neighbour, rested his wheelbarrow and said, 'Good morning Joe.'

'What are you doing?'

'Building a wall, hopefully.'

'Could be hard work?'

'It's lime mortar on these bricks – pre-1840 – so they're easy to clean. A bolster and hammer and it just falls off … not like cement mortar.'

Joe pulled a face. 'Have you seen that tallish woman cycling round here lately?'

'No.'

'Big-boned, flaxen hair … in her twenties … wearing a brown leather jacket?'

'No … why?'

'Tom wonders if she's watching your house.'

'Oh. But why?'

'Next time I see her, I'll stop her. "Good morning, Miss?

Are you lost? Can I help?" See what she says.'

Come mid-afternoon David went inside, washed his hands, changed and made more tea. Marion was in the kitchen baking, Sally was out on her new job and Sabine sat at the dining-table doing her mathematics homework.

The door-bell chimed.

A smart thinnish fellow in his thirties stood on the door-step. He wore gold-rimmed glasses and an expensive well-cut medium grey suit and carried a briefcase.

'Mr David Fairweather?'

'Er … yes.'

'My name's Lockett, of Lockett Lockett Pearson and Lockett, Solicitors in Northampton.'

Sir David nodded inquiringly at this.

'Er … would it be possible to come in?'

Fairweather led the way to his study where they both sat down.

'We are representing a Mr and Mrs Alan E. Doll of Charleston, West Virginia.'

The retired Air Vice-Marshal opened his palms. 'I am bemused.'

Lockett smiled professionally, but perhaps with a hint of humanity. 'All will become clear shortly.

I believe you have an adopted daughter named Sabine?'

'That is so … although we never officially adopted her.'

'May I ask her surname?'

'Well, she uses ours, "Fairweather".'

'Do you know her surname prior to your adopting her?'

'Er … "Engel". She's of German origin.'

'Mrs Doll – whose first name is "Ulrica" – believes she may be her natural mother.'

'Sabine's mother was called "Ulrica".'

'Mr and Mrs Doll would, I understand, like to invite yourself, your wife, your own daughter and Sabine to their ranch for a month in the summer holidays … all expenses paid.'

'My goodness. We've never been across the Atlantic.'

'It would be a splendid opportunity.' He paused. 'There is though one possibly thorny aspect … that Sabine might wish to stay with her own mother?'

David thought for some seconds. 'Well, if Sabine wished it, we would not oppose her.'

'Thank you, Mr Fairweather. I will ask Mr and Mrs Doll to contact you directly; if that is in order?'

'Er, yes.'

As he left, Sally came in. 'Daddy, it's Sunday tomorrow … have you any plans?'

'No, not unless Mummy has? She does not always disclose her plans in full.'

'You could have missed the last two words off that sentence,' Sally said, with feeling.

David smiled lightly. 'True … but with her I am never cynical. The touch of her hand makes me regret any unkind thought.'

Sally shook her head. 'You're very odd. That's very uncommon.'

'Maybe so … or perhaps I'm unusually lucky?'

THE END.